LYLE NICHOLSON
CAUGHT IN THE CROSSFIRE

By Lyle Nicholson

Bernadette Callahan Series

Polar Bear Dawn
Pipeline Killers
Climate Killers
Caught in the Crossfire
Deadly Ancestors
When the Devil Bird Cries
The Suspect from Berlin
Suspects and Liars

Vinci Books

vinci-books.com

Published by Vinci Books Ltd in 2025

1

Copyright © Lyle Nicholson 2019

The author has asserted their moral right to be identified as the author of this work in accordance with the Copyright, Designs and Patents Act 1988. This work is a work of fiction. Names, characters, places and incidents are the product of the author's imagination or are used fictitiously. Any resemblance to actual persons, living or dead, places and incidents is entirely coincidental.

All rights reserved. No part of this publication may be copied, reproduced, distributed, stored in any retrieval system, or transmitted in any form or by any means, including photocopying, recording, or other electronic or mechanical methods, nor used as a source for any form of machine learning including AI datasets, without the prior written permission of the publisher.

The publisher and the author have made every effort to obtain permissions for any third party material used in this book and to comply with copyright law. Any queries in this respect should be brought to the attention of the publisher and any omissions will be corrected in future editions.

A CIP catalogue record for this book is available from the British Library.

Paperback ISBN: 9781036703646

Printed and bound in Great Britain by Clays Ltd, Elcograf S.p.A.

Chapter One

Three Weeks Ago

Ghulam Nasim hurried along the darkened streets of Kandahar. Isha, the last call to prayer, had sounded several hours ago. The cleric's short legs moved as fast as they could over the recent snow; his leather shoes had become wet. He cursed leaving without his boots. But this was too important. A boy had appeared at his house telling him Imam Sardar Agha, the leader of Kandahar's largest mosque wanted him at the Shrine of the Cloak of the Prophet.

Something was wrong; Ghulam could feel it in his bones. The ancient cloak, once worn by the Prophet Mohammed, had been kept in the shrine for centuries. Ghulam's sole job was to keep the cloak he'd never seen safe in the shrine. It was kept in an ornate wooden box. The boy said the box had been broken, things in the shrine were scattered. He had to come quickly.

His mind raced over the possibilities, his breaths coming

in short bursts. His heart felt like it wanted to explode with fear.

The imam, Sardar, would have his head if the sacred cloak were missing. How would he explain such a thing? Last night after the fourth prayer, when the imam had been meeting with two foreigners, the box had been intact.

Ghulam had opened the shrine and let the imam and the foreigners in. One was a thin man with blond hair and blue eyes that darted around the room taking in the artifacts as if he was appraising them for sale. The other man was tall and dark with a thick chest and arms; he seemed to be the blond man's bodyguard.

The imam had dismissed Ghulam, telling him to leave the key with him. He could pick it up at the mosque next to the shrine in the morning.

Now, the cleric panted as he reached the stairs of the shrine. He could hardly make it up the stairs from his exertion.

He heaved himself through the front doors. It was, as he feared. The ornate box with the brass hinges that Ghulam had polished so lovingly for many years was in splinters.

He clutched his chest. "What happened? How did this happen?"

"I thought you could tell us, Ghulam Nasim," Imam Sardar said as he walked into the room. The imam was much taller and older than Ghulam. He always carried himself with an air of his religious office, however tonight he wore plain brown robes and only a cap. He looked as if he'd been pulled from bed. His fierce eyes penetrated into Ghulam's, making him feel smaller than his five feet three inches.

"But, but, I left you alone with the two gentlemen

tonight. You said you'd leave the key at the mosque for me this morning."

"Enough of your silly explanations, Ghulam. I locked the door myself when I left. I have the key with me. Did you make an extra key and give it to the foreigners?"

"Of course not. I could not, I would do no such thing," Ghulam protested.

"Are you sure? The little one, he seemed quite taken with you last night, asking you many questions. He didn't offer you some extra money to steal our precious cloak?" the imam asked. His eyebrows rose high in two accusing arches.

"No, no, no my Imam. I have been caretaker of the sacred cloak for many years. This shrine is my life, I would never sell it to Infidels—to anyone."

"Yes, we will see what the videos show. All will be revealed...ah, here is the chief of police. We will have an answer to this great tragedy soon, Ghulam. You had better hope that Allah is merciful."

Ghulam felt his heart growing smaller in his chest. How could this be? The sacred cloak, the only thing that mattered in his shrine, was gone. If by some hand of fate he was found at fault, his head would roll, not figuratively, but in the square of Kandahar at the hands of an executioner.

Chapter Two

Chris Christakos wasn't happy with this morning's mission. He'd been pulled from his room at 0500. His orders were to escort Jannick Lund, their personal protection client out of Kandahar, to a small village so he could do some recon of a water project he wanted to fund.

Jannick Lund was CEO of a Non-Government Agency; they called them NGO's here in the 'Stan, the short name for Afghanistan.

Chris had signed a three-month contract, leaving his fiancé Bernadette Callahan to come here and show his worth. This was the dumbest thing he'd ever done, he thought as he pulled on his bulletproof vest and strapped his Glock to his leg, then checked his MP5 Heckler and Koch 9 mm machine gun.

He was supposed to be heading for the airport the next day on a flight to Paris to meet Bernadette and rekindle their relationship. He couldn't count the number of times he'd apologized for being so brash and accepting this job. Sure, it was one thousand dollars a day, a cool ninety thousand good old US dollars tax-free for three months work. But the work! Damn, it was dangerous.

They'd been shot at and run over IED's, those lovely big 'improvised explosive devices' the Taliban liked to dig into the roads and blow up unsuspecting vehicles. Three of their team had gone back home with injuries. This job was getting more dangerous all the time.

And last night, doing the personal protection gig for Lund at the shrine with the crazy imam, that about settled the guy as bat shit crazy. Chris hoped they'd get out, check the village and be back in time for him to call Bernadette one more time before she left for Paris.

They mounted up into the trucks—three dark SUV's with heavy amour, which they hoped would protect them from IED's. Secretly, they all knew the trucks were toast if they were hit.

Stanhope, an ex-British paratrooper was in the lead vehicle with McEwan, a Scot who'd retired from the Black Watch Regiment. He had a wicked sense of humor, while Stanhope had none. With them was Max, his real name was Mahboobolah, which no one could pronounce, their interpreter who spoke Pashtun and Dari. His English was sometimes hard to understand, but they cut through translations with hand signals.

Lund, their asset, was in the second truck with his driver, Douglas, a young kid of 19, who never should have been hired but they were desperate for warm bodies. Douglas was a wash out from the armed forces but could drive anything. He was a big kid from rural Nebraska with a wide smile who didn't get rattled. He actually fit into the team quite well.

Chris was in the last truck, with Cameron who took the wheel. They sped out of their compound, shooting dust into the air. Afghans cursed the convoy as it sped by, scaring their donkeys and chickens. People dove out of the way to avoid being hit by the three large trucks that looked as if they would rather run over someone than stop.

"This is bullshit," Chris said to Cameron.

"Copy that," Cameron said. He was a young former marine from Ohio named Cameron Anderson. He'd done two tours with the Marines in Iraq and how the hell he ended up here took a two-hour story and six beers. His long story short was—insanity.

"Why the hell do we have to drive like we're protecting some five star general? Who does he think he is?"

"Yeah, total dumb ass. But his orders are we drive like hell for his protection. He's paying the bills and Stanhope takes him to the letter. Just like a true Brit," Cameron said. "And we got some kind of rendezvous with a big Afghan in a village."

"Sure, but this just draws attention to us. Kick up a lot of dust when we hit the outskirts of town, you alert every Taliban that you've got something important. Puts a target on us."

Cameron turned to Chris. "Hey, QC, you're finally thinking like a true military guy. Wow, from QC to jarhead in three months. Impressive."

Chris smiled and stared ahead. His nickname had become QC for "Queen's Cowboy" when the guys learned he'd been a constable with the Royal Canadian Mounted Police in Canada. He told them the force was once nicknamed the Queen's Cowboys by Canadians after Queen Elizabeth of England. The name stuck.

The convoy sailed past the markets then onto the main highway. They had several checkpoints to go through before they left the city of Kandahar. The ANP, Afghan National

Police, manned the checkpoints, took the bribes and made sure they got their cut of anything that was leaving the city. They did well.

In this case, they'd have to wave the convoy on, for no goods were being transported; Lund always made sure of that or he hid them well. Max showed their credentials and they went through each checkpoint without problem.

They were soon out in the open. Guard towers appeared on the sides of the roads. Machine guns tracked their progress with young Afghan kids barely out of puberty holding the trigger of a 50 MM machine gun. One slip of the finger and their truck would be toast.

The convoy sped on. Chris tensed up as they reached the hills. In his imagination, he saw Taliban behind every hill. The landscape looked like uneven brown pancake batter spread over ominous hills. Each hill could hide a Taliban with an AK47 Russian-made machine gun and a cell phone with a transmitter to an IED.

"We're approaching our first choke point," Cameron said. "Clench your cheeks QC 'cause this is the fun part."

Chris knew what he meant. Choke points were a narrowing of the road. When the road ran right through a hill, leaving a deep valley, they were vulnerable to attack from two sides. The Taliban loved these hills. They could sit there all day and take out anyone they wanted. The only thing that kept them away was U.S. helicopters and drones.

"Skies are clear, we should be okay," Chris said.

"Once again, QC, you're right on, true military thinking," Cameron said with a smile.

When the skies were clear, the drones were flying high on the perimeter of Kandahar. They were loaded with Hellfire missiles that made quick work of any Taliban who decided to linger over a hill staring down at the highway.

Clear skies were their friends; cloudy days made them want to cringe.

They relaxed as they came out the other side of the valley and into the clear open spaces of the Afghan countryside. There was one more hill left. As they approached, the lead truck started to slow.

"You think there's a problem?" Chris asked. He racked his machine gun, pulling off the safety and placing his finger on the side of the trigger.

Cameron spoke into his collar mic, "What's the situation?"

"Lund has to take a shit," Stanhope replied from the front vehicle.

Cameron muttered, "Copy that." He turned to Chris. "Well that's the biggest *brown star cluster* I've heard of in sometime."

"Which means?" Chris asked.

"Total bullshit," Cameron said. "You'd think the guy could clear his friggin' bowels before we left town."

"Stay frosty," Stanhope said over the radio. They knew he meant stay sharp.

Chris watched Lund walk towards some low hills. "Is he carrying something?"

"Damn if I know, let me get the binoculars—shit—incoming!

The whoosh of an RPG round streaked between the trucks and ignited Lund's vehicle. The truck lifted off the ground before dropping back in a ball of flames.

"Get out, get out!" Cameron yelled to Chris.

Chris grabbed his machine gun in one hand, pushing open the door and launching himself out of the truck. He turned on his stomach with his weapon ready. AK47 rounds pinged on the truck. Cameron followed him out the same door, his weapon hitting the ground with a crunching sound.

Cameron yelled, "QC, follow me—head for the BFR!"

Chris crawled behind Cameron. The BFR was military code for big friggin' rock. They got behind it and peered out.

"I make out ten hostiles from the weapons fire," Cameron said.

"Great, that gives us three each. Any chance we can move to that other rock and flank them?" Chris asked. He fired off a quick round of his MP5. It resulted in the other side of their rock being hit with a fusillade of AK47 fire.

"I think you made them mad, QC. I'll call in my friendly American chopper buddies. They'll send a Blackhawk in here to put some missiles up their butts," Cameron said.

"Go for it," Chris said. "This could get old real fast, they got us outnumbered."

Cameron took out his satellite cell and dialed a direct line he had to U.S. Forces, Afghanistan. "Lucky I still got friends there that owe me favors."

Chris fired off another round from his weapon and pulled his head back, "You mean you still haven't paid off your gambling debts to the heli pilots?"

Cameron smiled as he listened for his phone to ring. His smile fell to a frown, "Ah shit, we got no coverage here."

Chris shook his head. "Not possible, your sat phone doesn't work on relay stations, it bounces off satellites. The Taliban must be using cell frequency jammers."

"I hate it when the hostiles go all geeky on us. Do you see any of our crew? Can we communicate by visual?"

Chris looked back to the road. "Looks like they got the

lead truck as well. Maybe we can make it to our truck and head back for help."

Cameron was about to respond when an RPG round whooshed over their heads, striking their truck. A roar of flame threw the truck onto its roof. Cameron shrugged. "There goes our ride."

An Afghan voice yelled out. "Surrender to us and you will not be harmed."

Chris stared at Cameron. "What are our options? I'm out of ammo for my MP5. I got nine rounds in my Glock, which means I need them close in, and you don't have any weapons."

Cameron winced at the obvious. His weapon had jammed when he'd jumped out of the truck. It was useless. The sporadic weapons fire from their team in the other trucks who'd made it out had become silenced. They were all out of ammunition. With no cell coverage, they were done.

"Do you trust these bastards?" Chris asked.

"They don't get any ransom money if we're all dead. Kind of the law of the land," Cameron said in a dry tone.

"What about our interpreter?"

Cameron shook his head. "You know what the Taliban do to interpreters, they shoot them on the spot or torture them to death. There's no debate on that with them. Our interpreter Max knows that."

"Bullshit," Chris said. He moved his face towards the edge of the rock. "Does your promise of protection go to all of us?"

A laughing voice answered, "Of course, Allah is merciful to those who surrender to us, *inshallah*."

Cameron yelled to the others in the crew. "Guys, what's the call? I got no cell, no back up. If we surrender, we do it as a group. No one here does a cowboy and starts firing. You got that?"

A muffled 'copy that' came from a rock a hundred meters away and the other men in the crew put their hands up. Chris and Cameron did the same.

The Afghans came forward with their weapons trained on them. They were herded into a group. Cam looked around; McEwan and Stanhope looked okay.

"Where's Douglas?" Cam asked.

McEwan nodded in the direction of the flaming middle truck. "He didn't make it out."

"What about Lund?"

The question was answered with Lund coming towards them with his hands over his head. He looked pissed. Chris couldn't tell if it was his stupid decision to stop at this obvious choke point or if he thought his security team had failed them. He didn't care; staying alive was his main concern, not the health of this idiot who had gotten them captured.

Chris looked down at their interpreter; Max was sitting on his haunches, his hands cradling his head as if he expected the worst.

Max looked up at him. "You must kill me now, please, I beg of you. The Taliban kill all interpreters, after they torture them. Your bullet would be a mercy to me, please."

"Hey, don't worry, Max. They said they would be merciful to all who surrendered. You'll be fine," Chris said. He couldn't imagine putting a bullet in Max's head.

Max looked up with eyes filled with tears. "You do not understand the true translation of *inshallah*."

"Sure, I do, Max, it means God willing."

"Yes, my friend, and it also means, if God wills it. The Taliban can kill us all and say that God willed it."

Chapter Three

Present Time

Bernadette Callahan stared out the airplane window at the cold and barren mountains below. She'd be landing in Kandahar in the next half hour. The captain announced they were arriving on time. The weather was 3C/37 F, snow and wind—a normal January day in Afghanistan.

Nothing about her life was normal. She'd been waiting to hear if Chris had been located for weeks. They were supposed to have met in Paris; she'd even picked out an amazing hotel with a claw foot tub in the Latin Quarter.

All of that changed the moment she got the phone call that Chris was missing on his last security patrol in Afghanistan. She still had no answers. Countless phone calls to the Canadian Embassy and the security company he'd worked for in Kandahar turned up nothing. A series of dead ends led her to this plane flight.

Bernadette Callahan was a detective in the Royal Canadian Police Force in Western Canada. Thirty-five, five-foot eight and medium build with green eyes and red hair and a bronzed skin tone that proclaimed her Irish and Native Cree Indian heritage. The anger that seethed inside of her could come from either of her lineages at this moment.

She shouldn't have let the relationship get to the point that Chris had to prove his worth by taking such a hazardous assignment in Afghanistan, but his leaving was a symptom of the holes that were appearing in the fabric of their relationship.

They'd been together for over a year. He'd proposed to her one evening in December while they were on a trip to Banff National Park. Large snowflakes descended out of the darkness as he'd dropped to one knee and asked her to marry him. She'd said yes even as her heart had cried out in terror at her answer.

She never wanted to leave the police force. Being a detective was her life. For their relationship to work, he had to leave his job as constable for the RCMP on an idyllic island on the west coast of British Columbia. She'd always felt like she'd captured a bear and tried to tame it.

Chris was a Greek-Canadian with a wild nature. He loved the outdoors of Canada. The RCMP had become a way to spend his time at the office—outdoors.

Now, as the plane descended into one of the most dangerous places in the world, she wondered if she should have said yes to that good-looking Greek god with the curly black hair, almond brown eyes and easy smile. If she'd said no, none of this would have happened. He'd still be catching salmon poachers and tracking stolen fishing boats.

Getting to Afghanistan was her greatest challenge. She wanted to be here with every fiber in her body, but you needed a hard to obtain visa to get to Afghanistan. A business visa was the only option, there were no tourist visa's being issued, as the country was deemed too dangerous.

Bernadette had tried every angle with the Afghanistan Consulate. She needed to be working for or consulting for a legitimate agency in Afghanistan. After two weeks of calling in every favor she could think of, she called Agent Carla Winston with the FBI. They'd had some close calls together, and the end result was that neither of them, especially Winston, had suffered any harm, therefore she was willing to help.

Winston was able to procure a special visa for Bernadette as consultant for a company called Apex 5 Security. The company was a front to move FBI, CIA and Homeland Security personnel into Afghanistan without any special attention.

Bernadette was on her own as to her personnel protection and translator. She needed to hire both—the first was costly. A man named Bardulf Brandt, ex German military, would be her bodyguard; his fee was five hundred dollars a day in Kandahar and one thousand if they left the city limits. He had stressed repeatedly in emails that going out of Kandahar was too dangerous.

Her interpreter was a man named Reza. His fee was much less, fifty dollars a day in Kandahar. He gave no fee for leaving Kandahar, which seemed to imply he did not want to leave the city limits.

The plane landed on the tarmac with a thud. Bernadette watched out the window as they taxied past rows and rows of American Air Force planes and Black Hawk helicopters. It looked like a war zone.

She followed the rest of the passengers off the plane. Soldiers were everywhere with AK47 Russian machine guns. They stared hard at the stream of passengers as they walked past. Bernadette pulled on her overcoat and her headscarf as she made her way down the peeling gray walls with the fluorescent lighting. She'd been in prisons with better lighting. The sunglasses she wore made the hallway worse. They were her way of being able to look around her without being noticed. Women in Afghanistan were not to look directly at men. Bernadette was damned if she'd comply with such a custom. The sunglasses would allow her to see men's faces and eyes. Words could hide volumes; eyes could not, as far as she was concerned.

The line of passengers came to a halt at the customs hall. They inched slowly forward as a group of uniformed customs officers, all with beards, scrutinized passports and passengers as if a Taliban infiltrator or drug smuggler was present.

Bernadette's turn came. She marched forward to the officer.

"Sunglasses, off!" the bearded officer commanded.

"Oh, sorry," Bernadette said. She'd been so engrossed in watching all the passengers' interactions she had forgotten.

The officer stared at her Canadian passport and her American consultants' documents. "You are Canadian, yes?"

"Yes, I am Canadian."

"You are working for the Americans?"

"Yes, I am working for the Americans." She decided not to elaborate. She could have told the officer how she was a Canadian detective with the Serious Crimes Division of the Royal Canadian Mounted Police, but all of that was too much.

The officer took her passport and her document and a piece of paper. He wrote as much of her details as he could on the paper. His paper would be sent to the police chief of

Kandahar and to the security forces. They would know she was here.

He stamped her passport loudly and handed it back to her, waving her away and summoning the next person.

She felt relieved to have made it through customs. There was a moment when she thought they might refuse her entry, send her back. She put on her sunglasses and proceeded to baggage claim. After picking up her bag, she was checked three more times. Every five meters another bearded, officious looking officer stared at her passport, her visa, and ruffled through her bag.

She finally got through and found herself in a sea of Afghans on the other side. An anxious-looking smallish man, with a long black beard, held a sign that read B. Callahan.

He was dressed in the traditional Afghan style, which included a pakol hat, reminiscent of an oversized floppy beret. He wore the traditional perahan tunban, a baggy, loose fitting trouser that came high above his boots and an oversized shirt with short sleeves. Over the shirt with its long tail that came three quarters to the ground, he wore a quilted down vest.

The résumé that Bernadette read online for Reza, one name only, was that he had studied philosophy and linguistics at university. He'd been a teacher but moved into interpreting when the Taliban had overrun his school in rural Afghanistan.

"Hi, you must be Reza," Bernadette said as she strode towards him. She almost reached out her hand, and then quickly put it by her side. Reza saw the movement but made as if he did not notice it. Males and females were forbidden to touch one another in public. Bernadette's gesture would have infuriated the men in the airport.

"Yes, I am Reza. I trust you had a satisfactory flight?"

"Yes, thank you," Bernadette said. She really wanted to say she'd wanted a beer on the plane but knew there was none to be had. Not only was Afghanistan a non-joy for womankind, it was mostly without alcohol. A double buzz kill, as far as she was concerned.

"I will take you to your car and you'll be taken to your guesthouse. All of this has been arranged," Reza said. He took her duffle bag and began leading her out of the airport.

Bernadette caught up to him. "Thanks, but I want to be taken straight to Kandahar Police Headquarters. I need to speak with the chief of police. I want to start the search for my missing fiancé."

Reza stopped. "This is impossible."

"Why, is he not there today?"

"No, he will not meet with you. You are a woman he does not know; he cannot meet with you unless I am there. I cannot be with you today. I'm only here to greet you and see you to your escort."

"I see. Can we set up a meeting for tomorrow then? I want to see the American and Canadian Consulates after that."

"All will be done in the morning. I promise." Reza nodded his head and picked up her bag. "Now, please follow me to your transport."

Bernadette adjusted the headscarf, the hijab she'd been warned she would need, and followed Reza. They walked out to the curbside area of the airport. There was not the usual comings and goings of traffic. Cars were summoned when their passengers arrived and security was tight.

Reza called Bernadette's driver on his cell phone; a black SUV with dark tinted windows pulled up almost immediately. Reza opened the back door, Bernadette slid in. The door slammed behind her and the SUV took off.

Reza watched the truck drive away. He hurried away from the airport hoping no Taliban had seen him with the foreign lady. He'd told his wife he wouldn't take any more interpreter jobs. His need for money had finally surpassed his fear, for now.

"I am Bardulf Brandt," a Germanic sounding voice said from the driver's seat. "I see you met Reza. That man is a real pussy. I think maybe he's a fag."

"Thanks for your update. I have no problem with gay men, but if you do, you can keep it to yourself," Bernadette said.

She looked out the window as they left the airport. Two Afghans were staring at the SUV and dialing into their phones.

"I understand you are here to find your missing fiancé," Bardulf said as he maneuvered the car away from the airport. "You have wasted your time. The Taliban will send word of him in a week or two. You should have stayed in your country arranging his ransom. I hear he is Canadian. That is bad; Canada does not pay ransom, you'll need to do a lot of fundraising."

Bernadette stared into the rearview mirror. She could see only part of Bardulf. He was older, maybe 45, a blond with some streaking of gray in his short-cropped hair. He had blue eyes set in a wide face. He looked well built, someone who spent hours in the gym in his off hours. Thick arms with big hands guided the steering wheel.

"I thought maybe I'd come here, make some inquiries, and then do some recon in the countryside," Bernadette said.

"Ha, you are joking. To do that I need to get four more

men and two more trucks. Your cost will be five thousand U.S. per day to venture outside of Kandahar. You have no idea how dangerous it is in the countryside of Afghanistan."

Bernadette could feel her anger growing as her cheeks grew red and her lips set into a tight line. "Really, are all the extra men and trucks for my protection…or yours?"

"Again, you are funny. The Taliban would get special joy in taking a North American woman hostage. I will not tell you all the many things they do to her, but you can guess."

"The joke's on them. I'm Canadian, we don't pay hostage takers like you said…and we have ice cold hearts."

Bardulf laughed. "You'd better have some ice between your legs if you want to fend off the Taliban, lady." He looked into the rearview mirror. His smiling eyes turned to a leer as if he was trying to judge Bernadette's assets beneath all her clothing.

"Giant asshole," were the words she muttered as she turned to look out the window. This conversation with the large Germanic moron was getting boring. She'd dealt with many men just like him in the police force. It was best to stand up to them.

Bernadette turned towards the front and leaned forward. "Listen up, Bardulf, I'm not here in Afghanistan to listen to what you like or don't like about gays or to discuss the temperature of my vagina. In your own language, I believe the term is *Das geht mir am arsch vorbie.*"

Bardulf's eyes went wide. He started to laugh so hard he almost went off the road. "Who told you how to say kiss my ass in German?"

"I have German girlfriends back in Canada. Now that we understand each other, maybe you can help me get some intel on how to find my fiancé."

"You have a good sense of humor, maybe you'll keep

that if you're caught by the Taliban." Bardulf winked into the rearview mirror.

Bernadette saw his wink—then saw a flash of something alongside the road. She had only seconds to process what it was.

"Take cover!" she screamed.

Bernadette dove down onto the floorboards of the SUV as the rocket hit the right side of the vehicle. She covered her ears and tried to make her body as small as possible. The blast sucked all the air out of the passenger compartment.

She reached up and pushed on the SUV's back door, the blast had destroyed the locks—it was open. She pushed herself out the door as another explosion ripped through the vehicle. Stumbling to a ditch, she fell in. Then, there was darkness as she passed out.

Chapter Four

Bernadette dreamed that Chris was beside her. He was stroking her hair with one hand. His other big hand was on her stomach. He was rubbing her tummy. It was something he did when they lay in bed together after sex. She moaned softly with pleasure.

"Are you okay, Madame?" a voice asked.

Bernadette opened her eyes. She looked up to see a doctor and nurse standing over her. The nurse was adjusting the covers on her bed. She tried to sit up.

The doctor forced her back down with both his hands. "I am Doctor Ahmed, this is Nurse Sharbat. You've had a concussion from the explosion. You must lie back now."

"The explosion?" Bernadette asked. She wondered what they were talking about.

"A rocket propelled grenade struck your vehicle two days ago when you arrived. You have been asleep since then. The driver was not so fortunate. He was flown back to Germany with serious burns," the doctor said.

"Yes, now I remember…his name…was Arsh…"

"No, no, that is the German word for a person's backside. Your mind must be addled. His name was Brandt."

Bernadette closed and opened her eyes, "Yes, his name was Bardulf Brandt."

"Do you know your name?"

"Yes, it's Bernadette Callahan. I'm a detective from Canada."

"Excellent." The doctor checked her eyes and took her pulse. "You are coming along nicely. Someone from your consulate will be here to make preparations for your return home."

"My return home?"

"Yes, of course, with such a concussion you must return to your country as soon as possible. We have x-ray equipment here, but you'll need assessment from an MRI and possibly the attention of a neurosurgeon."

Bernadette tried to raise her head again. Her forehead exploded in pain as a sharp red light flashed before her eyes. She lowered her head back to the pillow.

"I'll have the nurse give you something for the pain," the doctor said. He gave instructions to the nurse and left the room.

As the nurse left the room, another person entered. It took Bernadette a minute to let her eyes focus on the female visitor. She looked East Indian and was dressed in a long blue coat with baggy pants. The traditional hijab surrounded her face; she wore a bright pink lipstick that set off her soft brown skin.

"Hi, I'm Chandra Gupta from the Canadian Embassy," she said.

Bernadette tried to raise her head, failed, and made a welcome smile. "Hi," is all she could manage.

"I know this is hard for you, Ms. Callahan. I read your

file in the consulate before I came here." Chandra dropped her eyes, trying to hide the disappointment she felt for Bernadette. "I know you've come here to try to find your fiancé. You must believe that we've done everything we can to locate him."

Chandra's words made Bernadette rise up. "You mean to say, you are doing everything, not you have done everything. The last term means the past, it means you've finished looking."

"I'm sorry, yes, we are still looking, but you have to realize how vast this country is and there are so many tribal conflicts here—the military can hardly manage what they have to deal with now."

"So, my Chris is just another statistic in the scheme of things? Just another foreigner gone missing into the desert?"

"No, of course not. We have pictures of him and his men. Every NATO soldier who leaves Kandahar has the information. They've checked numerous villages on every patrol, they've enquired to all the tribal chiefs, there's been nothing so far."

"But have your people made enquiries in Kandahar?" Bernadette asked.

"Why would we do that? They went missing in the country," Chandra said.

"Someone here knows where they were going, what they were up to. Has anyone in the consulate thought of that?"

"Yes, yes of course. All of this has been done."

Bernadette narrowed her eyes to look hard at Chandra, to see if she was giving her the whole story. "I'll want to see the complete report. Once I've seen that I'll have a basis for my own investigation."

Chandra shook her head. "You don't understand, Ms. Callahan, I have orders to get you on a plane back to

Canada as soon as you're fit to travel. The Canadian Consulate asked the Afghan Police to post a guard outside your room for your own safety. Once the doctor has deemed you fit to travel, you'll be flown back to Toronto. I'm sorry you came all this way and I'm so sorry for your injuries, but this is the situation."

"You speak any German?" Bernadette asked.

"No, I speak Punjabi, Urdu, Pashtun, and Tajik," she said with an arch of her eyebrow, clearly implying this job of dealing with Canadian travelers was beneath her.

"Well, find someone in your consulate who does, and tell them to translate kiss my ass in German."

"But I don't understand, you just said it," Chandra said.

"Oh, yes, I guess I did. Never mind. Now run along back to your lovely consulate. Tell them thanks for the offer of the flight home, but I'll be getting back on the hunt for my fiancé as soon as I can walk out of here."

Chandra turned on her heels and strode out of the room.

Bernadette let her head fall back on her pillow. She needed to think. How badly hurt was she? She knew about head trauma. She lifted her hand to her head and felt her entire forehead. She had no outward sign of injury. The bomb blast would have produced a wave that would have bounced off her body. She thought it would be similar to having three to four big 280-pound hockey guys hit her full force in the rink. She always thought in hockey terms.

She'd had a head trauma years ago when she was sixteen. Three girls had given her a beating. She survived, took up karate and never had to take another beating. But a rocket propelled grenade was different. She would have to wait and see and develop a plan. Bernadette always had plans. She let herself fall asleep.

Chapter Five

Sardar Agha walked into the grand hall and let his eyes slowly take in the room. This day was the Loya Jirga, the grand assembly of the tribes of Afghanistan.

Normally, it would be in Kabul, but the theft of the holy robe of the Prophet Mohammad made Kandahar the central focus. Sardar Agha was both blessed and cursed. His presence was sought after. He'd been the one who'd seen the robe last. He knew everything about it, but if he failed to have it returned…?

He moved confidently into the hall, his son, Barlas beside him. He'd picked out his name; it meant strong, powerful, and authoritative. Barlas was none of these. He suffered from a weak chin that his patchy beard did not cover, eyes that were too close together, and hunched over shoulders that seemed to be an apology when he spoke.

At 70, Sardar was tall for his years. His fierce eyes were hooded beneath bushy eyebrows that were still jet-black. The Koran was the cornerstone of his life, but politics and power coursed through his veins. It was how you survived in Afghanistan. He'd outlived the Russian occupation, their scurrying home, and then the warlords followed by the Taliban. Finally, here he was amongst the tribes while the last vestiges of the mighty American military camped on their doorstep.

His dream was to banish all foreigners from their soil. The Americans and their NATO allies would have to go, with their cursed government contractors that brought bribes and despair to the people. The Afghanis were pure people, when left alone they fought and haggled amongst themselves, but they left their blood in the soil of this desert and mountainous country. It made them strong.

He would bring the faithful back, banish the warlords, and bring the Taliban to their senses. To Sardar, the Taliban had been right to rise up against the warlords, but they went too far. If he could reason with them, he would make them once again the guardians of the faith. Afghanistan would be the great country it was meant to be.

"Come, Barlas," Sardar commanded. "Pull back your shoulders and follow me. We have much to talk about with the many tribes. See how I do this and take note."

Barlas pulled his shoulders back, stood ramrod straight and followed his father. As soon as his father turned his back, his shoulders slumped as if he really didn't have it in him.

They made their way across the sea of men, many in clusters of deep conversation. Barlas noted the men all looked as his father walked past. Some gave a nod. Some muttered a Muslim greeting of "Peace be upon you," casting their eyes down in reverence. Sardar muttered back a *wa'alaikum assalam*, the Muslim reply of "and unto you be peace," to some and nodded at others. To others, he gave no reply to show his indifference of their low position.

Sardar was seeking Jamshed Rabbini. He found him engrossed with three other men in heated conversation.

Rabbini lifted his head when he saw Sardar. "*As-salam alaykom.*"

Sardar touched Rabbini's sleeve. "*Wa'alaikum assalam.* We have much to discuss."

One of the men, Abdul-Bari, looked at Sardar in surprise. "I'm sure you have much to talk about. The sacred robe of Mohammed has gone missing right from under your nose. How do you intend to deal with such an insult to the Afghan people?"

Sardar looked at Abdul-Bari. He was an imam from the second largest mosque in Kabul. He was related to the president, so he could not be disrespectful to this man.

He bowed his head and placed his hand over his heart. "My revered brother, Abdul-Bari has made a good point. The robe was under the care of my disciples and it was stolen." He looked directly into the group of men. "You must know that I have already placed a fatwa on the men, the foreign infidels that stole the robe."

Abdul-Bari laughed "You have placed a death threat on the infidels? How will that see the return of the robe?" He looked at the other men to prove his point. They nodded in agreement.

Sardar's face turned red, and he sputtered, "The fatwa will have the many tribes give up the hiding place of the infidels and return the robe to its proper place in Kandahar."

Abdul-Bari raised his hand to Sardar to make a point. "My brother, if fatwas worked, then Jamshed Rabbini's uncle would still be alive today."

Sardar stared at Jamshed. He could see the hurt that the man's words had brought. In 2011, Taliban suicide bombers had assassinated his uncle, Burhanuddin Rabbani. His uncle had served as the President of Afghanistan from 1992 to 1996 and had tried to get a fatwa placed on all suicide bombers. He was not successful. The Taliban had approached him to make peace; one of them had a bomb in his turban. Sardar told himself to never embrace a Taliban with a turban.

Jamshed shook his head at Abdul-Bari's inference. "This reference makes no sense my brother, and it is not the same. Now, please excuse me, I must speak with Sardar."

They walked away from the other men. To Sardar, it couldn't have been a moment too soon. Abdul-Bari was a presumptuous little turd. He used his connection to the president for his benefit. Without the president as his protector he would be lucky to get a job as a goat herder.

His son, Barlas, correctly knowing he was not needed or wanted, melted away into the crowd.

"How is it with you, Sardar?" Jamshed asked.

"These are troubling times, my friend," Sardar said as he looked around the room. He limited his expressions and his gestures, as if he was discussing the weather.

"How will you deal with the missing robe? Do you have any leads?"

"Yes, I believe the infidels were put up to the theft."

"By whom?"

"Our friends in the Hazara tribe."

Jamshed adjusted his cap. He wore a black cap and black robe, similar to what his uncle had worn. Jamshed was a Tajik, the second largest ethnic group in Afghanistan. That Sardar, a Pashtun of the largest ethnic group and Jamshed were able to get along was a mystery to many.

There was distrust between the Tajiks and Pashtuns, as the Tajiks had always been in power when foreigners had ruled the land.

Sardar had sought out Jamshed many years ago; he told him it was to unite the tribes. He never told him it was because he could not get along with his uncle. Secretly he'd rejoiced when the Taliban had murdered him.

"You think the Hazara tribe is behind the theft. You have some proof of this?" Jamshed asked.

Sardar stroked his beard lightly; he had to be careful with these next words. "I heard a rumor that the Hazara would like more prominence in Loya Jirga. They feel that their voices are not heard. If they had the robe, they would have that power."

Jamshed rubbed his eye. "If this were true it would make sense. The Hazara are Shia Muslims. They believe they are left out of many of our sacred religious practices and not represented in our parliament."

"What if they used the stealing of the robe to unsettle our country? This might have all the tribes at war. A civil war might bring in our neighbors to the west," Sardar said.

Jamshed's eyes went wide. "You think that Iran would dare attack Afghanistan?"

"No, they would not need to attack. They would walk in to protect their fellow Shia Muslims. Where would we be if this happened?"

"The Americans would never let it happen."

Sardar looked around to see if they were being overheard. "If you were a student of history as I am, you'll remember that America supported South Vietnam for years until they got sick of hemorrhaging money and losing their sons and daughters. When North Vietnam attacked they did nothing but remove their army and as many of those who had been faithful to them."

Jamshed bowed his head, letting Sardar's words take hold. "Yes, you are right. There is much talk in America that they are tired of our wars. I cannot say I blame them."

They both looked across the room where Abdul Ali Balkihi was huddled with the others of his Hazara tribe. He looked just like the rest of his clan; a mixture of Mongolian and central Asian ancestry made them easily identifiable. There were close to three million Hazara in Afghanistan and much bad blood between the Hazara and the Pashtuns. The Hazara had been subjected to massive killings when they refused to be ruled and staged an uprising in 1883. Since then, mistrust, and that they followed the Shia and not the Sunni branch of Islam, kept many of them as outsiders.

"If the Hazara tribe is trying to incite the rest of Afghanistan, the stealing of the robe would be the thing to put the match to fuel," Sardar said.

"You must be very careful, Sardar," Jamshed said. "If you are right, you will have to do this quietly. We would have to strike quickly. But if you were wrong, it would be your head. You know that?"

Sardar made a tight smile and put his hand over his chest. "Jamshed, I am only a poor servant of God. I assure you, that everything I do is only for the good of Afghanistan. I will make sure I work in quiet until this is resolved."

"I have my faith in you, my friend. Let me know what you find."

"Yes, my friend, *inshallah*, I will have an answer soon," Sardar said. He walked back to the group of men and waved for his son to follow him. He tried not to show the feeling of joy that was brimming inside of him. He'd been able to place the theft onto the Hazara.

Jamshed would discuss this with others in his close family this evening. Afghanis could keep nothing secret. This rumor he'd started would be common knowledge by the end of week.

Chapter Six

Bernadette Callahan realized she had made a mistake and needed to fix it. For the past three days she had languished in the hospital, a police officer outside and the nurses watching her every move.

She would have to accept her return to Canada. That was all there was to it. The nurse arrived with her breakfast and Bernadette smiled.

"Nurse Sharbat, I want to apologize for my attitude. I'm truly sorry."

The nurse put down the breakfast tray. She looked at Bernadette's sad eyes and took her hand. "You have been through much trauma. I know you have come to search for your fiancé, and I cannot know what you must feel now that you must return to your country."

Bernadette brushed a tear from her eye. "Yes, it is sad, but you nurses and the doctor have been wonderful. I have not been the best patient, and for that I'm truly sorry."

"Please, do not be sorry. This will only hamper your

recovery. You must now eat and get better. We will have you back home to your own doctors soon."

She was a pretty, young woman of twenty-six with light brown skin, a cascade of dark brown hair peaking out under her hijab, and bright green eyes. For days she had tried to communicate with Bernadette, but to no avail. Now that Bernadette had accepted her fate, she seemed much happier.

"Will you try to walk a bit today?" Sharbat asked.

"Yes, of course, will you help me?"

"It will be my honor. Now you must eat your halleem and drink your tea."

Bernadette looked at the meal called halleem. It was oatmeal with chicken and cardamom. The tea was green with cardamom and ginger. Neither was appealing to her. Bacon and eggs with rye toast would be preferable. She smiled and took a large spoonful of halleem, put it in her mouth, and winked at Sharbat. Never had she eaten anything as weird as this. To add to the dish, the cook had put a dollop of oil on top.

She finished her tea and oatmeal; Sharbat cleared her tray and then helped her out of bed. Bernadette's feet were wobbly at first. She'd been in bed for five days. The headaches had ceased, but now she had vertigo and the room spun when she turned her head to one side.

Sometimes a crazy slow motion thing happened with her eyes, as if she was watching a movie screen in a jerky frame by frame. It made her sick to her stomach. She hadn't told the doctors or the nurses. She knew they'd keep her longer if she did.

With Nurse Sharbat at her side, she made it down the hall. Other patients, nurses, and a few doctors greeted her as she walked. They came to a stop at the nursing station.

Bernadette had to hold onto the counter to steady her trembling legs.

"I will get a wheel chair to take you back to your room," Sharbat said.

Bernadette smiled weakly. "Let me see how far I can get before you help me. I need to exercise these legs." She turned, walked four more steps, and collapsed.

Sharbat called to the other nurses, "Sisters, please help me get her back to her room."

Two nurses and an orderly picked up Bernadette, put her in a wheel chair, and got her back into bed. Bernadette thanked each of them as they tucked her in.

"Now, you must rest," Sharbat said.

Bernadette nodded and went to sleep.

That afternoon, she was pulling herself out of bed after lunch. She got to her feet and moved down the hall using a wheel chair in front for stability. She made it to the nursing station and halfway back before Nurse Sharbat found her and scolded her.

"You must wait for someone from physiotherapy to come and work with you. They will help to train your legs. Please let us do our job for you."

Bernadette nodded. "You all work so hard, you have so many patients that are much worse. I have only a mild head trauma. Many of your patients have the wounds of war. I'm trying to heal myself so I will not be a burden on you."

"My dear sister, please, you are so brave. Please let me help you," Sharbat said, helping her back into bed.

Bernadette let tears fall freely. Sharbat put her head on her shoulder and rubbed her back as Bernadette fell asleep.

The next day, Bernadette was up and walking without

the wheelchair. She was now going to and from the nursing station. The other nurses marveled at her quick recovery.

Chandra Gupta arrived that afternoon. "I've heard of your recovery and your attitude change." She was wearing the same blue overcoat as before with a different color headscarf, her lipstick a bright red.

Bernadette smiled at Gupta. "Yes, I'm so sorry for my attitude. I realized that in my condition, I should not be running around Afghanistan trying to find Chris. You're doing everything you can and I thank you for that."

Chandra let out a sigh of relief. "We so rarely get thanks in the consulate. Everyone thinks we move at a snail's pace. No one realizes what we are faced with here in Afghanistan."

"Yes, I'm sure you must have a massive task before you. I'll be on my way in a few days once I've made arrangements for my return. Now, if I could just have my passport and my clothes, I'll be getting myself ready."

Chandra stopped. She gave Bernadette a penetrating look as if trying to see into her mind. "Your passport and clothes will be returned to you on your day of departure and you will then be escorted to the airport by either myself or someone from our consulate."

Bernadette nodded and smiled. "Of course. I'm sorry to rush you on that. Thanks again for all of your help."

Chandra seemed to have expected a confrontation, but Bernadette gave her none. She shook hands with Bernadette and left the hospital.

Chandra met with a co-worker that evening for dinner. They were about to dig into a savory dish of lamb and rice when her cell phone rang. "Your Canadian detective has escaped our hospital." Dr. Ahmed said.

Chandra shook her head. "Doctor, she has no passport, she will not get far without that and her visa."

"She picked the lock and took her things from the nursing station. She somehow got past the police. We have no idea where she is."

Chandra rubbed her forehead. "You must alert the police to search for her."

"No," Dr. Ahmed said. "This is a Canadian Consulate matter. The police will not get involved. You will need to find her yourself. If she feels she is well enough to leave, then we cannot stop her. We are only a hospital, not a prison."

Chandra ended her call. Her friend looked at her. "What will you do?"

"Nothing. She has her passport and her visa. I would have to apply to the Afghanis to have her visa revoked. That could take weeks… She got past me with her lie. I underestimated her. I won't do that again."

Chapter Seven

Bernadette's escape had taken her three days to plan. The trips to and from the nursing station allowed her to find out that her passport and documents were in a locked cupboard under a counter.

The sturdy-looking lock on the cupboard had "American Lock" inscribed on it. A criminal she'd arrested many times had told her wiggling a paper clip might work on television, but it was a lie. You needed proper tools.

He'd also told her, "No lock is safe—it's only the time it takes to open it. All you need is time."

In the three days of roaming the halls, she found an unlocked room with surgical supplies. She picked up a surgical tool with a slight bend and a long wire. In the middle of the night, while the nurses did their rounds, she picked the lock. Her criminal acquaintance would have been proud of her.

She retrieved her passport, visa, and wallet with all of her cash and credit cards. Her clothes were a problem, but she'd found a solution.

On the day of her escape, she waited until the night shift change. She slipped out of bed and hurried to the supply room. Donning a set of surgical scrubs, she covered them with a lab coat. The hospital mosque and the evening prayer solved the shoe problem. The shoes were left outside the room.

Bernadette left the hospital with a shawl she found in a cloakroom for her hijab. She nodded to the policeman on duty and found a cab outside the hospital.

"Take me to the American Consulate," she instructed the driver.

The American Consulate bristled with security and two stern-looking U.S. Marines with machine guns stood guard. The cab could not park in front with the numerous metal bollards to keep away suicide bombers.

Bernadette paid the driver and approached the marines slowly. She knew that making sudden moves could get her shot. They were on high alert to protect their consulate.

"I'm here to see Christina Lackey," Bernadette said as she opened her lab coat to show she had no weapons.

"You have an appointment with her?" the marine asked. His name said Simons. He was large, black, and had a scowl that looked like he'd be happy to unleash a few rounds of M16 bullets into someone who pissed him off.

"No, but I was instructed to meet with her when I arrived in Kandahar."

The other marine, his name was Plinkton. He looked all of twenty-two with pink blotchy skin and pale blue eyes that stared at Bernadette as his finger covered his machine gun. He'd lowered the gun while Simons looked at her passport.

"I'll call her, see if she's here," Simons said.

He dialed a number, listened, and then spoke into the phone. All Bernadette could hear was some 'aha, yes ma'am's. A minute later he said she could enter. They took her behind the blast wall and searched her. She felt the chill of the night as they ran their hands over her in search of weapons or bombs. They cleared her, and a third marine came out to escort her inside.

Plinkton turned to Simons. "Who the hell is Lackey? I didn't know we had anyone inside by that name."

Simons turned his head back to the street, "You can forget you did, she's the resident spook for Kandahar."

"What the hell is a spook?" Plinkton asked.

"You are green. That's CIA."

Christina Lackey sat in a small barren room inside the American Consulate. She was forty-three, with a pale complexion and platinum blonde hair. Her features were non-descript; she could pass you on the street and you'd forget what she looked like moments later. In high school back in Bakersfield, California, her nickname was Flaky. The bitches on the cheerleading team gave it to her.

Christina never forgot their taunting. When she entered the CIA, she made sure all of them were put on the TSA's watch list. They had a hell of time flying anywhere and never knew why.

As Christina sat there in the room, she had been looking at the recent reports coming in from her operatives in the field. Rumors were circulating of a civil war between the Pashtuns, Tajik, and the Hazara. All of it seemed to be over the stolen robe. That this Bernadette Callahan had walked into her consulate this evening was a bonus; she had a lot of questions to ask her.

Bernadette was shown into her room. "Thanks for seeing me. I didn't know if you'd received word from

Carla Winston. She'd told me to look you up when I got here."

Lackey motioned for her to take a chair. "I had a report that you got your bell rung by an RPG. I thought you were headed home."

"I was sidelined, but now I'm back on the hunt for my fiancé."

Lackey opened a desk drawer, pulling out a bottle of Scotch and two glasses. She filled the glasses and pushed one towards Bernadette. "Winston said you had guts. I'm glad they didn't end up on the highway."

"Cheers to that," Bernadette said. She lifted her glass and let the Scotch slowly ebb its way down her throat. "You know how to make a girl feel welcome. This makes up for all that green tea."

Lackey swallowed hers. "Maybe you can solve some of the mystery we're having now that you're here."

"What's that?"

"Your fiancé, what was his position in the police force back in Canada?"

"He was a constable in the Royal Canadian Mounted Police."

Lackey leaned back in her chair and swished her Scotch in the glass. "In the major crimes division or working narcotics?"

Bernadette let out a chuckle. "God no. He was trained in police work, but he'd spent all of his time in small Canadian communities. His last posting was an island on Canada's west coast where he tracked down stolen fishing boats and intercepted the odd drug trafficker."

Bernadette took another long drink of her Scotch and put her glass down. "You want to tell me where this line of questioning is going?"

"I need to know how your man could be involved in the supposed theft of one of the most sacred robes in this country. As of right now, three tribes are ready to do battle in the streets of Kandahar."

Bernadette sat up. "What? I didn't know that Chris was implicated in any theft."

"That's the story we got from the sacred museum that held the robe. The imam of the mosque next door said he had given a viewing to a man named Lund and to someone who looked like your Chris. The imam said he locked up and came back to find the robe gone.

"Was there security footage?"

"Only for the meeting with the imam. Later that evening the footage was taped over," Lackey said.

"Sounds like a set-up."

"Could well be. Most things in this country are lies on top of lies. I need to find someone who knows what happened. I also need to find this robe and get it back to the museum before a civil war breaks out."

"Can I see the tape from that night?" Bernadette asked.

"It's with the police chief of Kandahar. I can set up a meeting for us tomorrow. Do you have a place to stay tonight?"

"Yes, the Continental Guest House. I'm a bit late for my check in, but I'm sure I'll get a room."

"You're right, this city doesn't have a flood of visitors, I'll have our marines take you there." Lackey allowed a slight smile. "Get some rest. And…get some clothes; I'm sure the hospital might want those back."

Bernadette got into an armored Humvee with two marines. They drove through the darkened streets to the guesthouse.

The place had a single light outside. Large walls surrounded it with a guard at the formidable door.

The guesthouse had high ceilings and ornate columns. It had once been the opulent home of a wealthy merchant of Kandahar who'd made his money off the Russians and fled when the Taliban arrived.

She entered, checked in, and was shown to a simple room with two single beds an ancient television, and a closet. There was shower and toilet that looked like they'd seen better days. She found a bottle of water in the small fridge and collapsed on the bed. She wondered how she was going to proceed the next day. She wanted to go to sleep so badly, but her dreams had been of Chris. Some of them were good, and in some she saw him dead.

She lay flat on her back and breathed slowly until she finally fell into a deep sleep. Tomorrow would come, and her hunt for Chris would finally begin.

Chapter Eight

Chris watched the sun come through the broken bricks of the hut he was in. How many days had he been here? He'd tried to scratch each day on a wall beside him. His captors found his markings and scraped it off. The days were registered from the sun coming through the bricks. A small beam of sunlight hit the far wall and moved across the room until darkness fell.

The only person who spoke to him was an Afghani named Gul. He brought him his two meals a day and took out his chamber pot. He had a small bed on the floor and a plastic jug for water. Chris was used to roughing it in the woods in Canada, but this was beyond anything he had experienced.

He'd lost weight. His clothes hung on him. His face had sprouted a beard and he could use a shower in the worst way. The room was cold. The wind blew snow and rain in through cracks in the walls. He finally convinced Gul to give him some firewood for the metal stove in the hut.

Gul came in, brought him more wood and water that morning. Chris watched him from the corner of the hut.

"You are well?" Gul asked.

"Yes, I am well," Chris replied. This was the same conversation they'd had for several weeks. Gul spoke reasonable English. He was in his mid-thirties with the standard Afghani beard and customary dress. He wore an army issue parka from the Afghan National Army. Chris wondered if he'd stolen it or killed for it.

"I have a question," Chris said. He watched Gul drop his daily wood supply by the stove.

Gul stopped and looked at Chris. "I am not sure I have answers."

"You have taken no video of me to prove I am alive. Why is that?" Chris asked. He watched Gul's eyes to see how the question resonated with him.

Gul busied himself with the firewood. "We will do it soon. We need someone to come with video machine. We do not have in this village."

Chris knew he was lying. They could use a cell phone to make a video. He'd seen several of his captors talking on cell phones in the village.

"Do not worry," Gul said. "We will take video of you, send to your government, they will pay ransom, you will be set free."

Chris shook his head. "I am Canadian, and my government does not pay ransom. I told your people weeks ago. Seems no one is listening."

Gul finished with the wood then brought in another large plastic jug of water and set it inside the hut. "You have wife?"

"I have a fiancé…yes, I have an almost wife," Chris said.

He realized Gul probably did not understand the word fiancé.

Gul smiled. "I have an almost wife."

"You are getting married?" Chris asked.

"No, no. I have relations with another man's wife in the village," Gul said.

"Ah I see. How is that working out?"

"Not good. The wife's husband has asked the warlord to have me killed," Gul said in a matter-of-fact tone.

Chris shook his head. In the time he'd been captive, this Gul had been the only one who spoke to him. The others treated him with disdain. Some spit in his direction. A dark-skinned young man named Aktar pulled his finger across his throat to signify his death whenever he was near him.

Gul, as crazy as his conversations were, was somewhat harmless compared to the others. Chris hoped the warlord didn't kill him.

"Do you have a way out of this?" Chris asked.

"I have gone to the village imam; he may give me a pardon. I have offered to pay him if he will come to my aid," Gul said.

"You can do that?"

Gul shrugged. "Sometimes, the imam will see someone's side. Under Sharia law, there must be four witnesses to adultery. We have only three now. The husband's two brothers and his uncle saw me leaving their hut."

"In Canada, that would be enough for a divorce. I've known lawyers that would have convicted you for much less."

"Yes, that is why we are ruled by our Sharia law."

Chris took his meal of lamb and rice and took a spoonful. The lamb was tough, the rice was cold, and with a gulp of water he was able to get it down. He did not want to get into discussion with Gul on Sharia law. This Afghani was the only one of his captors who treated him reasonably well. He wanted to keep it that way.

When Gul had learned that Chris was from Toronto, Canada, he asked him if he'd help Gul immigrate there. He had a cousin who lived there and operated a cleaning and delivery business.

"You will help me move to Canada?" Gul had asked just days after Chris's capture.

"Sure," Chris had replied. He didn't want to tell him that as a Taliban, he was the member of an organization that was listed as illegal and terrorist by almost every country in the world. If he did get to Canada, he'd be a guest in their prison system until he was deported back to Afghanistan to serve time in their prison.

"I go now," Gul said. "Be well." He walked out of the hut, closing the door behind him. A loud clang of metal on metal sounded as the lock was put in place.

Chris went back to his usual day of being captive. He could see out of a small peephole in the wall. It gave him a view of the center of the village. He'd watch every day to see if any of the other captives were there. They'd been separated as soon as they got to this village.

He tried to figure out where they were. They'd marched for three days into the mountains. A narrow pass with rocky walls was on either side as they came into a valley and this village. They arrived here at night so he didn't know how big the village was. Ten buildings with mud walls surrounded one large tree where the men congregated. They sat on their haunches, smoked cigarettes, and conversed in low tones.

Other than the sounds of some goats and chickens in the area there were almost no signs of life. A dog might bark at night, then silence. He'd strained to listen for sounds of a helicopter or a drone overhead. He'd heard nothing.

Until today. He saw a man he'd thought he'd seen before. He was dressed in robes similar to that of the village imam. He was tall, his beard trimmed, he walked with the air of someone who must be respected. The others lowered their eyes and put their hands over their hearts as a sign of respect and acknowledgement. The village imam and the warlord came forward to greet him. They moved off in a corner, away from the Taliban fighters.

They spoke in low tones. Their heads moved and gestured towards Chris' hut and then to several others in the square. Were they doing an inventory of their captives? Chris wondered what they were up to. Was this the day they would make the proof of live video? He breathed slowly as he watched them talk, wishing so much he'd taken the lessons in Pashtun that Max their interpreter had offered him. He thought that he was never coming back here. Now he was a prisoner with no translator. How stupid was he?

The warlord and the village imam were making a case for something. The other man finally agreed and they smiled at one another. The warlord walked over to his men, gave a command, and they followed him to a door of a hut.

Chris watched in horror as they dragged Max, their interpreter, out of the hut. Max screamed in Pashto; he knew what was coming. The Taliban took turns inflicting wounds on him, laughing as he screamed louder. His screams echoed into the silent valley. The torture seemed to go on forever, was it an hour? Was it more? Chris couldn't watch but the screams extended into the deepest reaches of his mind that even with his hands pressed tightly over his ears; he could not block it out.

The warlord seemed to think Max had been tortured

enough. He walked over to him, put his AK47 to his head, and pulled the trigger. Max's head jerked back as if kicked by a mule.

Chris retched on the floor of his hut. He couldn't believe what he was seeing, but Max had warned him that the Taliban would torture and murder him. This was their way. Chris remembered Max wished to be killed immediately rather than surrender to them.

Now, he wished he'd done it. A quick shot to the head would have been so much better for Max than what the Taliban had done to him.

He watched them drag his body away. Would they kill all the captives? What was happening here? Who were these crazy Taliban that made no proof of life videos and no demands of ransom?

He was trying not to lose his faith that Bernadette was out there somewhere trying to find him. She was the most determined person he'd ever met. He knew in his heart that she was doing everything in her power, but he hoped she wasn't foolish enough to come to Afghanistan to find him. Sooner or later, the Taliban would want money and they would send out a message for ransom. He hoped someone would find the money to pay it, but then again, he hoped they'd bargained lower. He wasn't feeling worth that much at this moment.

Chris went back to his bed and tried to muster his courage, hoping fleetingly that his death was quicker than Max's.

Chapter Nine

Bernadette awoke to the sound of a low wailing. She got out of bed, rubbing the sleep from her eyes. Her bare feet on the cold tile floor sent a chill up her body. She walked to the shuttered window. It would not open. Turning an ear to the sound, she realized it was the Muslim call to prayer.

A clock on the table displayed 0645 hours. She stretched, yawned, and looked around the room. It was just as barren as when she'd checked in just before midnight. A small computer sat on a corner table. A sign proclaimed *Free Internet to Guests*. This was a godsend to Bernadette. She had no idea where her iPad or cellphone that she'd brought with her were. They could still be under lock and key back in the hospital or bits of charred plastic if they'd burned up in the truck blast.

She would need to locate a cell phone at least. And clothes; the ones she'd brought with her were in the back of the truck. The surgical scrubs and white lab coat were sufficient to break out of the hospital, but not a good thing for the meeting with the police chief, if that ever happened.

The shower was cold, but not any colder than she expected, and the towels were coarse enough to exfoliate her skin. It left her with a healthy red glow afterwards.

By 0715 she found breakfast in the main dining hall of the guesthouse. No one said anything about her outfit. She'd read the Afghanis would never ask anything about you unless you offered it. They thought it rude to pry. At this moment, she was thankful for that. Only two other men occupied the dining room. They looked eastern European, dressed in ill-fitting suits.

The dining room server was a young boy of sixteen or seventeen. He had a large mop of hair and dark brown eyes, which he cast downward as he approached her.

"I have special Afghani breakfast if you wish, madam."

"Is it oatmeal with chicken?" Bernadette asked, hoping it wasn't.

The boy shook his head, "No madam, this is eggs, tomatoes, and potatoes with naan bread. Would you like tea or coffee?"

"Coffee, please," Bernadette said with almost too much enthusiasm. "And yes please, to your wonderful breakfast suggestion."

"My pleasure, madam."

"And may I know your name, please?"

"Aaron, madam." He bowed with one hand over his heart.

He brought back a steaming mug of hot coffee. Sugar and milk were on the table. Bernadette stirred in the sugar, added a splash of milk, and took a sip of caffeine that zoomed all the way to her solar plexus and struck her central nervous system in seconds. Everything was right with the world for the next few nanoseconds.

Aaron brought the steaming plate of food. Two eggs

had been cooked sunny side up in an aromatic stew of tomatoes, onion and potatoes. A large portion of naan bread was on the side. Bernadette had eaten naan bread in East Indian restaurants; it was usually baked in a clay oven and basted with butter. She tore into the bread. It was light, buttery and hot; she felt like her spirit was returning with every bite.

She finished her breakfast, thanking Aaron profusely for the fine meal. He brought her three more coffee refills, making her stomach virtually swimming in caffeine and the butter from the naan bread.

When Aaron came back to offer her more coffee, she raised her hand. "Thank you, I've had enough. Please tell me if there is a shop nearby where I might purchase some things? I need some clothes and a cell phone."

"Yes, Madame, there is a bazaar very close, only minutes to walk, but you must not go on your own. I will accompany you," Aaron said.

"But I can't impose on you. You have work to do here," Bernadette protested.

"No, my work is our guests. I will take you. I will also have my uncle from the front desk come as well. It is very dangerous on the streets right now. We will make sure you are safe." Aaron raised his eyes to look at Bernadette for the first time. The seriousness was evident in his eyes.

Aaron and his uncle, Jangi Shah, escorted Bernadette to the bazaar. She was able to purchase several items of clothing including some almost passable undergarments, a small bag to hold them in, and a cell phone. She realized the disposable cell phone was probably the same one the Taliban used, but she needed it. She paid in the Afghani currency she had and made it back to the guesthouse with Aaron and Jangi.

Back in her room, she changed out of her hospital scrubs and into the new clothes. A long mirror on the wall showed her looking like an Afghan woman. The pants billowed to hide the form of her legs, and the long overcoat covered almost all of her features. She would be fine.

She pulled on her hijab, tilting her head to one side. The room spun around her. Stumbling to the bed, she sat down. "Damn vertigo."

She straightened herself, letting the focus come back to her eyes. She would have to keep from looking down or to the side, as those motions seemed to set the vertigo off. When she had time, she would figure how to deal with this, but right now there was nothing to do but get back on the trail of finding Chris.

She dialed the number of Christina Lackey. She put the phone in front of her eyes to dial, not wanting another episode.

The phone rang several times before Lackey answered. "Lackey here, who's calling?"

"It's me, Bernadette Callahan."

"You need to put an identifier on your phone next time you call." Lackey said in terse tone.

"Ah, yeah, sure," Bernadette said. She'd forgotten to do that and realized that Lackey probably did not answer calls from people she did not know in Afghanistan.

"I have a meeting set for one hour from now with the police chief. He said we can see the tape of the museum theft, but he won't give us a copy."

"How long will we be able to study it for?"

"Knowing him, it won't be long," Lackey said. "But if

you're willing to go outside the normal procedures, I know how we can get a copy."

"No idea what you're talking about, but if it gets us a copy of the tape, I'm in."

"I had a feeling you'd say that. Be ready outside your place in a half hour, I'll be there to pick you up."

Bernadette closed her phone. She had no idea what outside normal procedures would be. Lackey was CIA, which meant she dealt outside of everything Bernadette was accustomed to; she just hoped it didn't get her into trouble with the Afghani Police.

Chapter Ten

Lackey pulled up in an old Toyota SUV with a bearded driver who looked more Afghani than American. He motioned for Bernadette to jump in the back seat. Lackey turned around in her seat.

"Here's the deal, Callahan, we'll be there in twenty minutes so listen up. The Afghani police station is like an armed camp. It's been attacked numerous times by the Taliban, and each time the Taliban have breached their security and killed numerous police and blown up part of the building."

"Sounds like they need to work on a new security system."

"They have, but it never works. Everyone knows there are Taliban infiltrators working in the police station; it's just a way of life. So, you need to be very careful what you say and what you ask the police chief when we're in there—you read me?"

"I totally get it. How do we get a copy of the video stream?"

Lackey pulled out a small, matte black device that was as thin as a dime. "This is remote copying device. It has a sticky on one side. You need to attach it to the police chief's computer while I distract him. This will give us instant access to his files."

"What if he finds it? Won't he know we placed it there?"

"I have an Afghani who works for us in the maintenance department in the police station. He'll remove it late tonight," Lackey said.

"Sounds good. Any idea how to distract him?"

"We'll think up something, just follow my lead," Lackey said.

Outside the police station, steel and concrete bollards rose from the pavement to stop a potential vehicle from ramming the building with bombs. The windows were covered with wire and metal sheeting to keep rocket propelled grenades from piercing them. The top of the building had several machine gun turrets lining the roof and the doorway had two behind sandbags.

Bernadette felt her body tense as she exited their vehicle and walked to the entrance. Two police pointed rifles at them, telling them to lift up their arms and open their coats. After a pat down and scan of IDs the police allowed them to enter the building once the police chief cleared them for their meeting.

They were introduced to Chief Ahmad Khan. He looked young, in his late 20's. He had short-cropped black hair with a light beard. He was thin and tall, wearing military fatigues with red markings on his collar that signified his rank.

Lackey had told Bernadette on the ride over that

Ahmad Khan had been a general in the Afghan forces, taking the position of police chief after the Taliban had murdered the previous one.

Khan greeted them. "*As-salam alaykom.*"

Lackey and Bernadette responded with *wa'alaikum assalam*.

"I am not used to being visited by the head of the CIA," Khan said. "Why am I being honored with your presence?"

Lackey didn't smile at his inference; the Afghani's sense of humor was known to be dry and he often threw in questions to catch his guests off guard. "Thank you for seeing us, I have brought Detective Callahan with me. Her fiancé was taken by the Taliban with Mr. Lund."

Khan focused his eyes on Bernadette. "I see—" He stopped himself, waiting for Lackey to continue.

Lackey hated the way Kahn did these cat and mouse interviews. She had two other meetings with him, and getting to the point was always a roundabout exercise.

"It seems that Mr. Lund and Ms. Callahan's fiancé are implicated in the theft of the robe from the museum." Lackey volunteered. She needed to move this along.

"Ah, yes." Khan turned to Bernadette. "Your man is in very grave trouble. We want to find him and charge him with theft."

Bernadette turned to Lackey. "Can we see the evidence they have?"

"Yes," Lackey said, turning back to Khan, "we'd like to see the video taken from the museum."

"You do not believe our police report?" Khan challenged.

"I saw the police report, it's just that the detective would like to see the video with her own eyes. She would also like to see that it was in fact her fiancé."

"I am a very busy man. Showing you evidence of a theft that we know has already taken place is a waste of my time."

"Please, Ahmed Khan, if you would indulge us, for this woman has traveled all this way to find her fiancé," Lackey said in a soft tone.

Bernadette watched this exchange. She could see Lackey was very good at her job. She made no demands, just reasoned. She hoped it worked.

Khan looked at both women, and sighed. "Very well." He turned and punched some keys on his laptop, found the video, and brought it up. He turned the laptop around and pushed it towards them. "You can see for yourselves, these two men are thieves."

The video came on. Bernadette stared at the laptop screen as the front of the museum came into view. The front door opened. Two men walked out. One of them was holding something.

"May we enlarge the screen?" Lackey asked.

"Please do." Khan replied.

Bernadette moved her hand forward to hit the button. Her other hand slid the thin receiver disk under the computer.

The enlarged screen showed Chris and Lund walking out of the building. Lund stopped. He was holding something then handed it to Chris. Someone was behind them. The lights in the square went out. Chris and Lund walked down to the SUV in semi-darkness.

Bernadette sat back in her chair. "How does this prove they stole the robe?"

"They were the only ones in the building with the Imam. He believes they picked the lock and forced open the sacred chest."

"There's no time stamp on this video," Bernadette said.

"But you can see the darkness of night. There are no streetlights on. It is after curfew. Therefore, they entered after the museum closed for the evening," Khan said.

"So you're saying Lund and Chris had a meeting with the Imam to figure out where the robe was, then picked the lock, smashed the case, and stole that night?"

"Yes, detective, you are clever. They did what you call 'case the joint'," Khan said with a smile.

"There's only one problem with your idea," Bernadette said.

"What is that?"

"Chris is not that stupid."

"Please explain…"

"Chris is a member of the Royal Canadian Mounted Police, trained in criminal investigation techniques. No one in their right mind would come into a museum the very night of a robbery, meet with the imam and then steal a high valued asset that same night."

Khan took the laptop back and turned it towards him. "But, as you can see, this is the evidence we have. Your fiancé was the last one seen holding the robe. I think that speaks for itself."

Bernadette was about to say something—she saw a hand signal from Lackey it was time to end this meeting.

"Thank you, Ahmed Khan, you have been most generous with your time. We will leave you to continue your duties," Lackey said.

Khan smiled. "It was my pleasure. I'm sorry that the evidence is so clear."

They walked out of the police station. Numerous police were milling around with AK47's and rifles. Bernadette didn't feel comfortable until they got back into their vehicle.

"What do you think?" Lackey asked Bernadette.

"Total bullshit," Bernadette said. "I think this is some kind of a setup. How soon can we view the tape again? I need to see real close-ups of the video."

Lackey turned to the driver of the vehicle. "What do you think?"

He smiled at the small device he had in his hands. It looked like a large phone with an antenna. "I just downloaded the video and a whole shit load of police files in the same folder. We'll need our translator to transcribe it, but we could have this inside of six hours."

"Will you call me when you have it?" Bernadette asked.

"I'll be happy to," Lackey said. "If we find the robe, I stop about a dozen tribes from killing each other, makes me happy. What's your next move?"

"I'm going to see Vincent Caprinski. He was the team leader of the security force. I want to find out where they were possibly headed. Maybe I'll know where to look."

Lackey's eyes narrowed. "You really believe your fiancé is alive? There's been no demand for ransom. This is so outside the Taliban norm. They fire off a ransom note inside a week tops. They start with an outrageous sum and we negotiate for about a month and get a release. They get their money, we get the person back."

Bernadette lowered her eyes. "Yeah, I read all this on the reports. I know it's crazy, but I just feel he's out there, still alive."

"Okay, you stay out of trouble until I get the downloads and video feed from my IT guys, then I'll call you for a meet-up."

They dropped Bernadette off at her guesthouse. She walked in to see Reza standing in the lobby.

"I thought you'd left me," Bernadette said.

Reza put his hand over his heart and bowed his head. "Please, I am sorry. I tried many times to see you in the hospital, but they would not let me in. I heard from my sister who works at the hospital that you had left. I came here today to enquire how you are."

"I'm fine," Bernadette said, aside from the vertigo, she thought. "I just had a meeting with the chief of police, it seems I did not need your assistance. Is it possible that you can go to the hospital and have your sister get my things? I had some clothes there, and maybe my phone and iPad survived the attack."

"Yes, of course. I will do this right away." Reza bowed and walked away.

"Good, meet me back here in three hours. I'll have need of your translation for someone I want to visit."

Reza stopped and turned. "This meeting will be in Kandahar?"

"Yes, it will be. But if we have to go into the country, do you have a problem with that?'

The color drained from Reza's face. "All the teachers in my country school were murdered by the Taliban. I alone escaped. They have an oath to torture and kill all translators that they find. You must understand the danger I'm under."

"Yes, Reza, I will make sure you are protected if we have to go to the country or I'll find someone else if you are not feeling up to it," Bernadette said.

Reza opened his mouth to say something, then stopped. He bowed with his hand over his heart and walked away.

Bernadette returned to her room. She wanted to lie down. Today had been more taxing on her than she would have thought. She opened her door and walked into the room. Something about the room was off. It looked like someone had been in it. She walked around and looked at the drawers. She hadn't anything to unpack so hadn't opened or closed them. They were slightly ajar.

She checked around the room and looked for any small devices similar to what she'd seen Lackey use. She couldn't see anything, but that didn't mean that someone hadn't left something in an air vent. She went back to the front desk and asked for a room change. She would be diligent when she left her room the next time.

Police Chief Khan was busy on his phone. The reports were coming in from all over the city of tribal battles. Men with rocket-propelled grenades had taken over the rooftops in the central market. He needed to coordinate with the Afghan National Army and the NATO troops. If this tribal warfare became worse they could cut off the main road to the airport, then the city would shut down.

He told his sergeant they would have a meeting in the conference room. As he grabbed his laptop, a small disk fell from the bottom, dropping to the floor and rolling until it stopped at the door.

He picked it up. It was thin with a smooth surface on one side. He swore under his breath. "Those women were very cunning. But they are playing with the wrong person."

Chapter Eleven

Bernadette was heading out the lobby of the guesthouse when Aaron caught up to her. "Where is madam going?"

She stopped and looked at the boy. "I have someone I need to see." Her mind was set on seeing Caprinski, and she did not want or need an interpreter in her way.

"You cannot go into the streets of Kandahar without some protection. I will arrange it for you. Wait here."

Aaron disappeared behind the front desk. There was some shouting and much conversation. He appeared holding the hand of an old man. He was hunched over, he limped slightly, and his face was withered with so many wrinkles and lines it was hard to see where his eyes unfolded out of the crevasses on his face.

Bernadette put up her hand. "Please, Aaron, I do not mean to offend, but this man looks like he should be lying down and taking a nap."

"No, madam, this is Fazel. He is old, but one of the fierce fighters of the Mujahedeen against the Russians."

"Mujahedeen," Fazel exclaimed with a smile that showed few teeth.

"But...I'm not sure if I need protection," Bernadette protested.

"The streets have become very dangerous, madam. Fazel will keep you safe. He is very low cost, only two thousand Afghanis per day."

Bernadette looked at Fazel. He held an AK47 that he used to keep himself upright. In his belt was a long knife. One of his eyes was partly clouded from a cataract the other bright blue and searching her face for approval.

She sighed and smiled. "Yes, Aaron, I will take Fazel as my bodyguard, thank you."

Fazel put his hand to his chest and bowed, saying something in Afghani.

"What did he say?" Bernadette asked.

"He said he will protect you with his life, as if you were his own daughter," Aaron said. "And I will accompany you as well. You will need me to translate to the driver."

They moved out of the guesthouse, which was slow going as Fazel could only shuffle using his weapon as a walking stick. Bernadette hoped that seeing a man in the the cab with a weapon might deter any would-be attacker. She hoped he didn't fall asleep on the journey.

With the help of Aaron, she gave instructions to the cab driver and they were on their way. Fazel perked up. He somehow became more upright in the back of the cab. His weapon was sitting across his hips. He racked the AK47, placing his finger across the trigger guard.

His one good eye watched every movement in the street. When he saw something he didn't like, he yelled to the cab driver to go around objects or take side streets. Bernadette felt more comfortable with Fazel. He might be old, but he still had the fire of the fighter in him.

The streets were crowded with heavily armed men. They carried AK47s and rocket propelled grenade launchers over their shoulders. They looked casual, like this was an everyday affair, just another day at war with each other. Some bodies lay on the ground, but no one seemed to tend to them, and the cab driver moved on without looking left or right.

They arrived at the headquarters of Chris's former security company. Bernadette had not called ahead. Phone conversations with Vince Caprinski had never gone well. She didn't expect to be greeted warmly.

The taxi pulled up in front of the high wall that shielded the building from the street. Two men stood outside in heavy body armor. They looked like the typical security types she'd seen in Kandahar. Large biceps, large chests, and some overlarge stomachs from long hours in the gym with weights and no time running laps like they used to in the military.

Bernadette got out and approached the men. "I'm here to meet with Caprinski."

The man with the nametag Vincent stared at her out of his Maui Jim sunglasses. "You got a meeting with him?"

"Yes, I do. Tell him Callahan is here to see him. I'm just a bit late." She didn't mention she was about six days late, but too much information would be lost on this hunk of beef.

"Okay," Vincent said. "You can follow me, but your old man and the kid stay out here."

Bernadette motioned for Fazel and Aaron to stay with the taxi. Fazel took up a position beside the cab, his AK47 now waist high. His limp was gone. He stared at the other security guard as if he was a mongoose eyeing a snake. The man shifted his stance and looked away.

Bernadette followed Vincent down a long barren hallway with bare bulbs and threadbare carpets. An old brown cat stared at them with mild curiosity then moved on.

Vincent arrived at a door, knocked twice, and shouted, "Caprinski, visitor." He walked back down the hall and back to his post.

Caprinski looked up as Bernadette entered, his eyes went from expectation to dismay then to disgust. "I thought you were done in by that RPG hit last week."

Bernadette walked into his office and took the unoffered chair in front of the desk. She looked around the room; there was a single poster on the wall. The poster was the Hotel California from the Eagles Album. The caption read, "You can check out, but you can never leave."

Caprinski glared at her, he was all of thirty-eight, tall with big chest and large arms. He didn't have the beer gut the others had. He hated beer, drank Scotch. He looked to Bernadette like the typical Jarhead, square jaw, high forehead with shaved head and a neck extended from his shoulders that looked like it was bulging with steroids.

"The rumors of my demise were greatly exaggerated," Bernadette said. She pulled her scarf off her head and stared at Caprinski. "I think that was Mark Twain who said that. But it doesn't matter. I spent some time in the hospital and here I am. I'm looking for information on Chris' disappearance."

Caprinski leaned back in his chair. "You could have saved yourself the trip. I told you everything on the phone. I have no idea where Lund was heading. I can't help you."

"Are you his chief security officer?"

"Yes, I am."

"He wouldn't tell you what village he was going to or the road he was taking to get there?"

"Nope, he was tight lipped on the whole thing."

Bernadette stared at Caprinski; his eyes flickered to the left. Such a tell-tale sign of a lie, even a rookie would have caught it.

"And you're the senior person here, am I right?"

"Yes, that's correct." His voice was getting tighter.

"Why didn't you go on the mission?"

"Look, I don't always go on every trip outside the wire, I mean out of town."

"I know what you meant."

"Good, I'm not on every trip, sometimes I just send out a team of whoever we have, and try not to mix in too many shit magnets," Caprinski said, crossing his arms.

He was getting defensive. She needed to relax him, so she paused before she spoke. "What's a shit magnet?"

"Guys that seem to always get shot at or run over IED's when they're out there."

"So, who was the shit magnet on the mission?"

"Well, hate to say it, your guy Chris. He had a way of getting himself into trouble."

"Care to elaborate?" Bernadette asked. She leaned forward; even though it was against her instincts, it got him to lean back further. "Sorry, I don't mean to sound hostile, it's just the first I've heard this term and my fiancé in the same sentence."

She leaned back in her chair, placing her arms by her side and looked down at the desk. Caprinski relaxed and unfolded his arms.

"Look, I know it's hard to hear your guy was constantly getting in trouble, but he had no sense of the danger he was in. He'd always go too far ahead of the team, start yacking it up with the locals, and before you know it, some Taliban would fire a couple of rounds in his direction. He was just goofy. I should have sent him back two months ago."

"And you didn't, why?"

Caprinski exhaled and placed both hands on the desk. "You have to understand that we've been desperate for personnel for some time. The thing about Chris was he had everyone's back. No matter how bad it was out there, he took all the shit that was thrown at him and stood his ground."

"Well, that's Chris, he could definitely take it, and yes he's quite the talker, always meeting people…"

Bernadette rose from her chair. "I think you've answered all my questions, for now. Would you mind giving me a list of the personnel who went missing with Chris?"

Caprinski eyed her for a moment then turned to his computer. "Sure, don't know what good it will do you." He printed it and handed her a copy.

"Thanks, you've been great. I'll let you know what I find," Bernadette said as she turned and wheeled out of the room. She tried to walk as softly as possible down the hall. Clenching and unclenching her fists helped her conceal her rage. She'd never heard a larger spiel of crap from anyone. Caprinski was lying his ass off. She needed to find out why.

The return trip back to the guesthouse was a blur to Bernadette. They made numerous diversions to avoid fighting in the streets. NATO forces had roadblocks to try to keep the warring tribes apart. It didn't seem to help. Fighters took to the rooftops to fire off rounds at each other.

They arrived at the guesthouse to find Reza waiting for them. Bernadette jumped out of the cab and ran to him.

"Reza, I need you to come with me."

"But, the curfew is soon. The army will be closing the streets."

Bernadette almost grabbed his arm, and then held back. "We're going to the shrine the robe was stolen from. I have some questions I need to ask the cleric. I need you to translate."

Chapter Twelve

The taxi moved into the street. Reza and Bernadette were in the back. Fazel sat beside the driver. He spoke constantly, telling the driver which streets to take, which ones to avoid. The sounds of gunfire and explosions were everywhere.

Reza sat beside Bernadette muttering how dangerous this was. He was also anxious about prayer time. They would be cutting it close. It was 1645 hours. The sunset prayer would happen at 1745 hours.

The Shrine of the Robe was only two kilometers from the guesthouse, but it took a half hour to get there with all the detours. The taxi parked, let them out, and sped away. The driver now cared more for his life than his cab fare.

Bernadette walked up to the wide staircase with Reza. Two policemen armed with AK-47's stood guard outside the shrine. Fazel had to stay in the street with this weapon. The police had already waved him off the moment he put one foot on the stairs.

The heavy door was open; they walked inside, where

they were greeted by a young boy. Reza asked the boy to get the cleric. The boy rushed off to find him.

"You must be very careful here. Please do not offend the cleric by talking to him directly. I will translate all questions you have. Be sure to keep your eyes on the ground as you speak," Reza cautioned.

"Do not tell him I'm related to the man accused of stealing the robe," Bernadette said. "Say I'm here to investigate on behalf of the Canadian Consulate."

"But is this true?" Reza asked.

"Of course," Bernadette said. She took a breath at the depth of her lie, but at this moment, telling the cleric she was related in any way to Chris would set him off.

When the cleric arrived he made his salaams to Reza and ignored her. Reza made his introduction and told him why they were there. The cleric exploded in a long stream of words that sounded like a man in state of panic.

Reza turned towards Bernadette. "The cleric says if the Canadian Consulate is concerned with the return of the robe, they should have been here weeks ago."

Bernadette nodded in the direction of Reza. "Yes, tell him we are very sorry for the loss, we seek to do everything possible to have the robe returned."

The cleric exploded again at Reza's translation. Bernadette could see this was getting nowhere.

"Reza, ask him if he saw either man leave with the robe."

There was more explosive words and hand waving of arms from the cleric.

"No, he did not. The robe was here under lock and key when he left."

"Then who was left here with the robe?"

"He claims that the imam was here. He said the imam let them out and locked the door after them."

"And the key, who had it?"

"He says the imam locked up."

"And the door was not forced open?"

"No, he says the door was perfectly fine."

Bernadette walked to the door they had entered. It was very old, very solid. The locks were old and sturdy, but could also be picked easily.

"Reza, one more thing. Ask him how long the police have guarded the shrine?"

Reza translated and turned to Bernadette. "They have been here ever since the theft. There is now twenty-four-hour security. He says this should have been done long ago."

"Thank him for his time," Bernadette said.

They turned and walked out of the shrine. Two lights came on overhead as the call to Muslim Prayer was sounding. A long shadow was cast by a large earthenware jar beside the door. Bernadette looked up to see where the CCTV camera was positioned.

"We must get you back to the guesthouse," Reza said.

Bernadette looked up and down the street and noted several taxis had arrived, the drivers getting out to go to prayer.

"Why don't Fazel and you go to prayer, I'll be okay. Then we can grab one of these taxis after."

"But it will not be safe in the streets for you." Reza said.

"I'll be fine. Tell Fazel I need to borrow his gun while he's at prayer, he can't take it into the mosque anyway."

Fazel was reluctant but handed over his prized Russian AK47. It felt heavy but sturdy in Bernadette's arms. She watched them enter the mosque next to the shrine then she took up a position inside a doorway across the street.

She could see the entire street and the front of the shrine. She watched as the last of the light faded from the sky. The shrine lit up.

There were few streetlights; the two policemen were backlit by the shrine. They huddled together for warmth and smoked cigarettes. They couldn't see her from the doorway she hid in. She let her eyes run over the entrance, then out into the street. No other CCTV cameras were visible.

When the men began streaming out of the mosque, Bernadette met up with Reza and Fazel. "I have found a taxi," Reza said.

The taxi looked like its better days were long behind it. It was a Russian-made Lada, hand painted in yellow and white, with bullet holes and rust spots that had been filled with several attempts of bondo body filler. The poor roads had shaken the body filler out to make the taxi's body look like something was trying to consume it from the inside. To Bernadette, the taxi looked like a prop for the night of the living dead.

"*Yalla, yalla,*" the young driver yelled to everyone, the words for move. He was young with curly hair and an easy smile. He looked at ease driving the dangerous streets. His eyes sparkled with a sense of adventure and excitement.

They squeezed into the tiny car, Fazel with his machine gun poking out the window taking the front and Bernadette and Reza in the back. Reza once again muttered under his breath how dangerous this was as Fazel gave instructions to the young man as to what streets to avoid.

A convoy of light armored vehicles appeared ahead. They took a side street under Fazel's direction. Bernadette wondered why they would do that, and then saw an explosion of rocket-propelled grenades hit the vehicles. The old fighter knew what he was doing. They needed to avoid the armored vehicles. They were a target.

The taxi turned onto the street of the guesthouse and Bernadette felt herself relax. A motorbike with two men on it came racing down the street towards them.

Fazel began screaming something. He jumped out of the cab and shouldered his weapon.

The man on the back of the bike was firing. Bullets hit the cab, shattered the glass. Bernadette felt shards of glass rain down on her.

She could hear Fazel screaming as he fired. The sound of the AK47 shattered the night. The motorcycle zoomed by. A crash sounded behind them.

Bernadette crawled out of the taxi. Fazel lay on the ground, his weapon across his chest, blood poured from his wounds. The motorcycle was burning behind them. One man was limping down the street; another lay dead on the ground.

Reza and the taxi driver rushed to Fazel. Aaron came out of the guesthouse. They spoke to Fazel in low tones. Aaron brushed the hair from his face and tried to comfort him.

Bernadette knelt by Fazel's side. She wanted to touch him, to soothe him somehow, but words were all she had. "I'm so sorry, I should never have taken us out. This is all my fault."

Fazel whispered something to Aaron, and then sighed. He was dead.

"No, madam, this is God's will. Fazel died a happy man. He died fighting like a true Mujahedeen. He told me to thank you."

Bernadette stood up, looking up and down the street. It was empty, except for the burning motorcycle. Her phone buzzed in her pocket. The call was from Lackey.

"Callahan here."

"Where are you?"

"In the front of the guest house where we've just come under hostile fire."

"I'm sending a team for you. Get packed."

Bernadette stared down at the dead body of Fazel. "Why? This whole place is a battle zone. I'm as safe here as anywhere else."

"Your picture and location just went viral on a website. Someone wants you dead. They put a price on your head. Get inside and stay there until an armored vehicle with marines comes to get you."

Chapter Thirteen

Bernadette grabbed the things that Reza brought back from the hospital for her and waited inside the guesthouse. She heard the noise of vehicle outside and guessed it must be her ride.

A marine came into the guesthouse. "I'm Private Savinsky. You need to put this on." He held out a helmet and body armor. He was young, still with peach fuzz and pimples on his face, barely nineteen.

"But I'm just going to the vehicle," Bernadette protested.

"Yes, ma'am, but we got hostiles out there."

Bernadette did as she was told. Savinsky helped with the body armor. She felt like a turtle as she walked behind the private to the vehicle. Two marines stood watch beside the vehicle. It was huge, with eight massive tires and heavy metal skin. The back door was open.

"You need to giddy up and get in that door ma'am," Savinsky said. Bullets hit the wall behind him.

Bernadette needed no more persuading. She ran the last

few steps. The other marines climbed in and secured the door. The vehicle lurched forward.

Savinsky turned and smiled, and explained that they were traveling in a Stryker M1128 mobile gun system with a 105 MM cannon, a 50 MM machine gun and a whole bunch of other weapons they could deploy to clear the road. "Welcome to your taxi. We call it the badass MAS. Top speed is sixty-two miles per hour, but today we'll be threading it carefully through some hostiles."

"Private, get your ass up here and man the heavy," a voice yelled from the forward seats.

"Aye, aye, Sergeant," Savinsky replied. He winked at Bernadette and went forward.

To Bernadette he looked like a kid who was about to jump into the seat of a video arcade. The bullets out there were real, she could hear them pinging off the armor.

The inside was cramped. She found a seat on the sidewall and strapped herself in. A marine with the nametag Hammerstein sat beside her.

"I'm Sergeant Hammerstein, you can call me Hammer for short. We'll be taking you to the American and NATO compound on the outskirts of the city. Much safer than this area."

"Thanks for the ride, Sergeant, I'm grateful for you guys sticking your necks out to come get me," Bernadette said.

"It's what we do," Hammer said. "But my *swag* tells me you're a high value asset to someone in our organization. We received special orders to pick you up."

"What's a swag?"

"That's a sophisticated wild ass guess."

"Thanks for clearing that up," Bernadette said. She leaned back and bounced along as the vehicle got up to speed. A machine gunner in the top turret was radioing targets to the driver and sergeant as they moved. Several times the 50 MM on the turret burst into action. The smell of cordite mixed with diesel fumes filled the vehicle. Bernadette gagged from the smell and placed her headscarf over her nose.

The journey took an hour. It was slow, some backing up, some turns, some more machine gun fire, and finally they stopped. The engine idled.

"We're almost there," Hammer said. "We've entered the green zone."

Bernadette had heard of the green zone, a total enclave of American and NATO buildings surrounded by high walls and armed forces.

The vehicle motored on. There was silence inside the vehicle, but outside Bernadette heard the strains of music. Was that rock and roll?

The vehicle stopped and the back ramp came down. Agent Lackey stood on the pavement to greet her.

"I'm glad you could make it," Lackey said.

Bernadette shuffled off the vehicle, her legs stiff from the cramped quarters. "Yeah, that was a hell of a ride."

"Well, Sergeant Hammer and his squad do that several times a day for hours on end. You got the compressed version," Lackey said. "Follow me, I'll take you to your new quarters."

Bernadette followed Lackey into a building that looked like a high-class boutique hotel. Plush carpets, muted walls in soft colors, and framed pictures of tasteful photographs adorned the walls. A bar with a Nespresso machine was on one side of the lobby with a mini fridge with a glass door that displayed a selection of Perrier and soft drinks.

Lackey nodded at the coffee bar. "That's for our Muslim friends. There's a full bar and bistro in the courtyard in the back. It's open at zero six hundred hours and closes at midnight. Good German and American beer and damn fine cocktails."

Bernadette felt like she'd just walked into an oasis after being in Kandahar for the past several days. "Maybe I can grab a shower before we meet. I want to talk you about several things."

"Sure, I'll take you to your room, and then I'll show you the video we downloaded."

Bernadette almost wanted to see the video first but realized she needed to change her clothes. She was covered in dirt and specks of blood. The ride over had jarred her; she needed a few minutes to catch her breath.

Her room was small but comfortable. No bare bed like the guesthouse. It contained two beds, both with down comforters and fluffy pillows. A forty-inch flat screen television hung on the wall over a small bureau. A door led to a full shower.

She stripped off her clothes and got into the shower. The water was hot and the soap had a pleasing scent. She felt like she'd checked into a Marriott Hotel. The towels were soft, no skin abrasion. She dressed in the jeans and t-shirt she'd salvaged from her duffle bag and went to find Lackey.

Lackey was sitting with a laptop in the courtyard bistro. "I ordered us a pitcher of beer and a pizza. I hope that's okay."

Bernadette sat down "Totally fine. What do you have for me on the video?"

"You are direct and to the point." Lackey turned the laptop towards her. "As you can see, here is Chris and Lund exiting the shrine."

As Bernadette stared hard at the video, the pitcher of

beer arrived, but she didn't notice it. "Is there any audio with this?"

"No, it's CCTV only. And no time stamp either. This is old tech," Lackey said as she poured both of them mugs of beer and pushed one towards Bernadette.

Bernadette took a sip of her beer and stared back at the video. She ran the feed back and forth with the cursor. She could see a small man who was Lund hand something to Chris. She zoomed in on the video. Her heart almost stopped. There was Chris, it really was him, she felt him now, and the contact she'd lost had been regained. She knew deep down he was still alive.

"There's nothing conclusive here," Bernadette said, looking at the video. You see the two men, there's someone behind them in the shadows, and then the lights go out. I was there today. The lights were shining brightly from the shrine."

Lackey looked at the video. "The lights go on and off all the time in this town. They have black outs, brown outs, and then just plain no electricity for days in some sections of town. Also, we didn't get much intel from Kahn's computer. The Afghani Police have no clues to follow."

Bernadette sat back, took a long pull of her beer. "What do you know of this Lund guy?"

Lackey pulled up her phone and scrolled it. "I got this memo from our agents in Europe. Jannick Lund is the president of a non-government organization called Mission South that was supposed to provide clean water and sanitation to Afghans in the south. In his time here, he hasn't spent a dime.

The pizza arrived, a steaming hot pie of salami, olives, onion and tomatoes. Lackey cut into it and served a slice to

Bernadette. Although her stomach felt like it was desperate for food, this conversation held her attention.

"Where was he before here?"

Lackey stared at her phone. "He's been everywhere from Syria to Egypt and even some time in Jordan."

"Did you ever check if there's been other thefts of ancient objects in any of the countries he's visited?"

"No, we never thought of that. But I'll run some enquiries."

Bernadette took a bite of pizza. It tasted just like Domino's back home, hot, cheesy, and the right amount of grease. She chewed for a moment. "The security chief named Caprinski, who ran Lund's protection, said he had no knowledge of where Lund was heading that day. I'm sure he's lying."

"Why do you think that?"

"Wouldn't the head security guy know of all movements of the person who's paying to protect him?" Bernadette said as she swallowed hard. The lump of pizza hit her empty stomach like a fat child doing a cannonball in the pool.

"Good point. I've never checked into Caprinski."

Bernadette eyed Lackey for a moment. She took another slice of pizza and stared at it as if that was her focus. She tried to reason why the head of the CIA in Kandahar wouldn't have run a profile on the entire security team, with Caprinski included.

"You've never run into Vincent Caprinski in your travels in Afghanistan. I hear he's been here for some time."

Lackey sipped her beer then took a slice of pizza. She looked directly at Bernadette. "It's a big country. Nope, never ran into him."

They stared at each other for a moment, silence descending over the table.

"Well, I guess I'll have to check into it then," Bernadette said, breaking the silence. She drained her beer, and placed a slice of pizza on a napkin. "I'll take this back to my room and do some research. Thanks again for the accommodations, your American hospitality is great."

"You're welcome. Do you have any ideas for a personal security person for your next trip out?" Lackey asked.

"No, I was going to place a posting in Kandahar for someone who wants a shit magnet as a protection client. Sorry, that's a bit of a joke," Bernadette said with a smile.

"I'll put the word out. There might be a few solo guys that you might be able to hire." Lackey smiled back. "And by the way, I'll give you a special code number for the front gates if you ever do find someone. It's the only way they can enter for you to interview them."

"Thanks for that. I seem to go through body guards pretty quickly so hopefully the next guy is good or can duck quickly," Bernadette said, getting up from the table.

She walked back to her room and started to do searches on the iPad that Reza had brought back for her. Some strange things were going on with Lackey, things did not get answered in their conversation. But one thing she never asked her—was she in fact a highly valued asset, and why?"

Chapter Fourteen

Bernadette did a search on her iPad on both Lund and Caprinski, but didn't find much. She knew what she had to do. As the game show says, "you need to call a friend." She pulled out the cellphone that Reza had returned to her, the one she'd brought from Canada, and dialed her friend, Anton De Luca.

Anton was with Canada's Security and Intelligence Agency. He was a young, good-looking Italian Canadian in his late twenties who made most women do a double take when he walked by. To Bernadette, he was like a brother.

Anton picked up after the first ring. "I was wondering when you were going to call. I just saw a heads up from the Canadian Consulate; a lady there named Chandra Gupta has put in a request to have you ejected from Kandahar. I see you're already making friends."

"Yeah, we're kind of at cross purposes here. They want me to go home, and me, not so much." Bernadette smiled into the phone. It was wonderful to hear his voice. "Look, I know you're busy, but I need to find whatever you got on

Vincent Caprinski and Jannick Lund. They were both with the NGO that Chris worked for."

"Sure, I can do that and send it to you. How are you doing there? You staying safe?"

"I think the word is staying alive," Bernadette said in a dry tone. "There's someone here that is throwing roadblocks in my way—not sure who it is."

"What kind of roadblocks?"

"A price on my head…"

"That's a hell of a roadblock. You sure you're okay there?"

"It's a war zone, everyone is trying to kill each other here, so yes, I'm fine. I'll just look over my shoulder more," Bernadette said.

Anton paused, then said, "I heard your security guy got injured. Do you have a replacement?"

"The American CIA agent here is trying to hook me up."

"Look, I think I got someone. He's a bit of a long shot, a bit off the wall, but I know he's good," Anton said.

"Nice build up. What is he, a cross between a Bruce Willis and Rambo?"

Anton chuckled. "No, he's a Canadian named Jason Radic. He was born in Yugoslavia back in seventy-eight. His parents immigrated to Canada and he grew up in Moose Jaw. Served time with Canada's elite JTF2 in Haiti and Croatia."

"Wow, the JTF2, they were so secretive not even the Prime Minister was informed of what they were doing. Radic is here in Kandahar?"

"Yeah, he did a bunch of tours in Afghanistan, was in Iraq for a while, and did some nasty stuff for our government in Syria. He didn't come home when his tour was over. He's living there."

"You sure he's stable after all those missions?" Bernadette asked.

"I know, exposure to war can get to people. Some crack and some survive but in a different headspace. I have some people who can track him down. He is one of the best there is. Knows the countryside inside and out."

"Sure, why not. I need someone who knows his way around this war zone. Have him call me. Look, I know it's early for you, and thanks tons for helping me out."

"Anytime. Stay safe, Bernadette." Anton clicked off.

Bernadette stared at her phone. Those were the words Chris always used. She felt a chill down her spine. She breathed deeply and made another phone call. There was one more person she had to talk to, her Grandmother Moses.

As the phone rang, she imagined her aged grandmother ambling to the phone. She was full Cree Indian and lived in a small house with a wood stove on the Lone Pine Reservation in Northern Canada. She wore the same print dress nearly every day, and her hair was always in braid, either single or double. The long gray hair graced her soft brown face and twinkling brown eyes.

"I was hoping you'd call," Grandma Moses said.

"Grandma, how'd you know it was me?" Bernadette asked. Her grandmother had an ancient landline with a rotary dial. The telephone company wanted it for their museum.

"I know your ring," Grandma answered in a matter-of-fact tone.

There was no arguing with Grandma Moses; she knew

what she knew. Her knowledge was halfway between mystical and common sense. Few ever challenged her.

"It's nice to hear your voice, Grandma. I just wanted let you know that I'm okay. Sorry, I should have called earlier. I've been busy hunting for Chris," Bernadette said biting her lip at the end of her lie.

"No, that's not true. I had a dream you were in a long sleep, and then when you woke up you were dizzy like you'd been on the Ferris Wheel, you know like when Grandpa took you to the fair."

Bernadette shook her head, there was no way getting around Grandma Moses, she saw things in her dreams that happened to people in real life. No one knew how she did it. Some on the reservation were afraid of her and some flocked to her door to get her visions.

"Okay, sorry, Grandma, I got in an accident when I arrived. I banged my head but I'm okay now," Bernadette admitted. She closed her eyes as her vision went into a set of spins. Her vertigo had returned.

"I saw a small fox last night outside the house in the moonlight, it was staring at me." Grandma Moses said, as if she already knew what had happened to Bernadette and accepted it.

"A fox? What's so unusual about a fox? You're in Northern Canada. They live all around you."

"This one wanted to tell me something. He wanted to give me a message about you and your journey."

Bernadette held onto her head with one hand. The vertigo was starting to subside like a merry-go-round slowing down. "I don't understand."

"Sometimes small animals lead the way. You need to look for them there, Bernadette. Remember who you are. You're half Indian. Use your senses, not just your mind."

Bernadette chuckled at Grandma Moses's words; she never called the Cree the Indigenous or First Nations People. She'd grown up being called an Indian, but to her it was badge of honor, of a people who felt in harmony with nature and the land. Distinctly opposite from the white settlers who as she once said, "couldn't find their ass from a hole in the ground." She meant they were out of touch.

"Okay, Grandma, I'll use my senses. I have to go now. I just wanted to tell you that I'm okay." Bernadette ended the call, took off her jeans, boots and socks and climbed into bed. In minutes she was asleep. A little fox appeared in her dream. It seemed to wink at her.

Chapter Fifteen

Chris looked out the crack in the hut as the dawn broke over the village square. The fate of Gul had been decided. In the past few days, after the murder of Max in the square, Gul had confided in him that his case for clemency with the imam was not going well.

Chris felt sorry for Gul. He was a sad character. Although a Taliban, he wasn't a very good one. He hadn't participated in the torture and killing of Max; Chris had seen him back away from the square so he wouldn't be involved.

Now, Gul the soft-spoken Afghan who'd become a Taliban because the pay was better than the Afghan Army, was being brought into the square by two of his compatriots. The law was the law. The imam had decreed that the husband of the wife that Gul had slept with would be allowed to shoot Gul, but just once, and from a distance.

"God willing, I will survive," Gul had said. His reasoning was that the husband would shoot him, but he claimed the husband was a bad shot. Gul thought if he were able to survive the bullet wound, he would recover and sneak off to Kandahar with the man's wife. He'd send word of where Chris was held captive and have him rescued. Chris would then apply to the Canadian Consulate to have Gul and his bride to be immigrated to Canada.

Chris agreed to the plan whole-heartedly. He didn't think Gul had much of a chance, but this was the only possible escape plan he had. The only thing that stood in the way of the plan was the husband's bullet.

Gul sat on a rug in the center of the square and began to make his prayers to Allah. The imam, warlord, and aggrieved husband walked into the square. The rest of the Taliban fighters formed a semi-circle around them. Chris had an unobstructed view.

The weapon the husband was given looked like a Lee-Enfield. Chris knew the weapon well. A friend of his owned one. They were built for the English Army in 1907, with a long barrel and heavy, around nine pounds.

Chris watched as the husband raised the rifle to his shoulder. He hoped the weight of the gun would make him drop his aim as he fired, missing Gul's head and hopefully his vital organs.

The gun fired. A loud echo reverberated through the village. Then the gun fired again and again.

"Damn it," Chris muttered, "That shithead knows how to fire the thing."

The husband kept ramming the bolt action and sending another bullet into the chamber as he walked closer to Gul. The warlord ran to his side and beat on his back commanding him to stop. He did stop—when the magazine was empty.

Chris watched them drag Gul's lifeless body from the square. The warlord and imam were discussing the husband's bad behavior. The husband had dropped the weapon. He stood there, arms crossed, defiant in his actions.

The door to Chris's hut opened. Chris spun around and sat on his bed. Aktar walked in. He smiled at Chris, giving him a look that told him he was to be his new jailer. He pulled his finger across his neck in motion that showed what he wanted to do to Chris, and then slammed the door closed as he left. His laughter could be heard outside the hut as he walked away.

Chris took a deep breath. "Well, if anyone is close by, this would be perfect time to come to the rescue," he said with a sigh.

Chapter Sixteen

Bernadette woke up and stared at the ceiling for a few minutes to let her eyes focus. Would her vertigo return this morning? She turned her head to the left, nothing, no spins. Maybe it was gone. She rolled out of bed to the right and her world went haywire.

The vertigo returned. There was only one thing she could do; she'd read about vertigo being the movement of crystals in the inner ear. There was a remedy for it called the Epley maneuver.

"Okay girl, this is not going to be pretty," Bernadette said. She took a few deep breaths to calm herself. "Let's not screw this up."

She got back on the bed and sat up, leaving herself enough room to let her head fall over the edge of the bed. "Turn head, forty-five degrees to the right, check. Lie on back with head over the edge of the bed—holy crap!"

The world spun violently before her eyes. She fought back nausea. She started to count, in French so it was slower, "Un, deux, trois, quatre, cinq, six, sept, huit, neuf, dix…oh I'm going to be sick…onze, douze, treize, quatorze, quinze, seize, dix-sept, dix-huit, dix-neuf…vingt…."

The spinning slowed. Just like the merry-go-round she'd been on with her friends back in school. Her eyes stopped spinning, stopped twitching, and then came to a stop. She pulled herself back from the edge of the bed and lay on her left side, turning her head straight down. This was supposed to flush out the crystals in her inner ear and restore balance. She counted another twenty seconds then sat up.

"Whew, now all you have to do is to keep your eyes straight ahead and your chin up for the next twenty-four hours."

She got slowly off the bed. Getting dressed while not looking down was a challenge. She somehow got into her jeans put on her bra and slipped her t-shirt over her head. Getting into her boots was interesting. She had to walk towards where she knew they were and kick around with her feet until she found them.

She decided to put a towel around her neck as a brace. That way if anyone asked why she wasn't lowering her head she could say she pulled a neck muscle during the night. She walked out of her room in search of coffee.

The smell of breakfast drew her to the bistro in the courtyard. It was another cool Afghanistan morning. A series of propane patio heaters kept the diners comfortable. Bernadette felt like she'd dropped into an outdoor patio in Palm Springs in January, not Kandahar.

Bernadette took a seat at a lone table. A young male waiter took her order of coffee and eggs, hash browns, bacon and rye toast. She asked if they had peanut butter and jam for her toast, they did, and a smile spread over her lips. She was going to fuel up before resuming her hunt for Chris. So far, everyone she'd talked to was lying to her. She wasn't even sure about Lackey.

She took out her phone, making sure to put it up to her eyes to punch the numbers. Then she realized she was going to have one hell of time eating breakfast.

Before she could call, her phone rang. She put it up to her ear, looking ahead at two men across from her. One stared back at her, probably thinking her actions only slightly weird.

"Callahan."

"I hear you're looking for me."

"And you are?"

"Jason Radic."

"Ah," Bernadette said. Her coffee arrived. She tried to put milk and sugar in the cup and failed. Realized it was futile and lifted it to her lips. She winced at the bitterness. "I was told you might call. Where are you?"

"I'm at the gates of paradise."

"Where?"

"The gates of the compound that you're in. The marines won't let me in without a word from an insider. That would be you."

"Sure, who do I have to talk to?"

"I'll put him on."

A gruff sounding voice asked if this man could gain entry, and Bernadette gave him the code she'd been given by Lackey.

Fifteen minutes later a tall muscular man with a long black beard, Arab headdress and scarf walked into the bistro. He walked towards Bernadette.

"Jason Radic, I'm here to lead you to your lost lover or the gates of paradise. I promise neither, but the rate is seven hundred fifty U.S. dollars per day, and a bonus of five grand when I find him."

Bernadette sipped her coffee and looked at him. He was good looking, maybe thirty years old, with a scar that slashed across his left eye and disappeared into his hairline. He wasn't tall, kind of square and stocky with muscles that bulged everywhere, including his neck. His eyes were a soft blue with specks of gray. But there was something about him. He had an odor of stale alcohol and hashish.

"You're confident you'll find my fiancé?"

"Bernie…can I call you that?

"Nope, Bernadette or Callahan, Bernie is saved for my grandmother and my lover. You're neither."

"Okay then, Callahan. Here are the goods. I live and breathe Afghanistan. I know every tribe and what every warlord is up to, and which donkey farted on Tuesday. I can track your guy down better than you could back in Canada with your Cree tracking ways following moose turds on a moonlight path. Lady, I'm the best there is."

Bernadette chuckled. "Well you certainly got balls."

"Yes, I do and you've had your bell rung. How long since you did the Epley maneuver to manage your vertigo?"

"How did you know that?"

"I took two sips of your coffee since we've been sitting here. It needs milk and sugar."

Bernadette sighed. "Okay, call me Bernadette. Please put two scoops of sugar and some cream in my coffee and yes I had my bell rung as you put it." She stared into his eyes. "Can you really find a lead on Chris?"

"I already have one," Jason said as he put sugar and cream into her coffee. He ordered himself a coffee from the waiter and another for her.

"What have you got?"

"Right after I got off the phone with Anton, I made some enquiries to all my contacts. There's a warlord some hundred klicks from here has been talking loud about how he has a hostage. Says he got one of the men who stole the robe."

"Holy shit, we need to get moving," Bernadette said.

Jason put up his hand where Bernadette's eyes could see it. "Not so fast. We head outside the wire tomorrow morning. I need to make some arrangements with some of my contacts. I want them to cover my ass, not shoot it off."

"I don't get it."

"If you want to travel to a warlord's area to pay him a visit, you let him know and he makes sure his little army of fighters, who are sometimes ex-Taliban or just some stoned Afghanis, don't try to shoot you or take you hostage. To do that we set up a payment for our visit."

"How much is that?"

"You're going to have to come up with about one thousand US dollars. That's just for the meeting. If he has someone, it's extra, in cash. He will not take anything else. Someone tried to do a crypto currency exchange once to pay him in bit coin—he shot the guy. You okay with that?"

"Absolutely. I'll have the money. How come the CIA and the marines don't know about this bit of information?"

Jason smiled and sipped his coffee. "Because they don't have the contacts I have. Most of my Afghani connections won't speak to Americans or any of the NATO soldiers for that matter. They consider them invaders, who should be gone, just like they wanted the Russians gone and the British before them."

"And they trust you?"

Jason shrugged. "I'm Muslim by birth in Croatia, I have

an Afghan wife. They consider me one of them, not an infidel like the rest of them."

"Okay, sounds good. What time do we roll tomorrow?"

"At zero seven hundred hours. Do you have an interpreter?" Jason asked.

Bernadette was taken aback. "I thought you were one of them, a Croatian Muslim. Don't you speak Pashto?"

Jason shook his head. "No I speak Croat, German, French, and my Pashto is limited. My Afghan wife speaks fluent English. We need someone who doesn't get any of the finer details of a warlord conversation and meanings wrong. That can mean a bullet in the head in the wilds of Afghanistan."

"Okay, I get it, I'll get in touch with Reza, he's been my interpreter since I've been here. I'll have to see if he's up for a visit outside the wire."

"Good, I'll see you tomorrow." Jason got up and started to walk out. He stopped and came back to her table. "Don't worry about what to wear to this meeting, I'll have something for you."

Bernadette put a piece of bacon up to her mouth and chewed on it thoughtfully. She wondered what Jason meant by something for her to wear and how she'd convince Reza he needed to come with her to do translations for a meeting with a warlord?

Chapter Seventeen

When morning came, Bernadette rolled carefully to her right side on the bed. No spins. A smile crossed her face—things were looking up. She pulled on her jeans, sports bra, t-shirt, and laced up her boots. She had no idea what kind of gear Jason had for her, but her mind went to full combat gear and body armor.

She grabbed a coffee and a muffin from the bistro and walked to the front gate of the large compound. The neighborhood looked like an upscale street in Miami, with large buildings surrounded by walls and gates. Each one housed a different nationality, either another American enclave or German or British personnel. A string of military vehicles from different NATO forces lined the streets with Army milling around getting ready for the day's duties.

The one thing that was a possible problem was Reza. She'd called him last night. They'd had a long talk, and she'd finally offered him four times his normal fee to come outside of Kandahar. He'd almost been killed with her last time, he was understandably gun shy, to say the least. He'd said he'd go with her, but his voice was not reassuring.

As she approached the gate, she saw Jason standing outside with Reza beside him. Things were coming together, she thought. Her heart skipped a beat. She felt like this was a positive omen that they'd find Chris or some information as to where he was today and bring him back.

"I see you two have met," Bernadette said when she passed through the gates.

Jason nodded, "We need to get you dressed and ready to roll."

"Sure, what type of fatigues have you got for me? Military issue or hunting style?"

He smiled. He took out a long blue garment and gave it to her.

Bernadette took the garment and looked at it. There was a hood at the top with an opening for the eyes that was covered in mesh. "What's this?"

"A burka."

"A what now? You want me to wear a frigging burka? Are you out of your mind?"

Jason shook his head. "You need to hear me out first."

"Sure, I'll hear you out, then you can stuff that thing back in the sack where it came from," Bernadette said crossing her arms.

"This is your disguise. A woman cannot be in a village meeting with a warlord, not going to happen," Jason said.

"Okay, uh, you think walking in wearing a burka doesn't clue him in that I'm a woman? What the hell have you been smoking?"

"No, that's why you don't understand their customs. You can't come to the meeting as a woman, but you can come to the meeting as a man, who is in the disguise as a woman."

"What the hell are you talking about?" Bernadette looked at Reza to see if he understood. He nodded his head in agreement as if this all made perfect sense.

"Okay, let me explain. In the Arab world a man may don a burka if he needs to conceal his identity. We'll tell them you're being hunted by the Taliban, you're a bad ass operative that is hunting for the robe."

Bernadette looked at Reza. "Is this true?"

"Yes, a man in grave danger goes to the imam and gets a… permission. He must pay something to the imam, but yes this is done."

Bernadette shook her head and looked at the garment. "Hard to believe that women would put up with these. And why is blue instead of black?"

"The special burka color of Afghanistan, now, I've got some special things for you to wear under it," Jason said.

"Better not be something crazier than this, cause I'm about hitting my limits on going native," Bernadette said.

"This you'll like." Jason produced a Glock with extended clip and an H&K MP5 submachine gun. "I'm got special holsters to strap the Glock to your leg and a harness for the MP-five."

"Now you're talking," Bernadette said. She strapped on the firearm and put the harness over her shoulders that came around and secured the submachine gun to her chest. "Okay," Bernadette said after strapping on the weapons and putting on the garment, which billowed around her. "Now, this burka is loaded. Let's go."

"My ride is back here," Jason said as he led them past a row of black SUV's with tinted windows. He opened the door of a well-aged Toyota Camry, its body rusted and dented. The once white paint job had blistered off some time ago, so it looked beige. The front window was cracked, a selection of Arab tassels hung from it, making it look like a local ride.

"This thing road worthy?" Bernadette asked.

Jason winked. "Yep, and paid for. You'll get a lot further in one of these than those black SUV's. The Taliban love to take shots at the corporate security wagons. Mine, they think it's one of theirs. They always let me pass."

Bernadette got in the back. An AK47 lay on the seat. "Is this your backup weapon?"

"Oh yeah, sorry about that. Just throw it on the floor," Jason said.

They got in, the engine fired up with a mild groan and a cough. Jason winked and patted the dash of the car, then drove the car away from the compound..

They moved towards the main highway and followed it out of town. At the various checkpoints, Reza talked them through, saying they were visiting a sick relative in a village in the south. The Afghan army took pity on the derelict vehicle and the obvious poor passengers and let them pass. Some even shook their heads at the condition of Jason's Toyota.

After a half hour on the road they came upon an American armored convoy. Jason slowed to a crawl behind them.

"Can't you pass them?" Bernadette asked.

"Only if you want a bunch of fifty millimeter lead in your car," Jason said. "You see that big sign on the back in Arabic, it says *do not pass on pain of death*."

"What do we do? These guys are moving at twenty kilometers per hour. It'll take all day at this rate, we'll never make our meeting," Bernadette said.

"We wait until the top gunner sees us and we wave like crazy," Jason said.

Bernadette had no idea what Jason was talking about.

The machine gunner on the top of the last vehicle turned and looked at them. He moved the gun turret around and trained it on them.

Bernadette felt her stomach turn to mush and she broke out into a sweat.

"Okay, everyone, start waving, wave like the guy with the machine gun is your long-lost friend," Jason said as he waved his hand out the window.

Reza leaned out the side window and waved, Bernadette followed suit. Waving frantically as if she'd just seen Chris, her lost lover, on the top of the hulk of armor with the largest caliber machine ever pointed at her.

The machine gunner spoke into his mike, and then waved at them to pass. Jason gunned the ancient Toyota and they sped passed the column.

"What the hell was that about? How come they let us pass them?" Bernadette asked.

"Simple. The Taliban don't wave. Next time you have any NATO soldier point a gun at you, wave like hell, it will save your life," Jason said.

Bernadette sat back in silence, watching the desolate countryside pass by them. There were few trees, mostly rocks, and then a small farm would appear in the distance, like a slash of green, an oasis in a barren landscape.

The road became rougher; they bounced over the ruts on the poor shocks of the Camry. A motorcycle approached from behind. Bernadette tensed. She pulled up her Burka to ready her weapon. A motorcycle had carried an attacker a few days ago. She didn't trust this one.

"Relax," Jason said. "Put your weapon down. This is our escort."

Chapter Eighteen

They followed the Afghan on the motorcycle, the road narrowed, becoming more of a track used for goats. The Camry bounced wildly in the ruts. Bernadette felt the jarring into her back teeth. She leaned forward to speak with Jason over the creaking and moaning of the rusted out car.

"What's the story of this warlord we're meeting?" she asked.

Jason steered hard to avoid a rut that looked like a deep hole. "His name is Mohammad Mirwais. He's a crafty old fossil, all of sixty-three I'm told, but that's old for Afghanistan where the men die in battles long before old age hits them. He was a legend in fighting Russians when he was young, then he took on the Taliban. Most of them won't mess with him. They even pay him to leave them alone."

"Sounds like quite the racket. He could teach the Mafia something."

"These Afghan's learned their corruption from the

Russians, the Brits before them, and every other nation that has tried to defeat them. Genghis Khan was one of the first ones to try, and his people were assimilated into their culture. Warlord Mirwais is one of the best when it comes to playing all sides. He'll work for NATO if they provide him guns and money, then he uses that power to provide protection to the Taliban to secure their opium fields."

"So, how do we play this meeting?"

"Speak very low and only to Reza if you have something to ask. They'll respect your need for privacy once I've set up your cover. Make sure your face is covered at all times. This should be quite cordial and friendly."

"Then why am I packing weapons?"

"So that we make it back from the meeting alive. The Afghans are well known for attacking the very visitors that come to see them. In their meeting, we are safe, it's the leaving part that can get a bit dicey."

"Got it," Bernadette said as she leaned back in her seat.

They approached a small village of mud and brick houses surrounded by high walls. The motorcycle stopped in the middle of the village square, which was little more than a lone tree with a wooden bench.

Bernadette watched as a group of Afghan men carrying machine guns appeared. One balanced a rocket propelled grenade launcher over his shoulder like it was nothing more than a beach umbrella.

They got out of the car. Jason and Reza approached the first man in the group. Half his face was scarred by burn marks. He seemed to be the mouthpiece for the warlord. Bernadette could see much waving of arms and pointing in her direction.

Jason came back to Bernadette, he kept his voice low. "I gave them your story, the guy there wants to see under your

Burka. I told him it's not happening. I called him the ass of a sheep and that we are here to pay for information."

"Is he buying the story?"

"So far, yes. He took the one thousand dollar meeting, so we're good. He'll relay it all to Mirwais."

The half-faced man went into a house and returned with an older man. From his stature, Bernadette could see it was the warlord. He walked with his head held high. He wasn't big but he filled the square with his presence and attitude.

Warlord Mirwais wore the traditional dress of the Afghans with a black turban and black tunic and pants. A bandolier of bullets was slung across his chest and two small grenades bounced off his belt as he walked.

A small boy walked behind him. He was dressed in a style like he was there to perform. He wore a green turban with a sash that flowed down his trimmed hair. His perfectly pressed blue tunic was set off with a red vest adorned with little mirrors that glittered in the sun. He walked gingerly in flowing white pants with red shoes that bounced with tassels.

"Is that Mirwais?" Bernadette whispered to Reza, nodding in the direction of the man in black.

"Yes."

"Who is the boy? Is that his grandson?"

Reza coughed in his hand. "No, that's his boy."

"What kind of boy?"

Reza dropped his head and his voice went to a whisper that Bernadette could almost not hear. "That is the boy the warlord has for sex—this is frowned upon by Afghanis. They steal these boys from their parents or threaten them with death."

"That old son of a bitch…"

Jason put up his hand for the two of them to focus. "Reza, ask Mirwais if he has some information on any of the men that went missing a few weeks ago."

Reza made the translation and waited for the reply.

"He said he will tell us in time. First we must have tea," Reza said.

"Of course," Jason said. "Nothing happens in Afghanistan without tea."

The boy wandered around the circle of men and poured tea. As he came closer to Bernadette, she could see he was nervous. He approached, handed her a teacup.

She realized she had to take it. There was no way she could refuse. But the boy would see her hand was not a man's hand. She never wore nail polish, but still, how could she offer her hairless hands? But she had to try.

Taking the cup in both hands like the others, she bowed her head, but made no sound. The boy poured the tea from the large copper pot, staring at her hands as he did.

A small amount of tea spilled onto Bernadette's hands, she yelped softly. Then she swore under breath.

"*Ssedze*," the boy muttered. He walked away offering cups and pouring tea.

"What did he say?" Bernadette whispered to Reza.

"He said the word 'woman,'" Reza said.

Bernadette tried not to panic. If the boy went to the warlord and told him the supposed man in the burka was really a woman, they were done for. She watched the boy pour tea and then sit back down beside his warlord. He put his head down then looked up at her. Did she see him wink?

The warlord began talking loudly. Reza began to translate.

"He says he has something valuable, something we

want. For two thousand US dollars he will bring this out to show us," Reza said.

"Ask him if it is a man," Bernadette said.

"Yes, he says it is a man."

"How do we know if this man is from Chris's team?"

"He will not give that information," Reza said. He waited for a moment while the warlord continued, then turned to Bernadette. "He says if we have no interest in seeing this man alive, he will have him shot. You can see his body for no price."

"I don't understand," Bernadette said.

"Standard warlord bullshit," Jason added. "He figures you're here to see someone. He may or may not have him. You don't pay, he has one of his men shoot him and drag him out. Afghani poker."

"Tell him I will pay," Bernadette said. The thought of them killing an innocent man sickened her. She handed another two thousand dollars she had to Reza. He walked it over and placed it front of the warlord.

The warlord yelled something to the man with half a face; he walked into a hut and dragged a man out. The man was dressed in black fatigues, similar to what security personnel wore in Chris's unit. Bernadette had seen Chris wearing the same style of uniform in the video from the mosque. He looked the same size as Chris, but his head was covered in a black hood.

The warlord spoke to Reza, then pointed to the man and back to Bernadette and Jason. They could see he was bargaining.

"What does he want?" Bernadette asked.

"He wants us to give him five thousand dollars to take this man away," Reza said.

Bernadette stared hard at the man with the hood. Now,

in the sunlight, he looked nothing like Chris. His stature was slumped, no shoulders like Chris, and then she looked at his hands. They were brown.

"Do you speak Pakistani?" Bernadette asked Reza.

"Yes, I do."

"Say a greeting to the man in Pakistani. Ask him who he is."

Reza spoke a greeting in Pakistani, the man's head snapped up. He screamed a reply. The man with half a face slapped him in the back of the head.

"Looks like we've been had," Bernadette said. "All the men in Chris's team were Caucasian from the U.S. This guy is probably a Pakistan border guard they captured to make some extra cash. Tell him we have no interest in taking this man away. They should call Pakistan."

"But they will kill him," Reza protested.

"He's bluffing," Bernadette said. "It's cost me two thousand dollars to find we've been duped. I'm not shelling out anything more. Besides, he needs to keep him alive to scam someone else."

Reza told the warlord they did not want to take the captive.

The warlord shrugged his shoulders and laughed. He pulled out his handgun, placed it against the captive's head and fired.

"Holy shit. He killed him," Bernadette said.

Jason shook his head. "I should have warned you—these guys don't bluff."

The rest of the fighters laughed. The half-faced man pulled off the captive's hood. A young man with dark skin and dark hair lay on the ground. His blood oozed into the ground.

"Time to say our goodbyes," Jason said.

Reza thanked the warlord for his hospitality and the wonderful joke he had played on them. The fighters were jubilant; this would be a story they could tell for years.

They rose up from the ground. Bernadette felt the tension in her legs from squatting on the ground. The warlord's killing of the man sickened her. She realized if she hadn't been so bold, she could have saved the man. There was another one thousand US dollars in her pocket—she could have bargained him down.

Jason pulled the Camry around the side of the village, and they followed. As Bernadette got to the car, she saw a small figure by the wheel. It was the boy.

He said something in Pashto, and Bernadette turned to Reza for translation.

"He says, please dear lady, take me with you, save me," Reza said.

At that point, Bernadette needed no thoughts, no conversations in her mind. She opened the back door, pulled the boy inside and put him on the floor. She had him squat down then covered him with her burka. She perched her submachine on his head. It was the only place for it.

"You didn't just do what I think you did?" Jason asked from the front seat.

"Damn straight, Jason. Now drive this piece of shit car like you stole it."

Jason put the car in gear and drove as fast as he could back down the rutted road. The car bucked even more. Bernadette was thrown around in the back. The boy wrapped his hands around her legs to keep from being bounced off the floor.

Jason looked into his rearview mirror. "I think we're okay, there's no one following us. I saw one of the locals pull out a hash pipe to celebrate their warlord's scam over us. By the time we reach Kandahar the old man will be looking for his boy to tuck him in, then all hell will break loose."

Reza looked into the back seat. "This is very dangerous what you are doing. The warlord will kill us all when he finds us. All of our lives will be in danger."

Bernadette glared back at Reza. "I let a man be killed back there because I called the warlords bluff. Well, guess what, I'm taking his boy with me. This is a little boy, not a sex toy. And I will defend him with my life if I have to."

Jason looked over his shoulder. "Well, Bernadette, it looks like you might get your chance. There's a roadblock up ahead."

Chapter Nineteen

Four heavily armed Afghanis stood by the side of the road. A white Toyota pickup truck was pulled half way across the road acting as a roadblock. One leaned on the truck, a grenade launcher by his side, as if he was in a golf foursome and waiting to hit off the next tee with his oversized driver.

"What's our move?" Bernadette asked.

"Stay calm," Jason cautioned.

"Do you think they're the warlord's men?"

"I'm not sure. If they were, I'd expect them to have already have that RPG trained on us and their weapons ready." Jason turned to Reza. "Tell the boy to be very quiet."

Reza repeated Jason's words to the boy. He began to whimper. Bernadette put her hand on his neck and massaged it. She didn't know what to do. She made soothing sounds like she'd done with her hunting dogs when they were approaching caribou in Northern Canada. She was out of her depth with a child.

The child muttered something.

"What did he say?" Bernadette asked.

"He is pleading with us not to give him up," Reza said.

"Tell him I will defend him with my life," Bernadette said. She took her hand off the child's neck and racked her machine gun.

She felt his tears drench her pant legs. She put her hand down and touched his face. He grew quiet.

The Camry drew alongside the Afghan fighters. Reza greeted them.

"They want to look in our trunk," Reza said.

Jason pulled the trunk lever. Two of them walked to the back and rummaged around in it, then slammed it. One of them walked up to the car. He wore sunglasses and Adidas tennis shoes. His fatigues looked fashionable like he'd picked these up in a Bass Outlet store in the United States. He stood looking down at Bernadette. She dropped her head, remembering that Afghan women were not to make eye contact with men. In this case it was a good thing.

He wandered back to the man leaning on the truck with the grenade launcher. They entered a muted conversation, then broke into laughter.

"Any idea what's happening? I can roll out this door and take out the two by the truck. You think you can get the two in the back before they have to time to raise their weapons?" Bernadette asked.

"Just hold on," Jason said.

The two men from the back walked back to Reza and motioned to Jason to put the car in gear, and they headed back onto the road.

"What was that all about?" Bernadette asked turning her head slightly to look behind her.

"That was a shake down for dope. They were hoping to get some free hash or weed from some locals. That's something I never carry. I do put a small stash of Afghan money in the back, about a hundred dollars' worth. I saw the two guys put it in their pockets, I'm sure they'll be happy with their day," Jason said.

"You think those were the warlords men?"

Jason laughed. "Probably. And they were too stoned to pick up their cell phones and check for messages. If he ever finds out we passed by he'll shorten their life spans. But my guess is they'll say they never saw us to save their skins."

They continued on to Kandahar in silence, with the boy keeping hidden at each checkpoint. Bernadette didn't draw an easy breath until they reached the city. They breezed through the final checkpoint and drove to the special secure compound.

Jason put the Camry in park in front of the gates and turned to Bernadette. "Sorry we didn't really find any intel today. But that's the way you do things in this country, you turn over a lot of rocks and many times, like today, you find a scorpion."

"That's fine, I'm used to this in detective work. Now, what do I do with the boy?" Bernadette asked.

"He's yours. You stole him, you keep him," Jason said.

"But I don't speak Pashto," Bernadette protested. "How will I communicate with him?"

Jason winked "Look, he's a little boy, just like all human little boys, he needs food, sleep, and some love. You give him that, you'll be fine."

"But you have a wife, wouldn't she want—?"

"Oh no." Jason put up his hand. "My wife barely puts up with my childlike antics, and she works full time for an Afghan relief agency."

"And I cannot bring this child to my house," Reza said.

"When my wife finds out he is the warlord's boy she would wail that I have brought disaster to our home."

Bernadette lifted the Burka off her head and pulled the boy up from the floor of the car. "Reza, ask him his name, and tell him that he'll be coming with me. I'll try to figure out where he's to go once I've had some time to think. Maybe I can find his relatives somewhere."

The boy moved onto the seat and looked around his surroundings with interest. His bright eyes took in the soldiers and the heavy armored tanks at the front gate. He smiled at Bernadette. It was a smile of relief. He conversed back and forth with Reza.

"He says his name is Almas. He wants you to know his name means diamond in Dari and Persian. He has only one name. He is twelve years old, he has only five years of schooling, and he was taken from his village when the warlord attacked. He wants to study medicine and the stars," Reza said.

"Okay, Reza, thanks for giving me his background. Now tell him to come with me," Bernadette said. She looked at Jason. "You have any idea how I get this kid through security and into my compound?"

"There are two ways. One, you use the Jedi Mind Trick where you say, *you don't need to see his papers,* or you just lie your ass off and see what happens, that's way number two," Jason said.

Bernadette unstrapped the Glock from her leg and the machine gun from her chest. She placed both weapons in the back seat and draped the burka over them. "Thanks for the unhelpful info. I'll see what happens."

She took the child by the hand and approached two large soldiers at the gates of the compound. She showed her

ID to them and ushered the child in front of her. "Who's the kid?" one of them asked.

"He's with me," Bernadette said, staring back into his eyes.

They let her pass.

She walked with the boy to her compound. The front door attendant buzzed her in. The attendant was a little man with a thin mustache. His eyes had a furrowed haunted look. His name badge claimed he was Massoud.

"Massoud, do you know where I can get something for this boy to wear?"

"Yes, in the market. It is close by. Do you want I get you transport to take you there?"

"Ah, no, he's kind of tired, I was hoping to get someone to pick them up for him."

Massoud stood there and looked at the boy. It was if he saw him for the first time. He looked at his fine features and costume; a light of understanding came into his eyes. "I will do it myself. My shift is over soon, it will be my pleasure to do this."

"Thank you, Massoud. That is very kind of you," Bernadette said. She took the boy with her to her room. He thanked her many times in his native language and was asleep on one of the beds in minutes. She covered him with a blanket.

Bernadette took a long hot shower and changed. She crept out of the room so as not to wake the boy and found a small carafe of coffee. She started to scroll through her voice mails on her phone, noting one from Anton. *I have some intel on Caprinski and Lund. You won't like it, Call me.*

Chapter Twenty

Bernadette looked at her watch. It was 1800 hours. The light was fading from the sky, the call to prayer was sounding from a mosque, and she was beyond tired, but she needed to call Anton. She took another sip of her coffee and dialed his number. It was 0630 in Edmonton, Canada, but Anton was an early riser; she knew he'd be awake.

"Hey, Bernadette, how goes it out there," Anton answered with a cheery sounding voice.

"I'm staying alive. How are you?"

"I've been watching all the intel we're getting from Afghanistan. There are now two theories of thought from the world's governments. You want to hear them?"

Bernadette sipped her coffee. "Sure, I'm all ears, fire away."

"Several European countries want to pull out completely. They've had enough of Afghan's squabbles and want nothing more to do with them. And the other one isn't good either…"

"Is it worse than everyone pulling out?"

"Maybe. It's to have all the NATO forces step aside and let the tribes fight until they've exhausted themselves, then work with the winner."

"I'm not sure that would be a good idea. Everyone here has more weapons than a Los Angeles street gang. I wonder how the NATO troops could stay out of it. Anyway, what do you have on my two stars, Caprinski and Lund?"

"Sure, let's start with Caprinski first." Bernadette waited while Anton pulled up the file on his computer.

"Vincent Caprinski is an ex-marine. He has a home in Butte, Montana, but hasn't returned there in years. He served in Iraq and Afghanistan until he was brought up on charges of killing civilians in Kabul."

"What kind of charges?"

"An entire family was killed in a sweep of a compound. They had no links to any terrorists. The CIA and Homeland Security think it was a hit paid for by one tribe on another and they used Caprinski to do it," Anton said.

"And of course, they couldn't prove it?"

"You got it. There were no witnesses, only dead bodies and Caprinski and his men to tell the tale. He left the marines and signed up with the personal security company."

"What does he do in his spare time?"

"He heads off to Dubai. That's a pretty happening city for those with money who want to spend it and party."

"How's our next contestant, Jannick Lund doing in the clandestine department?"

"You guessed it. He doesn't have a head office in Denmark, never has. His NGO is a sham. I checked out all the other places he's been and in each one there are sacred missing artifacts. Looks like there's a pattern with this guy."

"I wonder how this guy ever got into this country. Oh

don't tell me, he bribed someone. Yep, asked and answered," Bernadette said. She poured herself another coffee and went back to her chair.

"There's something else I wanted to tell you," Anton said. "I got a copy of the incident report from the NATO military that investigated the attack on Chris's unit. There's something I don't get."

"What's that?"

"There's no satellite or drone images for the time that attack took place. I watched their convoy leave Kandahar and go through several checkpoints, then there's no footage. One hour later you see the burned out vehicles and the missing men."

"How unusual is that?"

"Satellites do take breaks to take pictures elsewhere and drones need to land to refuel. Could be a coincidence."

"You know what I think of the 'c' word. There are no coincidences, just connections I haven't found yet," Bernadette said. "Who makes the decisions about satellites and drones in Kandahar?"

"U.S. Military Intelligence and the good people in the CIA. That's kind of the command chain. However, there's also a representative from Homeland Security as well as an FBI agent, but to my knowledge, the head spook…that be the CIA Station Chief has the ultimate say on getting intel from drones and satellites."

"Don't you think it's convenient that one of the busiest roads in Kandahar Province that's known to be heavily targeted by Taliban would have no drone that time of day?" Bernadette asked.

Anton paused on the line. "I know what you're thinking Bernadette. You see shadows behind every tree and intricate plots in every action, but I can't prove it."

"Okay, how closely does the Canadian Embassy monitor the U.S. Embassy here in Kandahar?"

"Whoa, now you're asking me to give up our most important stream of intel," Anton said with a halting tone.

"And just exactly what is your most important stream of intel?"

"Okay, we all spy on each other. The Americans on the Canadians, likewise the Brits, the Germans, and of course everyone spies on the Russians and Chinese and vice versa."

"The typical den of thieves out there for you guys, isn't it?" Bernadette said sarcastically.

"Everyone is afraid the other country is going to find out something deeply critical to the others' survival…"

"What do they find?"

Anton sighed. "Mostly gossip. Like if a British agent or consul aide is having an affair with someone in the Danish Consulate. It's pretty mundane stuff really. It keeps the staff up at night when they can't binge on House of Cards on Netflix."

"And I thought so much better of you, Anton."

"Sorry, I wear the title of security analyst, and with that comes taking out the trash."

"While we're at it, can you see what you can find on Kandahar's CIA Chief?"

"Really, what do you want to know?"

"Just any interesting affiliations she might have. There's something about her that gets my senses tingling."

"Okay, Bernadette, this may take a few days. This kind of investigation has to be done through back channels and pulling a lot of favors."

"Sorry for the hassle, but the only way I know how to find Chris is to uncover what his mission was about. I've just been out to a village and blindsided by a warlord who thought it was joke to kill a man in front of me—" Bernadette stopped and put her head down. "Sorry, Anton, I'm babbling."

"No, no, it's okay. look, I'll get this done. I know the stress you're under. If it's of any comfort, I have a person checking the wires for any traffic on Chris or his people and I have nothing so far, but we'll keep looking."

Bernadette wiped a tear from her eye. "Thanks, Anton, you're the best. I'll call you again in a day or two."

She ended her call and then started to scroll for voice messages. She'd always hoped she'd see a message from people who'd captured Chris and his team. There was nothing.

Scrolling down voice mails and texts from friends and fellow police officers that'd left messages of hope and concern, she came across the voice mails she dreaded—the ones from Chris's mother.

She had six of them. She listened to the first, got the gist of it and sat back in her chair. The thought of talking to Maroula Christakos, Chris' Greek-Canadian mother, made her stomach churn. Should she go to the bistro and get herself a beer first? Would that be enough—maybe a double scotch? The woman hated Bernadette. She'd never hidden the fact that Bernadette, an *xeonos*, which was Greek for stranger was not good enough for her son. She was too old, she would never bear him children, and she was not Greek. Bernadette thought she'd said that maybe a million times or it felt like it.

Maroula had been born in Athens and met her husband, Andreas, when she was seventeen, after an arranged marriage. She immigrated to Canada with Andreas where he got a job in a coat factory. Andreas died of a heart attack at work when she was only twenty-seven.

With a child to raise, she became a dressmaker; it was all she knew. She remained dressed in black and grieving for her husband and fiercely loyal to her Greek traditions. Bernadette had been a pox on her family and traditions from the moment they'd met.

On one trip to Toronto with Chris, Maroula trapped Bernadette in the kitchen as she was desperately trying to get her morning coffee. She pulled out pictures of every young and beautiful Greek girl Chris had ever gone out with. The message was simple: Why he chose Bernadette over these girls was a mystery to the old woman. Maybe she thought Bernadette held some kind of spell over her son?

She took a deep breath and called Maroula, who lived in Toronto. It would be 0830 hours there. The fiery old woman would have had three Turkish coffees by now and be ready for action. The phone rang three times before she answered.

"*Ya su*, hello, Maroula Christakos here."

"Maroula, it's me, Bernadette."

"Where are you? Why are you not looking from my Christos?"

"I'm in Kandahar, Afghanistan right now searching for him, Maroula."

"Why you no find him yet? You say you are detective? What kind of detective you are, you cannot find my son?"

Bernadette put her hand to her forehead, "Maroula, things are different here, I cannot go to the countryside without security…"

"Yes, things different there. My Christos should never have gone there. He go there for you. To show you how big man he is, to make money for you. You are the reason he gets captured there. You hear me? You are the reason!" Maroula yelled into the phone. Her voice ended in sobs.

"Look, Maroula, I know, you're right, okay? But I'm doing everything I can. I will not leave here until I find him. You must believe me."

"I believe you. I know you are good police officer—you will try hard. But you must promise me one thing."

"What's that?"

"When you find him, you bring him back to me, then you let him go. You are too dangerous for him to be around. He will get killed from being around you. You promise me?"

Bernadette was stunned. She knew Maroula's word were true. "Yes, Maroula, I promise you." She clicked off the cell and let the tears flow.

Composing herself, she headed for her room. The front desk clerk had left some clothes for the boy by the door. She picked them up and entered the room and found the boy sitting up in bed.

"Clothes," Bernadette said with a smile, raising the pile up in the air.

The boy smiled, he said the word in Pashto, which Bernadette didn't understand, and she repeated the words "clothes."

"Clothes," he said, he smiled broadly showing perfect white teeth.

Bernadette took him by the hand and ushered him into the bathroom. She put the clothes there and turned on the shower for him, showing him the soap and shampoo. She did everything in sign language while saying the English words for soap and shampoo. He repeated everything.

She closed the door and waited for him. What was she to do with this little boy? How would she find him a home? What was it that Jason had said? All little boys need is some food, some sleep, and some love.

The shower stopped, and a few minutes later, Almas

emerged, looking like any little boy. He was freshly scrubbed; his clothes were now those of a regular Afghan child of his age. Gone was the garish costume the warlord had made him wear.

He got back on the bed, smiled at her, and lay down again. Bernadette curled up beside him and put her arm around him. Soon they were both fast asleep.

Chapter Twenty-One

The Loya Jirga was still in session. The many tribes milled around the room trying to make some sense of what was happening. Rumors were raging. Some said the Shia Militia in Iran was massing at the border for an attack. Some said they were already inside the walls of Kandahar City disguised as tribesmen. How would they know?

Imam Sardar Agha surveyed the room. He tried not to smile—he wanted to look grim like all the rest. Things were going his way, the police chief had looked at the tape and it could only be the infidels who had stolen the robe. Sardar Agha had proclaimed the fatwa, the pronouncement of death for them that morning. Soon all the faithful of Afghanistan would be out for their blood, and they would find their precious robe.

The head of the Hazara Tribe, Abdal Ali Balkihi, walked by and threw a glance in Sardar's direction. They had a mutual hate for each other. He wandered off to another side of the room and went into a deep discussion with another man dressed in white robes. Sardar knew him, his name was Basir Nasab, and considered the worst of the vipers of the Hazara Tribe as far as Sardar was concerned. He watched out of the corner of his eye, he wished he knew what the two were saying.

The two men wandered away out of Sardar's hearing.

"How goes it with you?" Balkihi asked Nasab.

"Good my friend, by the will of Allah, we will prevail. Do you have any word?" Nasab asked.

He looked quickly from side to side to see if he was being overheard. "Yes, Iran's elite Ansar-al-Mahide force has offered to come to our aid," Balkihi said.

"But, how can they? The moment they cross the border, the Americans will proclaim war with them?" Nasab protested.

"They will dress as Pashto tribesmen. They can be here in three days."

Nasab lowered his head. "How do they think they can defeat the Americans and the British? They have helicopter gunships and armored vehicles. This would be suicide."

"Once they get inside the gates of the city our tribe will revolt and come to their side. We have thirty thousand fighters; the Americans and British are a small force. They will fall back to the airfield where we will hem them in like rats. Soon they will be leaving the country in droves." Balkihi laughed. "With our permission."

Across the room, Sardar watched the two Hazara's share a joke. He could only imagine what they were up to. He needed to act fast on his own plans.

Police Chief Khan stared across his desk at his three top sergeants. He leafed through their reports and threw them on the desk. "You mean to tell me that in all this time you have come with—nothing?"

The first sergeant, a man with a large moustache and bulbous eyes that seemed to protrude from his head, nodded furiously. "No, Chief, we cannot find the robe as it is not in Kandahar. If it was here, we would have found it."

Khan shook his head and pounded his fist on the desk. "Not good enough." The men jumped in their chairs.

The first sergeant put his hand over his heart. "Believe me, Chief, this robe has left Kandahar and is in the hands of the infidels. If it were in our power, we would bring it back. The infidels now hold our precious robe. We can only look to the tribal leaders to help us to get it back."

Khan wanted to choke the first sergeant. He was a buffoon. He'd bought his commission with the help of the mayor, his first cousin. The man had no sense of police practice and spent his time in coffee shops while his men roamed the streets and got shot at by the Taliban and the warring tribes.

"And how do you expect the tribal leaders will help in this regard?" Khan asked.

"Ah, because of the fatwa, that our great imam, Sardar Agha, has placed on the infidels who stole it, this will bring the tribes together, they will search him out and bring him to us."

"Excellent. While you have your coffee and stuff yourself with pastries? Is that how it works?" Khan asked with his hands clasped together as he stared at the lump of incompetence before him.

The first sergeant did not reply. His large body

squirmed in his chair. He dropped his eyes to his hands as if an answer lay there.

"Get out of my office—all of you," Khan yelled.

They rose as one. Chairs clattered as they raced away from the wrath of their chief.

Khan sat there and fumed. Why had he taken this job? The last police chief was murdered for standing up to the Taliban and the tribes. He thought of his options. He needed to do some police work, and that required getting all the facts.

The one fact he needed to know, was what did the CIA and the Canadian detective find of interest on his computer? He could not touch the lady from the CIA, but the Canadian detective, she was fair game.

He massaged his temple for a moment as a plan came into mind. He needed to discover what these people had found interesting on the tape and why they wanted it. He would set a trap and see how they would get out of it.

Chapter Twenty-Two

Bernadette opened her eyes. The boy was not beside her. A thin stream of light through the window told her it was morning. Rolling over she checked her watch—zero seven hundred. Where was the boy?

She washed her face and went down the hall to the front desk. Almas was sitting on the back counter of the desk, a sticky bun in his hands while laughing in a discussion with Massoud.

"Hi, Massoud. Thanks for looking after Almas. I didn't know where he had gone," Bernadette said.

"Ah, no problem, Madame, this little one is a joy. I know he has been through a lot…" Massoud put his hand to his mouth as if he'd said too much.

"Then you know of what he's been through—did he tell you?"

"Oh, no, Madame, but the moment I saw him in the costume I knew he was the prize of someone. Then last night at home there is a rumor that the Warlord

Mohammad Mirwais is looking for his boy that he says was stolen from him. Sorry if I assumed this is him."

Bernadette looked around the room; there was no one there. "Do you promise you will tell no one?"

Massoud put his hand over his heart. "Please, your secret is safe with me. You must tell everyone that his boy is with you as you are planning to adopt him. It happens all the time, and..." He looked around, "...Do not say his name is Almas, that is the name the warlord is looking for. Tell people his name is Aimal, it will be easy for Almas to remember."

"Would you tell him that, please?" Bernadette asked. "My Pashto is at please and thank you."

"Of course," Massoud said. He turned to Almas and told him of the name, Aimal. The boy shook his head violently. "He doesn't like the name," Massoud said looking up in resignation.

"Tell him it is his secret name. This is a game we are playing," Bernadette said.

Massoud translated to Almas. The boy smiled and took a big bite of his sticky bun.

"I take it we have a winner," Bernadette said. She stared hard at the boy for a moment. "Did he happen to tell you where he is from, and if his parents are still alive?"

Massoud said something to Almas and the boy jumped off the back counter and shot off down the hallway.

"I told him to get another bun," Massoud said. "The boy comes from a village in the north near the Iran border. Six months ago he says a night letter was posted on his parents door."

"What's a night letter?"

"This is something the Taliban puts on a door in the

middle of the night. The letter will warn the people that they need to stop doing something or to obey to their will. The consequences of disobeying the letter are always the same—death."

"I take it that Almas' parents did not comply?"

"The boy is not clear on that. He says when he came home from school, his parents were not there. The whole village had been deserted. He says some men took him away. I did not need him to fill in the rest," Massoud said.

Bernadette blew out a breath, "I can't imagine what he's been through."

Almas ran back into the lobby with his second bun and began munching on it. In between bites he started to talk excitedly to Massoud. He laughed out loud at the boy's words.

"What's so funny?" Bernadette asked.

"He says if he is to have a secret name, why can it not be of the pendant around his neck?"

"Tell him to show us."

The boy wiped his hands on his trousers and unbuttoned his shirt. He pulled out a shiny silver medallion. On the back was an inscription. He looked at Massoud and said something in Pashto.

"He says you should read it for him, he thinks it's in English."

Bernadette looked at the Pendant, a Saint Christopher Medal. On the back was the English word, Christos.

"Where did he get this?" Bernadette asked. Her eyes narrowed—the boy jumped back in fear.

"He thinks you are mad at him."

"No, no, tell him I'm not angry at him, I just need to know where this came from."

Massoud asked Almas. The boy spoke quietly making signs of a house with his hands, turning to Bernadette with a smile.

"He says the warlord took them to a village that was close to his own. The warlord said that a secret man was inside. He gave him this pendant, said it was from the man, and that Almas now contained the man's power as the man would die soon."

Bernadette looked at the pendant and her hand started to shake. She clasped both her hands together to get a grip on herself. There was only one explanation. This was the pendant that Chris's mother had given him years ago. He always wore it. The inscription was to Christos, the only name his mother called him by.

"Can he tell me the name of the village?" Bernadette asked softly.

The boy paused. He looked from Massoud to Bernadette and back to Massoud and began speaking quickly.

"If you promise to protect him from the warlord who held him captive, he will take you to the village. He never wants to be near him again."

"Tell him I understand, but he doesn't have to go with me, he can give me the name of the village, and I will go there myself."

The boy shook his head after Massoud translated Bernadette's words.

"He will give you the name of the village, but he will do so only if he gets to come with you," Massoud said.

"Why?"

"He feels he wants to give the pendant back to the man in the house. He thinks the reason he is safe now is because he has the pendant. It belongs to the man and he took his power. He needs to return it to him."

Bernadette hugged Almas. "Never have truer words been spoken. Thank him for his bravery. We will go together to find the man."

Chapter Twenty-Three

Bernadette rushed back to her room and grabbed her computer. The only source for information she had was Wikipedia. The village that Almas gave her was Azau in Farah Province. According to the listing, it was a little village of some thirty families on the Azaw River. All her other Google searches turned up nothing. She needed to call Lackey at the CIA.

Lackey answered on the first ring. "I heard you had some fun with a warlord outside the wire yesterday," she said.

"You heard about that?"

"You forget, I'm CIA, we have our ears everywhere. I also heard you snatched the warlord's boy toy. How very noble of you. You just put my relations with him on hold for the next month," Lackey said sarcastically.

"But you know what he was using the boy for, don't you? You can't possibly condone that?" Bernadette said.

"Look, I don't agree with ninety-nine-percent of the bullshit that goes on in this country. But the Warlord

Mirwais keeps the Taliban in check in his area. Without him we'd have to commit an entire battalion of marines and a squadron of the air force to look after the Taliban he keeps control over."

"So, that's the price of the boy?"

"Don't get high and mighty on me, Callahan, we've got men and women risking their lives every day in this country —yes, damn straight—it's the price of the boy until we get those bastard Taliban under control."

Bernadette shook her head. There was no way to win this. "I'm sorry, Lackey, I know I don't understand the politics and what you're going through…"

"I guess I kind of unloaded on you. Sorry, I'm having a shit day. You called me for something, what's up?"

"You're right, I do have the boy. He gave me a lead of a village where he thinks they have Chris. Actually I'm pretty sure he's there."

"What's the village?"

"Azau, in the Farah Province."

"Holy shit, you might as well have said on the moon."

"Why is that?"

"The Taliban took it over last October. The whole place from the town of Farah to Anar Darreh is teaming with those black turbaned bastards. We only have fifteen thousand American soldiers for the entire country, which is not nearly enough to get them out. If you go in there, you're going to your death."

"Well, that sucks because I have to go there," Bernadette said.

"I had a feeling you might say that. Look I can't make it back to the compound for the next few days. I'll be bunking here at the embassy working on some projects. Is there anyway your security guy can get you here in the next two hours. I have some intel I can give you on the place. I don't want to send it over email as I don't trust the server at the compound."

"Sure, I'll call you when I'm on my way," Bernadette said and ended her call.

Checking her watch, she wondered how long it would take to get Jason from where he lived on the other side of Kandahar; she called him to find out.

"Jason here." The line was sketchy, gunfire sounded in the background.

"Hey, Jason, I hope this isn't a bad time, but I need your help to get me to the American Embassy."

An explosion reverberated through the phone, almost like it was next door.

"Are you alright, Jason?"

"…Ah…yeah, I'm fine…" Jason answered. "There's a fire fight between two tribes outside my door. It might be some time before I can get to you. Do you have to leave right away?"

"I got a lead on Chris—I think I know where he is. Lackey is going to give me intel on the village—got to be within two hours." Bernadette said. She found herself toying with the cross around her neck that her mother had given her. It was something she rarely did.

"I think I can set you up with an alternative. Hold tight. I'll be back to you shortly," Jason said and went off the call.

Bernadette sat in her room and shut her eyes. She was a somewhat practicing Catholic. Her mother, who had died when she was young, had made her promise to keep the faith on her deathbed. She'd done so begrudgingly. The faith in God never seemed to equal the depths of despair humanity could reach. But just this time, she sent a prayer up to whoever might listen. She needed a vehicle to get to the American Embassy—perhaps someone was listening.

Her cell phone rang—it was Jason. "What have you got?" Bernadette asked, almost forgetting to breathe.

"I got a real ace. He will get you there. Go to the front gates of the compound, make sure you wear some Afghan style women's clothes, doesn't have to be a burka, but a hijab that covers your hair. The guy's name is Mohammad. He may look a bit rough, but he's the best there is, with the best Taxi service in Kandahar."

"I thought you were the best?" Bernadette said with a chuckle.

"He's my Afghan equivalent, he'll be there in thirty minutes. I'll get to your compound as soon as the tribes stop shooting the asses off each other, you copy that?"

"Yes, loud and clear. Stay safe, I'll see you soon," Bernadette said. She put her phone down and let another prayer go upward and chuckled to herself, "You're becoming a religious fanatic in this country."

She went to her closet and looked at the clothes she'd purchased at the bazaar. She took out the long overcoat and the large hijab. She made sure she wrapped the hijab properly over her head so she covered her hair. She would pull it up over her face when she was in the back of whatever car Mohammad was driving to ensure she did not look like a westerner.

She went back to the front desk; Masood was standing there while Almas drew pictures on a piece of paper.

"Massoud, I'm going out to the American Embassy by taxi, can you take care of Almas for a while?"

His eyes widened in disbelief. "You going to take a taxi in the craziness that is going on in Kandahar? You must have a death wish."

"I'm getting that question a lot lately. I need to meet someone there."

Massoud shook his head and put his hand to his chest. "I hope Allah will protect you. I will take care of Almas, do not worry about him."

"Tell him I will be back for him," Bernadette said.

Massoud translated to Almas. The boy jumped off the counter and rushed to Bernadette. He hugged her hard and talked excitedly.

"He thinks you are leaving him behind," Massoud said.

"Tell him I am going to find some information for our journey," Bernadette said holding Almas and stroking his head. She knelt and kissed both his cheeks and dried his eyes. He smiled and hugged her again and said something.

"He said, God willing, you will return and you will begin your journey together," Masood said.

"Yes, *inshallah*, if god wills it, I will return, Almas." She kissed his forehead and walked away. In just forty-eight hours she had become attached to this little boy. The whole idea of motherhood while becoming a detective had been pushed aside. She thought she had crushed it to become the fierce female she thought she was. This little boy's hugs had breached all of her defenses.

Bernadette's thoughts on children were clear—they were good for other people, not for her. Her parents had semi-raised her along with five brothers and then left them as they pursued a life on the road seeking fame as musicians. Her father had turned to alcohol and drugs and died young. Her mother had died of a broken heart. Bernadette wished none of that on any child.

She walked to the front gates trying to suppress her emotions. She needed to get clear to focus. The soldiers at the front gate were waiting for her. They had smirks on their faces.

"Are you the Callahan that ordered a taxi?" one of the soldiers asked.

"Yes, is it here?" Bernadette asked straining her neck to see over the soldiers and the barricade.

"Oh, yeah, it's here all right. A guy named Mohammed is out there waiting for you." he said, waving his hand towards the outside.

Bernadette walked out and looked around for the taxi. Instead of a car, she saw what looked like a bright red motorized rickshaw with tassels on the front window and an old man who looked all of eighty hunched over and using the dilapidated vehicle to hold his body up.

"Callahan—Yalla, Yalla, come now, come now!" the old man yelled and motioned with his hands.

Bernadette couldn't help noticing that one hand had only two fingers left and he wore an eye patch over one eye. As she approached the rickshaw, she saw the old man wore the usual Afghan garments but looked like they'd been cleaned sometime last year. The man looked older than Fazal, her previous bodyguard, who had died protecting her.

"Mohammad?" Bernadette asked tentatively as she approached.

"Yes, come—get in—we go," the old man responded.

Bernadette squeezed into the back of the rickshaw. Mohammad pulled a cord several times in front that ignited the two-piston motorcycle engine and the little chariot sputtered to life.

The rickshaw lurched into motion. For a moment, Bernadette realized the strange predicament she was in. She thought Jason was sending her a crack Afghan security guy.

He had sent her a perfect disguise. What Taliban would suspect any foreigner to be traveling in one of these? At least she hoped his reasoning was right on this.

The back of the rickshaw was totally closed in. She could only see out the front over the head and shoulders of Mohammed. They weaved through narrow side streets with doors shut tight against the fighting that could be heard around the city.

Mohammed seemed to have sixth sense about the journey. Sometimes they went towards the fighting and sometimes he turned away from it. His hands deftly turned the motorcycle handlebars that were the rickshaw's steering device.

Shocks were none existent. Every pothole in Kandahar radiated upward through Bernadette's butt and jarred her brain. She wondered just why she'd thought of this scheme and recalled that for the first time in days she had a lead as to the location of Chris. She could feel it in her bones that he was in the village that Almas had named. She had to get there.

The rickshaw putt-putted along, drowning out almost any thought that entered her mind until it came to a screeching stop. The old man muttered, "Taliban."

Bernadette sat upright and pulled her hijab tighter around her face.

Chapter Twenty-Four

Loud voices sounded outside the rickshaw. Mohammed muttered at the Taliban and then began to shout at them. A gun muzzle appeared in the cab, the end of the muzzle resting beside Mohammed's head. He pushed the muzzle away and yelled at them louder.

She heard laughter outside the rickshaw. The little vehicle revved back into gear and resumed its journey. Fifteen minutes later, it stopped again and Mohammed turned to Bernadette. "America—America Embassy."

He stepped out of the rickshaw and helped her out. She reached into her pocket to pay him. He motioned her hand away.

"After, after…I wait."

They were in front of the embassy. Two tanks with a squad of marines behind sandbags now guarded the embassy.

Bernadette walked up to the front gate, opening her jacket as she did to show no weapons. A marine checked her ID and called into the embassy to clear her.

As he handed her back her ID, he said, "Lady, you got some kind of balls traveling in that frigging rickshaw to get here."

Bernadette took her ID back. "No, the driver does, he stared down the Taliban on the way, I just went along for the ride."

She walked into the embassy, trying not to show the marine that her legs were still shaking. Lackey was waiting for her just inside the embassy door.

"That's quite the ride you took. You know who your driver is?" Lackey asked when Bernadette approached.

"No idea. Someone my guy put me in touch with. Said he was good," Bernadette said.

Lackey nodded in his direction. "Yeah, he was one of the key leaders of the Mujahedeen. I thought he was dead until now. Apparently, he came out of retirement."

Bernadette looked at the old man. He'd taken out a cigarette, placed it between his lips, and lit it. He leaned back against the rickshaw and exhaled smoke into the air. He seemed relaxed, as if he'd just taken a joy ride through Kandahar.

"Follow me," Lackey commanded. "I don't have much time."

Bernadette followed her down the embassy hallway and then upstairs to her office. The embassy was more barricaded and on alert than usual. Sandbags bracketed the doors and windows. Heavily armed marines quick marched down the halls to take up positions behind them.

Lackey sat at her desk and typed on her computer. "I'm glad you made it here. I can give you a copy of the SSE intel I have, that's the sensitive site exploration document. It contains photographs and bios on most of the occupants of the village you're going to."

She sat back from her computer as the printer began to shoot out pages. "Not that I think this will do you any good." She pulled her bottle of scotch out of the desk drawer and poured two glasses. "You have a snowball's chance in hell of reaching your destination—as a Canadian you should know what that means." She threw back her scotch in one swig. "Bad joke, but you get my drift."

"I'm not leaving this country without Chris. I'll take whatever chance I need to get him back."

"You can't be certain he's in that village." Lackey said. She poured herself another stiff one and threw it back.

"No, I can't, but this is the only lead I've had since I've been here. I've had two attempts on my life since I've been here—I have strong feeling none of that was a coincidence. Someone knows I'm on the trail to find Chris and is trying to stop me. Not going to happen." Bernadette pushed her Scotch towards Lackey. "Thanks for the intel, I'd best be going."

Lackey took Bernadette's scotch and threw it back wiping her mouth with the back of her hand. "Suit yourself. As for people making attacks on your life, an Afghan will kill you for looking sideways at him. I have no idea who you've pissed off since you arrived here. Could have been the imam, or even someone who saw you outside the mosque. Remember—they hate women here."

"Again, thanks for the heads up," Bernadette said as she stood.

Lackey escorted her back towards the front entrance. "I wanted to warn you that with all the shit that's going on, your Canadian Embassy is talking about pulling out, and we Americans won't be far behind."

Bernadette stopped and turned to Lackey. "I thought you CIA types hung around no matter what?"

Lackey laughed. "Yeah, you're right, we just pull the earth over ourselves and hide deeper." She patted Bernadette's shoulder. "Now, if you'll excuse me, we captured a high value Taliban asset. It's essential we interrogate him in the first twenty-four hours before his buddies have time to flee their locations."

Bernadette walked out into the street. Mohammed was waiting for her beside the rickshaw. She got in the back, taking the document she had received from Lackey and stuffing it into the inner pocket of her coat. The gunfire had ceased.

The rickshaw fired up in a cloud of blue smoke and they began their return journey. She wondered if finally she was on the road to find Chris. Everything in her gut was telling her she was on the right path. All she needed to do now was get back to the compound, get together with Jason and Almas, and they'd be on their way.

The rickshaw rounded a narrow corner and stopped. Bernadette looked over Mohammed's shoulders and saw a green army truck. Men in helmets and weapons advanced on the rickshaw.

Mohammed said, "Police."

Bernadette hoped Mohammed could talk their way out of this stop. She put her hand in her pocket and pulled out a wad of Afghani bills. Perhaps this would be enough to bribe their way through.

The police spoke to Mohammed. He gestured back and forth, finally he turned to Bernadette. "You need show papers—you must get out."

Bernadette stepped into the ring of police officers. She'd placed the Afghani bills inside her passport. It looked ridiculous, there were so many there they made a bulge in her passport.

A sergeant with bulging eyes and stomach took the passport. He pocketed the money and stared at her. Then he yelled to his men. They grabbed her from behind and lifted her into the back of the truck.

She heard Mohammed yelling behind her. Gun butts sounded, the dull thud of wood on bone as the soldiers beat him into the ground. She lay face down as the truck sped away. She closed her eyes tightly and said a prayer to Saint Christopher, the one who supposedly guarded all travelers. "Okay," she whispered, "now would be time for a little help."

Chapter Twenty-Five

To Bernadette, being on the other side of the law was never pretty. She'd taken many people into custody. Sometimes it was rough when the person resisted, but most often, it was a matter of restraining and placing the person somewhere to calm them down.

None of that happened with the Afghani Police. From the moment she was thrown in the back of the truck, she was treated like the most dangerous criminal on the planet. They manhandled her out of the truck at the police station and pushed her down the corridors as if she'd committed the worst crime in the world.

They stopped at a solid wooden door, opened it, and threw her inside. The room was dark, only a small ray of light shone from the outside through a slit in the window.

"Damn it," Bernadette said. "I don't think I'll be getting a phone call." She crawled to the wall, put her back against it, and sighed.

A voice out of the dark said, "You are English?"

Bernadette turned to the voice, "Hi, I didn't know anyone was in here."

"My name is Safiya Durani, and you are?"

"Bernadette Callahan."

"Why have they arrested you, Bernadette Callahan?"

"I have no idea?"

"Oh, yes, you do, the first thing you need to know is that you are a woman. As a woman in Afghanistan you have already committed a crime."

"And that is?"

"You have not been born a man," Safiya said with a dry laugh.

"From what I've seen so far in this country it does seem a definite disadvantage. So, Safiya, what have you been arrested for?"

"Mine is the worst of all crimes in Afghanistan…"

"You were the one that murdered the last police chief?"

"No, worse, I have been accused of a moral crime."

"And, that is?"

"I am, or was, a professor of English studies at the university. My husband is also a professor there. His brother is a low life rat who wanted to have an affair with me. I told him I would have nothing to do with him, he went to the police, told them I had committed adultery with him…and here I am," Safiya said with a sigh.

"What about a lawyer, your due process under the law? When will your case be heard?" Bernadette asked.

"I will be shuffled off to prison and the court, which is often made up of a bunch of imam's who will hear the case in six months or a year from now. In the meantime, I will remain in prison."

"What about your husband, can't he intervene on your behalf?"

"His brother, my accuser, is a very powerful man in the government. If he is not careful in his protests on my behalf, his brother will ensure that he meets with an unfortunate accident."

"His brother would kill him?"

"Yes, that is what they call the triangle of love in English literature, is it not?"

"Yes, I'm a police detective back in Canada and I've seen more murders over love than just about anything else."

"Are you the fiancé of the man that stole the robe of Mohammed?"

"Wow, word gets around. And no, he did not steal it. I think someone is framing him for the theft."

"I like the word…framing. In English it sounds like someone is mounting a picture. You think then, your man is innocent?"

"I know it, I just haven't been able to prove it yet."

"*Inshallah*, you will be able to do so, Bernadette Callahan…"

The door opened to reveal two policemen. They walked into the room and hauled Bernadette to her feet.

"Looks like I've been invited for my interview. Good luck Safiya."

"The same to you, Bernadette Callahan."

Bernadette got only a quick glance of Safiya as light flooded the room. She was a beautiful woman from what she could see in the blinding light and what was revealed of her face under her hijab. Dark blue eyes, milky white perfect skin, full lips and dark hair that showed itself in one wisp from her head covering. Safiya had the curse of being too beautiful and the desire of her husband's powerful brother. To Bernadette it was if she'd stepped into a medieval kingdom, but with modern weapons of destruction.

They marched her down a long hallway and into the police chief's office. She was placed in a chair with the two officers on each side of her.

Khan sat at his desk. He took a handful of pistachio nuts from a bowl, cracked one, and began to munch on it while he stared at her. Bernadette stared back.

"You seem to think this is a joke," Khan said as he swallowed his nut and cracked another shell.

"Do you hear me laughing?" Bernadette asked.

"I could have you shot, for what you have done."

"And that is what exactly?"

Khan brushed the shells off his desk and picked up a disk from beside his computer. "I found this on my computer after you left my office with your CIA friend. You want to tell me what you learned from my files?"

Bernadette shook her head. "I know you hear this a lot, but I have no idea what you're talking about."

"You are working for the CIA. You know I cannot touch them, but you, you are nothing. I can throw you in my cells forever. Your Canada government is too weak to touch me. They will make protests and nothing will happen. You will sit and rot while they write letters to our president. The rats in my jail will crawl over you night and day."

Bernadette sat quietly and took a deep breath. This was the time to not show fear or say too much. She'd broken many a suspect the way Khan was acting.

"I'm sure you hold the power to do what you wish with me. I am only telling you that I did not place the device you have in your hand on your computer, nor do I know of any files that you are speaking of. I will be happy to enquire with Ms. Lackey of the American CIA when I see her."

"You will not be leaving here until you give me information," Khan commanded.

Bernadette had a sinking feeling. None of this was going well. Her thoughts raced to a way out. She couldn't call Lackey at the embassy; she would deny any knowledge and leave Bernadette hanging. The CIA could never be accused of spying on the police they were supposed to be working with.

"What if I just tell you that I did hear from my friend at the CIA that they may have some information, but that they were not able to get any clear answer from the information they received."

Khan smiled and cracked another pistachio nut. He took the nutmeat and squeezed it between his teeth. "So, you admit you know something of the theft of my data?"

"No, I only said I heard about some information, not the same thing," Bernadette said. She realized she'd just backed herself into a corner. Damn, a total rookie mistake.

"If you heard something, then you know what they are up to. You know they took files from my computer. You were in on this," Khan yelled, pieces of nut spewing from his mouth.

Bernadette breathed deeply and watched Khan escalate into a frenzy, how could she tell him they'd viewed the CCTV footage and found nothing there? Maybe Lackey hadn't shown her everything on the file. Maybe she'd set Bernadette up to take the fall in case Khan found out his computer had been accessed.

"Well? What do you wish to tell me or do I send you off to jail?"

"What am I being charged with?"

Khan shrugged and wiped the pieces of nut from his mouth. "It doesn't matter, I can put theft, I can put obstruction of police, I can put nothing and say you are person of interest in my investigation. It will all be the same."

Bernadette knew there was no way out. She was trapped. Anything she told Khan of the tape she'd seen would mean nothing to him. She was going to be sent to prison no matter what she said.

"I guess I'm ready to become a guest of your prison," Bernadette said. "Do I get to make a phone call before I'm sent away?"

"Of course not. You are in Afghanistan. You think this is something like your Canada or in America? When you get to prison, bribe one of the guards, and you will be able to make as many calls as you like. Until your money runs out." He repeated his words in Afghani to his men. They laughed loud and hard.

Bernadette was pulled out of the chair and taken down a hallway and several flights of stairs. A door opened and she was pushed into a large holding cell with a crowd of women.

Safiya walked towards her. "I see my sister Bernadette Callahan has come to join us for our journey to the prison. I take it that your interview did not go well?"

Bernadette smiled at Safiya. "Not my best, but I think the result would have been the same no matter what I said. Khan wants me in jail."

"You are right. The Afghani prison system is the way the men hold power over the women here. Even if we are given a release order from prison, unless a husband or male relative comes to collect us, we have to stay. Some women are there for years as their husbands or brothers are mad at them and they cannot leave."

"My God, that sounds archaic," Bernadette said.

"Yes, it has been this way since ancient times, and we

seem powerless to change it. Maybe in time, *inshallah*, we will change it."

Bernadette looked around the room. "Are all these women being sent to prison for moral crimes?"

"Many of them. Some have committed a '*zina*,' which under Islamic law is illegal for women to run away from home from a forced marriage. If they are raped and have an involuntary pregnancy, they have committed a crime, and are sent to prison with their child. The child is then sent back to the families when they are five years old."

"And if the family doesn't want the child?"

"You have seen the many children in the streets of Kandahar? Many of them are orphans, released from the prisons," Safiya said.

"This is sad," Bernadette said looking around the room.

"The worst thing is, that the women accused of moral crimes will be sent to prison with women who have committed real crimes. You see that woman in the corner with her head down? She is a violent one."

"What did she do?"

"She is a convicted serial killer. Together with her three brothers, the police found they had murdered over one hundred people in and around Kandahar. She was the victim of much abuse by her brothers from a very young age, she ended up doing their bidding by attracting men and women into their ring of death."

Bernadette looked in the direction of the woman. She swayed back and forth. A strange sound emanated from her mouth that had something between an animal and human noise.

"I think I'll stay clear of her."

"Yes, and there are several other women here who are petty thieves but several who have murdered their husbands when they could not take any more abuse," Safiya said.

"I think your *zina* law could use some divorce laws and lawyers," Bernadette said. "You'd save the prison system from overcrowding. And some Afghan men might live longer."

Safiya nodded. "Yes, our system of ancient laws has placed us in a strange pattern of behavior."

The doors opened, and guards came in shouting.

"It is time to board the bus," Safiya said, "Follow me."

They were herded out of the room and onto a green prison bus with bars over the windows. Each prisoner was handcuffed to the seat in front of them; Bernadette and Safiya were seated together. The muttering serial killer was placed at the back with two guards beside her.

The bus lurched forward, leaving the police compound with two police trucks as an escort. Bernadette watched out the window. Children and women looked up at the bus from the streets. Their faces looked blank, as if they'd accepted the fate of the women passengers. Perhaps they had relatives or mothers who were in the prison they were being sent to or feeling lucky they were not on that bus.

Bernadette tried to steel herself for what was to happen next. She'd visited prisons many times in her years in the police force. There was a culture there. You had to fit into it and never stand out. A person who stood out had to either take over as the leader or be taken out. Her objective was to survive until she could get release and look for Chris again. She felt the CIA documents in her coat. She needed to keep them safe and hidden.

The convoy rounded a corner onto a wide street and stopped. There was much shouting from the Afghan Police.

Bernadette looked up to see two American army tanks and an old Toyota Camry blocking their path.

Chapter Twenty-Six

The police on the bus started yelling. The women put their heads down. Bernadette raised her head to see what was happening. A policeman slapped her in the head, yelling at her.

"You must keep your head down, my sister," Safiya said. "The guards are very excited."

Bernadette put her head down. She was sitting in the seat beside the window. She moved over slightly so she could peek out the side. Two men walked towards the bus. She could see one was Jason the other was Reza with a megaphone in his hand. He lifted it to his mouth and began speaking to the police.

"What's he saying?" Bernadette whispered to Safiya.

"He says that the police have a prisoner they want. If they deliver her—it's you Bernadette—they will let them proceed without harm."

The policemen on the bus erupted in shouts and curses. The man in the lead police truck threw up his arms. He had his handgun in one hand, pointed at Jason and Reza threatening to shoot them.

Jason rose up one hand. A spray of machine gun fire erupted from one of the tanks. It hit the engine of the first truck. The policeman hit the ground as the police on the bus spread-eagled onto the floor. Their curses took on a more muted tone.

Reza came over the megaphone again. This time he sounded more calming.

"What's he saying? Bernadette asked.

"He says they must understand the tank will put an artillery shell through the truck next. They do not need to be harmed, if they release you now, they can go to their evening tea. If not, the tank will usher them into paradise where they can meet Allah."

"I had no idea Reza was so poetical in his speech," Bernadette said.

The police on the bus started to argue, one ran off the bus to consult with the officer, then ran back on the bus and began discussing the situation with the other policemen.

"What's going on?" Bernadette asked.

"The guards are debating how they can give you up and not be destroyed by Khan when he finds out what happened."

"He would murder them?"

"This is a metaphor. They think Khan would fire them all and their lives ruined. He would make sure they never worked in the police force. They'd end up in the Afghan Army where they'd have to fight the Taliban. Many of these men are cowards who only know how to push women around." Safiya said.

The megaphone sounded again. This time Reza's voice sounded quite loud and commanding.

"What now?"

"He's telling them their time is up."

A rhythmic sound came from Reza's megaphone.

"Is that counting down I'm hearing?"

"Yes, it is, I suggest you put your head lower, there could be some explosions."

Bernadette dropped her head below the seat. All the women did the same. The policemen muttered back and forth on the floor.

A policeman yelled from inside the bus.

"It's okay," Safiya said. "They are going to give you up."

A policeman came behind Bernadette; he unshackled Safiya's cuffs and then took off Bernadette's and motioned for her to get off the bus. This time he did not touch her—he was apologetic in his actions.

Bernadette grabbed Safiya by the arm. "I want you to come with me, and as many of these women that you think we can take with us."

Safiya put her hand on Bernadette's. "My dear sister, if I were to come with you, I would be a fugitive. Kandahar is not safe for women right now. You go, we will be safe in prison. I wish you a safe journey and, *inshallah*, you will find your man and the robe."

Bernadette hugged Safiya and got off the bus. The doors of the bus closed, its engines revved and it sped off down the street with police following in the remaining truck. Some of them stared at Bernadette as if she was the vilest criminal they'd ever seen.

Jason approached her smiling. "Sorry I couldn't get to you sooner. Mohammed told me he was surrounded by police and couldn't do anything. The only good thing is this police convoy to the prison leaves every day at the same time. You'd think these guys would learn."

"And your tank escort? How did you round up this kind of heavy American hardware?"

"Oh, these guys?" Jason said pointing with his thumb and fist over his shoulder. "I did some sniper work with their unit back in the day. I was able to save a lot of their hides and they returned the favor. Now, I got to say my goodbyes to them." He turned towards the tanks.

Bernadette walked to the Camry to see Reza there with the megaphone.

"I want to thank you for coming here. This was very dangerous," Bernadette said. She wanted to hug him, but placed her hand over her heart and bowed to him.

Reza adjusted his glasses and put the megaphone in the car. "Jason called me last night. He told me the police took you. I could not let that happen after what you did yesterday with the boy."

"What do you mean?"

Reza took off his glasses and wiped them slowly, bowing his head. "You had the courage to save the boy. When I came home last night I saw my own boy. He is the age of Almas. You stood up with your courage to help him…save him."

"I couldn't do anything else. It's just how I'm wired, Reza."

"I know, I see that in you." Reza raised his head to put on his glasses. His eyes were moist. "I told you I escaped from the Taliban when they killed my fellow teachers—I hid under a desk."

"That's the same as escaping in my books," Bernadette said.

"There was a gun on the floor. I could have done something," Reza said.

Bernadette shook her head. "It's never that simple. If

there were many Taliban in the room, you would have died with the others. The time to stand and fight is not always clear."

"Thank you, Bernadette, I hope I will know when the time comes on our journey."

"You are coming with us?"

"Yes. Jason told me you are going to the west to find your fiancé. You will need my services. I will go with you," Reza said bowing his head.

"I will do everything in my power to keep you safe, Reza."

Reza smiled. "It is the will of Allah that will keep me safe, but I thank you for your offer."

Jason came back to the car. Reza got in the front and Bernadette jumped in the back. Jason threw the car in reverse and spun it around, heading the other way down the street.

"I'm going to get us to a safe house I have," Jason said. "I have provisions stashed there for our journey. I hope you got some good intel from your CIA friend."

"She gave me everything: the village, it's Azau in Farah Province, and the amount of people and the names of the villagers."

"Did she give you name of the warlord or tribal leader that runs the village?" Jason asked.

"Yes." She pulled the sheaf of papers out of her inside coat pocket and leafed through it. "Here it is. Ramin Rasul. Does that sound like someone you've heard of?"

"Oh my god," Jason said, almost swerving the car into a market stall. "He is one of the toughest warlords in the western provinces. He is also a personal friend of our imam, Sardar Agha."

"Is he one of those child molesters, like that jerk, Mirwais?" Bernadette asked.

"No, he's hardliner. A real Muslim's Muslim and he's a Taliban. But he could be in league with anyone who furthers his hold on his territory."

Reza looked over his shoulder to Bernadette. "It seems like we are looking to have a bit of hard luck on our journey to find your Chris."

"Why is that?" Bernadette asked.

"The tribe or clan of Ramin Rasul is very fierce. The International Fighters thought they had fought them into submission, but that is never the case with them. They will lie down, but they will never die. They are an offshoot of the Durrani Pashtuns tribe."

"How many different tribes are there?" Bernadette asked.

"There are major ones, like the Baluchis, Turkmens and Aimakes, and dozens of small ethnic, like the Jats, who are gypsies. One of my Hazara friends told me of a tribe called the Dumdor, dum means tail, in Dari, I believe. He may have been right—there is no reason that, with cousin marriage, some would develop a tail," Reza said.

Reza continued in a serious note. "It is impossible to tell the exact boundaries of a tribe, since they break down into sub tribes. They learn to fight each other for dominance over the land as their clan grows"

"Kind of like the Hatfield's and the McCoy's of the West Virginia in America," Bernadette said.

"I don't know who that is," Reza said.

"They were two clans that were at war with each other for years," Bernadette said.

"Yes, I see," Reza said, shaking his head. "But you must

understand, some of these tribes, they have been at war for centuries."

Jason turned the Camry into a narrow laneway besides a building and stopped. He jumped out, pulling a canvas awning over the back of the vehicle. They looked like a market stall had just covered them in.

"We're here," Jason said.

Bernadette got out of the car, following Jason into the building with Reza behind her. They heard the shouts of Almas as he came racing around a corner. He jumped into Bernadette's arms.

"I am here, I am here," Almas said.

Bernadette hugged him hard. "Yes you are Almas. I am so happy to see you."

"I here, I here, I happy…" Almas said.

"That's all the English I had time to teach him," Jason said. "The rest is up to you." He motioned for Bernadette to follow him into the other room of the building. "Follow me and I'll show you what our trip is going to be. Not quite the Michelin Guide trip, but it will be interesting."

Chapter Twenty-Seven

Bernadette stood beside Jason as he spread a large map out over a table. He pointed to the different sections and placed some markers on the map for reference.

"Here we are in Kandahar and our first destination is the city of Farah," Jason said with his finger on the destination. "It's only three hundred forty-nine klicks from here, but it's got Taliban checkpoints as we get close to the city."

"Why so many Taliban?" Bernadette asked.

Jason winked at her. "They took the city of Farah back in October of last year. They've got the police and the government holed up in the center of the city trying to hold out, but it's not looking good."

"How do we get around it?"

"We don't, we have to go through it, because if we go around, we are in barren countryside. The Taliban will suspect we're up to something. I got us some fake Afghan ID papers, and you Bernadette, sorry but you've got to do the burka thing again."

"Damn, I hate that thing. Will I be heavily armed once again?"

"I will load you up with so much firepower that you will be one hell of a battling burka…if that's what you want."

"I'm in," Bernadette said with a small smile. "What's the distance to our next objective?"

"Assuming we get out of Farah, we have only a seventy klick trek to Anar Darreh on pretty crap roads."

"Is that town under Taliban control too?" Bernadette asked.

"Not yet," Jason replied.

Bernadette let one eyebrow arch as she looked at Jason. "You're awfully cool about this. It seems the situation is compounding by the hour."

Jason shrugged his shoulders. "This is Afghanistan. The Taliban have taken or been pushed out of every city in the country. They make it their goal to mount a spring and summer offensive. Right now, they are trying to hold onto what they have during the winter season so they use the bases to strike at Kandahar and Kabul, but as long as the Americans are here with their airpower, they can't hold onto anything for very long."

"And what if the Americans ever pulled out?" Bernadette asked.

"This place would fold so fast you'd be hard pressed to get a flight out before the Taliban hit the gates. Of course, they'd have to come through some tribes that hate their guts, but that's the way it is here."

Bernadette shook her head at Jason's candor. "So, we get passed Anar Darreh, how far to our little village and objective?"

Jason looked down at the map. "It's only fifty klicks

outside of Anar Darreh. There's a small river to cross, and little mountain pass to get over but if we make no wrong turns and stay away from the Iranian border, we'll be fine."

"The Iranian's, how close are they to Azau?"

Jason pointed a large finger at the map. "They're almost kissing distance. One wrong step and we cross the border. The Iranian special units have been posted along the border. They don't like what's going on in Afghanistan now. There's a rumor they could come over the border to keep things under control for their Shia compatriots."

"Sorry, what now is a Shia?"

Jason picked up a bottle of water and took a drink. "In the Muslim's, there's two groups, the Sunni's and the Shia's. Almost like Catholics and Protestants. They view the succession of Mohammed differently."

"That sounds like most Christians and the succession of Christ. So much confusion, sad to know they caught some of our bad ways."

"Well, they did it on their own. Afghanistan is mostly Sunni, and Iran is all Shia. Most of the Muslims in the world are Sunni, the Shia make up only twenty percent," Jason said.

"Hmm, I'm wondering if the Iranians are feeling threatened with all the unrest here in Afghanistan?" Bernadette remarked.

Jason rolled up the map. "Could be, then I've been here for many years, just about anything seems to set the people off here." He stuffed the map into a case. "You know there was a tale about Alexander the Great. His wife asked him how things were going in his conquest of Afghanistan. He sent her back some dirt and told her to spread it around their home in Greece. She did that. Soon every one of the staff in their villa was fighting and quarreling. She asked Alexander what the reason was. He said, even the dirt is angry and causes fights here."

Bernadette sighed. "Yes, I think that sums this place up. Now, I need to find the facilities to take some kind of a shower. I smell of prison."

Jason pointed her in the direction of a crude washing facility. It was a toilet with a hole in the floor. Beside it was a cold bucket of water with soap. Bernadette stood to the side of the toilet, being careful not to step too close to it or smell it. The soap had a pleasant rose water smell. She doused a rag in the bucket, lathered some soap on the rag and did a quick bucket wash.

She was reminded of all the times she'd done this by a lake in Northern Canada. A memory of a canoe trip she'd taken with Chris came to her. She'd been washing herself by the lake naked from the waist up. Chris had come up behind her and folded his arms around her. He taken the washcloth and caressed her with it until they'd fallen into each other's arms, making love on the beach.

Shaking her head to get rid of the vision she put her t-shirt back on and walked back into the room. Jason and Reza were making dinner. The smell of rice with aromatic spices and goat meat filled the air. They gave her a plate and she sat with Almas on the ground and devoured the meal.

Later that night, they rolled some bedding onto the floor, threw down blankets, and lay down to sleep. The sound of gunfire and explosions punctuated the night air.

Bernadette lay there with Almas beside her, wondering if she'd find Chris in this violent country. Lackey had told her she had a death wish in going after him. But she had to find him. She was the reason he'd come here, to prove himself worthy. Her prominence as a detective and his inability to find a job had driven him here. Now, she had to find him to take him back home, even if, as his mother wished, that she was to never see him again. Exhaustion pulled her eyes shut and sent her to sleep.

Chapter Twenty-Eight

Jason woke everyone at 0500 hours. Bernadette rolled off her mat and shook her head. Almas lay there, looking around. He smiled at her and started to speak excitedly to her.

"What is Almas saying?" Bernadette asked Reza.

"He said he is happy you are here. When he closed his eyes, he prayed to Allah that he would see you again in the morning. Allah has granted his prayers. He is happy," Reza said.

Bernadette tousled the boy's hair. "I am happy too."

She got off the floor and went to the crude room that was called the toilet. Or as she'd named it "hole in the floor room," did her morning business and washed her hands in the bucket.

Jason was walking back and forth putting packs near the door. He picked up a machine gun and threw it in Bernadette's direction.

Bernadette grabbed it, checking the bolt action and safety. "This is the famed Russian AK-forty-seven?"

"It sure is. The best weapon the Russians ever made. The thing will fire almost anywhere. It's the core weapon for the Taliban and the Afghan National Army. Every time the NATO forces give the Afghan's one of their fancy weapons, they try to lose it so they can go back to that weapon."

Bernadette felt the weight and looked down the sights. "Why is that?"

"The thing just doesn't jam. You could go through a dust storm with it or drop it off a mountain, its damn near indestructible. You'd have to drive a tank over it to break it."

"Is that why you prefer to have it with you?"

"Sure, that and if you have an AK-forty-seven and every Afghan has one, all you need to do to get more ammo is kill or take it from your enemy. There's no Wal-Mart or Costco out there for resupply—know what I mean?"

Bernadette handed the weapon back to Jason. "Sounds good, when do I get one?"

"That one is yours. I have one for Reza, and one for Almas," Jason said.

"Almas, how could he know how to fire one of these?"

Jason turned to Almas. He said something to him in Afghani, nodding to the weapon. Almas ran to Bernadette taking the gun from her. He racked the chamber, put the stock to his shoulder and smiled.

"The children learn to fire AK-forty-sevens at their father's knee. They don't mess with toy weapons here. Why would you when the real thing is available? If a boy's father falls, his son picks up his gun and keeps on firing," Jason said.

Bernadette looked at Almas. The boy had taken on a new stature. He looked older, more deadly. She took the gun from him and pressed her hand on his cheek. He smiled, turning back into a boy again.

Jason gave Bernadette a set of army fatigues to put on. They were a bit snug, but she wriggled into them. She pulled a protective vest over that, and then strapped a combat knife to one leg and a Glock handgun to the other leg.

She took a web belt from the table, attaching two flash grenades and a fragmentation grenade to it. Jason handed her a small shotgun to hide under her burka. She felt ready.

"Once again, this burka is loaded," Bernadette said. She adjusted her weapons and pulled the long blue garment over her. "Does anything show?"

Jason looked her up and down. "No, you're good to go. I hope I look half as good as you when I put mine on."

"What? You're going to put one on?" Bernadette asked from under the burka.

Jason winced. "Yeah, once we get into Taliban territory, Reza here is going to be our front man. I can make like I'm a Muslim from Croatia who's taken up their cause, but they'll ask too many questions."

"I welcome you to the tribe of the battling burka's," Bernadette said with a laugh. "Now when and how do we get out of Kandahar?"

"I booked us a trip out by shadowing a NATO convoy. I know a bunch of guys in the unit. They got some heavy armored units going to Delaram. We hitch a ride on the back of the convoy, then we're on our own to Farah."

"Won't they think we're a bunch of terrorists trying to follow them? Especially me in this burka?"

"Nope, I got it covered. Now, let's move out. The convoy is moving at zero six fifteen hours from their forward location. We've got some city streets to navigate. I'm just hoping warring factions are still asleep right now or have gone to the mosque to pray."

As if on cue, the first call to prayer sounded. It was echoed from one mosque to another until the entire city sounded like a wave of clerics calling the faithful.

"Okay, load up. Once everyone is in the mosques we got a window of opportunity to haul ass," Jason said.

"But, I have a problem," Reza said. "I must pray."

Jason and Bernadette stopped in their tracks. They had packs slung over their shoulders, ready for the door. They looked at each other. Dropping their packs, they nodded their heads in agreement.

There was nothing else they could do. Reza and Almas needed to pray. Jason stared at his watch.

Bernadette moved closer, and whispered, "Are we going to make the rendezvous with the convoy?"

"It's going to be tight," Jason said as he watched Reza and Almas put down their prayer rugs and begin their prayers.

Bernadette and Jason stood in the doorway with their gear while the two stood shoulder to shoulder.

"I've never seen this, what does it mean?" Bernadette asked Jason in low whisper.

Jason looked at the two of them. "This is the *fajr*, this prayer starts off the day and is performed before sunrise. The first motion is the *takbir*, worshippers stand with raised hands at shoulder level, proclaiming *Allahu akbar*, God is great."

They watched as Reza and Almas proclaimed *Allahu akbar* in unison, the little voice of the boy pitched higher than Reza.

The voices of Reza and Almas rose up softly into the room; it became a beautiful melody as they repeated it together.

When the prayers were completed, Reza and Almas got up slowly and smiled at Bernadette and Jason. "We must go now," Reza said.

"Do we still have time?" Bernadette asked. She looked at her watch. The time was 0545.

Jason smiled. "Let's hope Allah will be merciful. And we need to haul ass."

They hurried out of the room, throwing their bags in the back of the car. Jason pulled the canvas cover off the car and with everyone inside, he spun the car in reverse.

The alleyway was vacant. A lone vendor with fresh bread watched the beaten-up car sped down the street.

The narrow alley opened up onto a large road. Jason stopped, looking left and right.

"What are you looking for?" Bernadette asked from the back seat.

"I'm trying to see if the army or police have put up any checkpoints yet," Jason said.

"Do you think they're looking for me?" Bernadette asked.

"Could be or just their normal squeeze point to rake off money from innocent people," Jason said. "There's a saying in Afghanistan, that the ordinary person cannot do anything. But a government person, which includes the military and police can do what he wants—killing, stealing… anything."

Reza turned his head. "We often say the Afghan government is a criminal syndicate."

"Well put." Jason nodded in agreement.

Bernadette leaned forward. "Well, that's great. If the Afghan government is totally corrupt and the Taliban is corrupt in a different way, how does a regular person exist here?"

Reza flashed a smile. "This here, in Afghanistan, is Allah's greatest test. You will see, that Allah will prevail."

Jason shook his head, put the car in gear, and turned right. They blew past a police checkpoint that had not set up yet. The policemen were sitting beside their car having their morning tea. They looked up with mild interest at the passing car. They would stop the next one.

"You see?" Reza said. "Allah has taken care of us."

They turned another corner and straight into the barrel of an Afghan Army tank.

Bernadette nodded her head to the front. "You best have some divine help with this one, Reza. I don't see them letting us slip by."

"That's a T-sixty-two Russian tank," Jason said.

"Great, nice to know what's about to make this little car disappear into bits," Bernadette replied.

The tank sat there, motionless and ominous, its very presence threatening the occupants of the little Toyota Camry. It was painted in a sand and brown camouflage. Its long gun barrel hung down and slightly to the left as if it needed a target to aim at. Two hatches were open on the top turret, both hatch lids opened towards them, but they couldn't see if there was anyone behind them.

One large machine gun pointed skyward beside one of the hatches, as if you needed more weaponry than the big gun on this forty-plus ton of steel mounted on two wide tracks.

A hatch opened in the front of the tank below the turret. A soldier stared at the Toyota and began to speak into his radio.

"What do we do now?" Bernadette asked.

"We get the hell out of here," Jason said, throwing the car in reverse and accelerating.

Bernadette stared at the gun on the turret. "Won't they fire at us?"

"They can't move the turret while the drivers hatch is open."

The car accelerated. The tank's engines revved. A cloud of smoke erupted from its rear. It started to come after them.

"The tanks coming after us."

Jason stared over his shoulder maneuvering the car backwards. "Don't worry, it's only got a top speed of fifty kilometers per hour. We can outrun it."

Bernadette looked behind them, then back to the tank. A head appeared beside the machine gun. The man grabbed the weapon and began to rack the ammunition chamber. "The machine gunner woke up. How fast can you back up to avoid the bullets?"

Jason yelled, "Get down."

Reza threw himself onto the floor of the car. Bernadette grabbed Almas, pushing him to the floor and covering him with her body. A stream of tracer shells flew by the car hitting the buildings on the right side. A cloud of dust and dirt showered the car.

Jason threw the car into a sharp left turn. They were in the cross street. Making a three-point turn he headed the car forward. Residents came out of their homes to see what had happened perhaps wondering if the Taliban were making a final attack, and many pointed at the car.

"It's okay," Jason said. "We're in the clear."

Bernadette sat up. Almas shook his head and sat beside her. "That was way more excitement than I needed for the morning. How soon until we get to the convoy?"

Jason reduced speed and turned into a large market where the shops were beginning to open. The smell of fresh

Caught in the Crossfire

bread and coffee wafted into the air. If they weren't in such a hurry, and if Bernadette wasn't wanted by the Afghan police, it would have been wonderful to have stopped for warm bread and coffee filled with fresh milk and sugar. Bernadette let the thoughts flit through her brain and then descend into the depths. She needed to concentrate on here and now—on staying alive.

Making their way through the market, they came to a plaza. Heavy walls banked both sides. There was an opening with several military personnel standing in front.

"This is the meet up point," Jason said.

"There's no one here. Have they left already?" Bernadette asked.

Jason checked his watch. "It's zero six-thirty hours. They were to assemble at zero six-fifteen. There's no way they've left unless they went out early. That usually never happens with the military."

Jason stopped the car a long distance from the soldiers. He walked towards them with his hands raised. He smiled and waved his hands in a greeting to them.

The soldiers watched him walk towards them, they tracked his movements through the sights of their weapons.

Bernadette watched from the car. Tension gripped the back of her neck. One pull of a trigger finger, and Jason's life would be over. He got within two meters of the soldiers and stopped. With his hands still raised he explained he was there to join the convoy.

The soldier on the radio checked Jason's story. Bernadette watched with relief as they lowered their weapons and Jason put his hands down by his sides.

The first vehicle in the convoy nosed out of the gate. A Humvee with a machine gun turret on top roared out into the square, screeching to a stop a few meters from the

Toyota. The young soldier on top trained the large bore machine gun down on the car.

Jason waved at the gunner and called over to him, "Hey, it's okay, they're with me. We're your escort for the trip."

The gunner looked back at Jason, then down at the car. He lifted the weapon up and gave Jason the thumbs up sign.

Bernadette let her heart go back down into her chest. She could imagine the large caliber bullets tearing through the thin metaled car and ripping them to shreds. Almas stared up at the Humvee with amazement.

Several more vehicles came out of the gate. Large armored vehicles bristling weapons, painted in sand color with the NATO flag fluttering from their antennas roared into the plaza. The entire area became a cloud of diesel fumes and dust with the loud hum of the massive engines.

Jason walked up to one of the vehicles. The man on the top of the vehicle smiled and waved at him, they talked, laughed, and gave each other an okay sign. Jason walked back to the car smiling.

"It's all good," Jason said, getting back into the car. "We're going to take the second from last spot, that way we don't stick out of the convoy."

"I didn't know that was possible in a military convoy, having a civilian vehicle inside the unit. They'll let us do that?" Bernadette asked.

Jason laughed. "This is Afghanistan, all things are possible or probable." He turned back and started the engine. The car's engine coughed a few times and caught. "Damn, should have replaced the spark plugs last month."

He pulled the car into formation behind an armored vehicle to wait for the convoy to start. "You'll be happy to know that this unit had a listening trawl out. There's been little phone traffic from the Taliban on our route."

"And a listening trawl is?" Bernadette enquired from the back seat while trying to adjust the firearm on her leg that had slipped down to her ankle.

"That, Bernadette, is all the information scooped up from satellites and phone calls or Internet portals. There's a whole team of guys that sit in a room and pull up everything that's going on. Then they do an analysis and pass it to the troops daily."

"That's super. Do you know if my name has come up anywhere? You, know, something about the crazy Canadian detective searching for her fiancé who supposedly stole their sacred robe of Mohammed?"

Jason winked. "Nobody mentioned it. But if they did, I'm sure the Taliban, the Afghan Police and the Afghan Army all want you dead. Don't take it personally."

"Thanks, I won't." Bernadette adjusted the handgun, pulling it back to her thigh. She stared out the window of the car as they roared by the streets of the town. A small boy watched the convoy. Both his hands covered his ears to block out the noise. A mangy dog cowered at his feet.

Bernadette wondered if this was such a good idea. The convoy had fifteen vehicles, it made noise, it was a large moving target, and they were now stuck inside it. But if Jason thought this was the best way to travel, she'd go with it.

Chapter Twenty-Nine

Large snowflakes started to fall as the convoy thundered out of Kandahar. A patch of blue light pushed its way into the dark morning sky. Bernadette breathed a sigh of relief. No rocket propelled grenades, and no gunfire—perhaps this convoy would be fine.

The ramshackle dwellings started to thin out. The countryside with sparse dwellings, mounds of dirt, and snow dusted mountains became the monotonous backdrop to their journey west.

There was a time when Bernadette had taken a trip with her grandmother from the far north of Canada all the way down to Wyoming. They had left the poplar and tamarack trees of Northern Alberta, ventured straight south down to Calgary, and Bernadette had marveled at the big sky and wide-open plains. This was different. All of western Canada and Montana and Wyoming had seemed peaceful. Sure, her Cree ancestors had fought over the land with the settlers, but that had been two hundred years ago.

This land, though, everything about it had a mixture of

blood in it. Bernadette could feel it, just the way her Native Cree Grandmother Moses had told her, "The native people can sense the land, they know when it is in harmony and when it is not."

None of this land felt in harmony to Bernadette. The small dwellings disappeared. They were in open countryside with little foliage, mostly rocks. The snow increased.

A squadron of fighter jets screamed overhead in formation. They left a stream of white contrails against the sky. Two Blackhawk helicopters came in low keeping pace with the convoy. One pilot gave a salute then both helicopters veered off.

Bernadette watched the Blackhawks float off into the distance and wondered if having them around would have any deterrent on the Taliban. She leaned forward to Jason.

"Don't these convoys usually have air cover?"

Jason looked over his shoulder. "You'd think it would be something they needed, but this is a small country. They have jets in the air all the time and the heli gunships are usually no more than ten minutes out. The Taliban would have to be pretty agile to strike and get out fast enough. Most of them, that be the non-crazy ones, want to shoot off their weapons and go home at night."

"You think the bad guys will stay away from the convoy?"

"Hell, yeah. The Taliban don't like doing anything like a major frontal attack, it gets them killed faster. They like to blow up convoys with IED's, throw some RPG's at the remaining vehicles, then run like hell when the they hear the fast-air—that being the jet fighters coming after them."

"And we're safe on this road from IED's?" Bernadette asked as she stared at out the window at the potholed asphalt road.

Jason tilted his head and winked. "NATO has snipers out all night with night vision goggles from several units. That's what I used to do. We'd stake out different patches of road near culverts. The Taliban would come there almost every night. We'd pick them off and leave their bodies for their buddies to find in the morning. They seemed to tire of doing it after a while."

Bernadette sat back and tried to find comfort in Jason's words. Maybe this road was clear of the IED's. She'd heard they were getting bigger, that they could reach three to five hundred pounds.

A tense feeling came over her—the burka felt restrictive—and she pulled it off. Jason looked at her in the rear view mirror. He just shook his head. She rubbed her forehead, finally feeling free.

Almas looked at her and smiled, she smiled back. A wave of sound blew over them. The ground lifted. A wall of smoke mixed with dust engulfed them.

Bernadette felt her brain move backwards then shift forward, as if a large train had shot by and she was still feeling the motion. She knew the convoy had been hit by an IED, but where?

"Everyone stay here!" Jason commanded. Reza translated the words to Almas. He took hold of Bernadette's hand and she squeezed it.

Jason jumped from the car and ran toward the front of the convoy. Bernadette looked out the window through the clearing dust. She could see figures running towards the convoy from the hills.

"Reza, Almas, come with me," Bernadette yelled. She took Almas by the hand and bent down for the AK47. "Reza get your weapon. We have Taliban on the right side."

Reza picked up an AK47 from the floor and rolled out

of the car. He joined Bernadette and Almas on the ground beside the car. Bernadette flipped off the safety on the machine gun. The Taliban charged over the hills firing their weapons as they advanced.

Bullets pinged off the armor of the vehicles. The soldiers returned fire at the Taliban. A large caliber machine gun opened up. Its spent cartridges flew off the side of the vehicle and rained hot brass down on Bernadette and she yelled for them to move.

The Taliban realized the force they were attacking wasn't going to back down. They turned and fled. Bernadette let a few rounds in their direction and closed her eyes in relief. She'd known in her core this was going to happen. Had her senses foretold this or was she paranoid and this was a coincidence?

Just seconds before the blast took place—she'd known it would, but how? She stood up beside the car and looked down at Almas. "You okay?"

"Okay," Almas said. His smile said everything.

Jason came back to the car. "They got the second vehicle. That was lucky; they are the most heavily armored. The guys are a bit shaken, but they had all their ports and window closed so no percussion damage. They'll still need to medevac them out, 'cause they got their bells rung pretty bad."

Bernadette walked to the front of the convoy with her weapon over her shoulder. She came to the vehicle that had been hit. The large armored vehicle was leaning to one side in the bomb crater beneath it. Three men and a woman sat on the side of the road. A medic tended to a young man, who looked no more than nineteen or twenty.

Bernadette sat beside the lone woman in the group. She had her helmet off, her head cradled in her hands, as if she was still hearing the sound wave that bounced off their thick amour.

Bernadette grabbed a water bottle and gave her a drink. "You okay?"

The woman looked up. She appeared all of twenty-five, with a simple complexion of freckles that highlighted her blue eyes and blonde hair. "I think I'll be fine. You know, this is the third time I've been in one of these—you never get used to it. I'd love to fight those bastard Taliban face to face, but this…" She let her word trail off and looked back down at the ground.

Two helicopters appeared overhead. They dropped down on the side of the road. Bernadette helped the soldiers get the shaken crew into the helicopter and evacuated.

Jason came up beside her. "It's the best thing to do, get the crew back to base. There's no telling what kind of trauma they've been through. A near miss from massive IEDs can still damage internal organs."

Bernadette looked up and down the convoy. The soldiers were getting ready to move again. "What's the plan? Do they just leave the wrecked vehicle?"

"They'll strip the vehicle of any ammunition, then have a heavy tow truck come in to deal with it. If they can't salvage it, they blow it up. Never leave anything for the Taliban, those bastards are scavengers."

Time seemed to drag. The sun kept dropping lower in the sky. The last of the light was being drained from the landscape before the convoy moved again. This time they moved faster as if the closing darkness was their new enemy. And it was. In the darkness, the Taliban could easily hide. They could fire from anywhere—the side of the road, the nearest hill.

Caught in the Crossfire

Bernadette felt the tension close in on her once again. She still hadn't donned the Burka. She clutched the large AK47 in her lap, leaving the window open in case she needed to fire the weapon or exit in a hurry. Her concern was Almas. How could she protect him and fire at Taliban at the same time?

Deep inside, the question was forming: How had she become so attached to protecting this boy? She'd thought she had no maternal instincts. Maybe she didn't, maybe this was just her being the cop, doing her duty and trying to protect the innocent. She let that thought keep her company as she watched out the window for signs of hostiles.

Lights shone up ahead, and they stopped at an army checkpoint. Jason turned and smiled. "We're just outside of Delaram. I'll buy the cold beer tonight."

Bernadette didn't let herself relax until the convoy entered the town. The place looked no different than Kandahar, just smaller. They found accommodations in a guesthouse in the center of the town.

The place had a real shower with an almost passable toilet. Bernadette felt revived after a shower and change of clothes. She came out of her room to join the others. The smell of roasted meat and spices filled the air. Reza, Almas, and Jason were sitting on the floor with plates of food, cups of tea, and a large platter of bread before them.

A woman dressed in a floral dress, her hands and face covered in henna tattoos, served her a plate of chicken and rice. Bernadette devoured the meal. The day's events had drained her. No, she hadn't been hit by the IED, but the proximity and the aftermath of seeing the young woman who'd had the earth beneath her rise up in an explosion, had rattled her to her core.

Between mouthfuls of chicken, rice, and bread washed down with tea, she managed to get a question to Jason. "What's the plan for tomorrow?"

Jason mopped up the last bits of rice with his bread and swallowed his tea. "Tomorrow we head out of this town on our own. We're okay until we hit Khormaleg. That's about seventy-five klicks from here, then we have Taliban country until we hit Farah."

"Which is in total control by the Taliban," Bernadette said.

"Ah yeah, pretty much," Jason said, taking a hard swallow of his bread and draining his tea.

"So, balls to the walls, and we take our lives in our own hands to get through the maze of bad guys. Have I summed that up?"

"Yeah, you've got it. Any questions?" Jason asked, putting his plate aside and resting his hands on his knees.

Bernadette looked at Jason and noted something in him that was defiant. She wanted to probe that. "My question is, why?"

"Why what?'

"Why would you risk your life for this? I mean, you could have found several other charities that needed hand-holding. Why did you take me on? Is the five thousand dollars really worth your life?"

Jason leaned against the wall, and he threw his head back. "Okay, you got me, you're one hell of a detective. I'm in it for the buzz, the thrill of the chase, the fight or whatever you call it." He leaned forward and pointed his finger in the air. "Look, I've done so many tours of the badass areas, that I've gotten addicted to conflict. I tried going home to my old hometown in Moose Jaw. I hated it. My old friends, and they were great, but they never seemed alive.

They hadn't seen what I had, lived like I had. My options back there were the Asphalt Factory or Starbucks. My PTSD would've had me hanging myself. Here, I'm still relevant, I'm real. Does that answer your question?"

Bernadette lowered her eyes then looked up at Jason. "You're a scary man."

"Yes, I know. My wife tells me that all the time."

Bernadette got up and went to bed. Almas was asleep already in a small cot beside hers. She checked her cell phone. The text message almost stopped her heart.

Chapter Thirty

Bernadette stared at her phone. The text was from Lackey.

I heard you'd been arrested by Kahn and got yourself released. Not good being wanted by the Afghan Police. You need to know I saw a report from your Canadian Consulate. They found a headless body near Herat. It's a close match to Chris. I can get you out of the country without problem. Turn yourself into our US military or the embassy. You'll be home in two days.

That mention of the headless body knocked the air out her. She sat on the edge of her bed and tried to fight back tears. How could this be? She took a deep breath to relax so she could think. If Chris was dead, she knew in every part of her being that she would have felt it.

She walked out of the room and found Jason. He was sitting with his back against the wall with his ear buds plugged into his iPhone, a beer in one hand. He looked totally relaxed; she almost didn't want to disturb him.

He sensed her presence and opened his eyes. "You look stressed, can I get you a beer?"

"Sure," Bernadette said, sitting down beside him.

Jason popped the top on a beer can and passed it to her. "It's Tuborg. I got it from the wrecked vehicle. The crew was Danish, they told me to take it, good bunch of guys." He leveled his gaze at her. "Now, what's up? You looked like someone jumped on your grave."

Bernadette took the beer and sniffed. "Yeah, some shits got me rattled. Here, look at this." She passed him her phone with the text message.

Jason read it, then put down his beer and put his hand on Bernadette's shoulder. "Look, the Taliban leave headless soldiers all over this place. They have no idea if this is Chris."

Bernadette swigged her beer and wiped her mouth with her hand. "Yeah, I know, it just got me rattled." She shook her head. "You know, what the hell am I thinking? Chris and his guys were taken hostage near Lashkar Gah, Herat is way the hell north of here. And, damn it, if he was dead, I would have felt it."

"You mean you two are that tight or you're some kind of Jedi Princess?" Jason asked with a wry smile.

She looked at him for a moment. "Asshole, that remark will cost you another beer." She drained her beer and tossed the can to the side.

Jason pulled the tab from another one and passed it to her. She drank the beer and sat back against the wall.

They sat, drinking their beer in silence. A small cat appeared, looked them over, found nothing of interest, and disappeared.

"Are you done tying yourself up in knots over that text?"

"Yeah, I think so. But I have to wonder, why would Lackey send something like that to me. Would she be trying to get me to stop my search?"

"The one thing I've never figured out all the time I've

been in this country is the CIA. They do things differently than we do. We'd go into a village to wipe out some bad guys and they'd appear and tell us they wanted those bad guys left alive, something about valuable assets they needed to work with."

"Yeah, I found the same thing in my detective work. We had criminals that were worth more outside of prison as informants than inside doing time like they should have."

"You going to get some sleep tonight, detective?"

Bernadette downed the last of her beer. "Yeah, I'll be up peeing a lot with all this beer, but thanks for the talk and the beer. I'm going to get some shuteye."

She went into her room, and sat cross-legged on her cot. Almas turned over, looked at her from his cot and went back to sleep. A small window with a semi clean pane of glass showed a blanket of stars in the cloudless sky. She wondered what stars she was looking at. One star shone brighter than the rest and she wondered if it was Sirius. Her grandmother had called it the "dog star." To some of the natives it was a bright star that lit the way to a good hunt.

Bernadette sat there and put her hand to her heart. "Okay, Chris, I know you're out there. Don't die on me. Don't even think about it, okay? I'm coming for you—you hear me?"

She wiped a tear from her eye and lay on the cot. In a minute she was fast asleep from her exhaustion.

Chris had been sleeping when something woke him up. He felt like someone had nudged him. He sat up on his mat. No one was around. The guard had been by several hours ago, dropped off a bowl of rice with a few stale bits of bread in it, and left him.

Ever since Gul had been murdered in the courtyard, conditions had deteriorated. His new jailer hated him. He made it known every time he fed him. His chamber pot was hardly ever removed and the delivery of firewood was almost nonexistent. The last embers of the fire in the stove were starting to die. Soon, his little hut would be unbearable.

Chris pulled the small woolen blanket around him that Gul had given him. Gul had wanted him to live. His new jailer wanted him dead. Each time he closed the door; he made the sign of his hand cutting across his throat, telling Chris he would like to be the one to behead him.

The thought of death from beheading shook Chris. He was normally a positive man. Nothing he could do would make this death seem any less gruesome. He was trying to be as brave as he could, but, each day, the circumstances of his capture seemed to be getting worse. The Afghans in the village were preparing something. It looked like they were getting ready to leave. Would they take him with them or execute him before they left?

He got up and looked out the crack in the wall at the stars overhead, concentrating on the brightest one. He was sure it was Sirius. The name meant 'glowing' in Greek. His mother had said the star would light his way if he ever got lost.

He stared at it. "Well, Bernadette," he said quietly, "if you're out there, I hope this star will light your way to me, because if you don't get here soon, these guys plan on separating my head from my body."

He lay back down on his mat, pulling the blanket as tightly around him as he could. Footsteps sounded outside the door. They stopped at the door, and then moved away.

Chapter Thirty-One

The morning came with low hanging clouds. They were thick and dark, as if they wanted to unleash a storm or blanket of snow. Bernadette got Almas off to the bathroom then did a quick wash and joined the others for breakfast.

They were all sitting cross-legged on cushions with steaming bowls of porridge, laden with cardamom, oil, and chicken. The smell of it almost put Bernadette off her appetite, but she was hungry. She took a bowl of the stuff that almost made her gag and thanked the soft-spoken lady with the flashing brown eyes.

The stuff brought back memories of her stay in hospital. If she took a big spoonful, chewed quickly and swallowed it she could handle it. She washed it down with tea, telling her stomach to accept this, as it was food.

After Jason finished his meal, he scrolled his cell phone as he talked to Reza in half Afghani half English.

"What's our plan for today?" Bernadette asked as she swallowed her last mouthful of the strange concoction.

Jason looked up at Bernadette. "We're going to head out

towards Farah on route 606. The road is pretty good. It was built with help by India to avoid travelling through Pakistan back in 2009. It's a nice two-lane highway, unfortunately the Taliban killed a lot of people making it, and it's not your safest place for daily travel. I doubt if Rick Steves has it on his travel guide."

"How do we stay safe on the road?" Bernadette asked.

"Well," Jason continued, "we're okay to Bakwa, that's about halfway to Farah, then by the time we get to Bayak, we got Taliban control pretty much all the way. You and I will be in burkas and Reza here will be our driver."

"Sounds like fun."

"Yeah, a real party. During our route, Reza will keep watch on Facebook, Twitter and Instagram to see what our Taliban buddies are up to."

"How's that help?"

Reza took out his phone. "The Taliban are always posting selfies on those sites. I just keep an eye on them to see how close they are. Sometimes they even post locations so their families can keep in touch with them."

"Seriously?" Bernadette said, looking at Reza's phone. "How did you get on their sites?"

"I know a guy from my old village. He decided to join the Taliban when the army rejected him. I sent him a friend request and here I am, I'm in the Taliban Facebook group."

Bernadette said. "You know, sometimes I wonder if I'll wake up tomorrow and all of this will just be a crazy dream?"

Jason laughed. "If you live through this, you can tell everyone you were in the strangest land in the world. No one knows if this place dropped back in time or it's some time warp that we've all fallen into and can't get out of until we board a jetliner and find ourselves back in the real world."

They went back to their rooms, packed up their gear, and went to the car. The clouds opened up with large flakes of snow. By the time the car was loaded, the roads were carpeted in a blanket of white.

"This could be good for us. The Taliban hate fighting in bad conditions. They can't see anything," Jason said.

"Yeah, and neither can we," Bernadette responded.

They drove down the road with the little Camry doing some slipping and sliding on the snow covered roads but mostly holding its own. NATO troops were stationed along the highway in heavily armored vehicles and tanks.

The snow kept falling and the road became harder to navigate. Bernadette thought she would welcome the sight of a snowplow but they were non-existent here. If they saw a troop transport truck, Jason would follow behind it, as its large wheels would provide a clearing. But the trucks weren't always going all the way to their destination.

By late morning, they saw the town of Bakwa appear out of the driving snow. The drive that should have been just over an hour had been three. They climbed out of the vehicle near an army checkpoint.

"I'm going to go inside and get some intel," Jason said. He walked into the operations tent. A corporal standing guard pointed him in the direction of the sergeant in charge of operations.

Jason knew the man, a German named Kaufer; they'd served in several campaigns together. He approached Kaufer, throwing him a quick salute. "Hey, Kaufer, what's the shit out there?"

Kaufer looked up from his maps, "*Auch, mein got*, what the hell are you doing here, you dumb Canuck? Don't you know we are about to unleash some serious hurt on the Taliban?"

"What, is that something new?" Jason replied with a grin. They had been in some serious conflicts in both Croatia and Kabul. The German loved the words 'serious hurt,' he thought it made him sound funky.

"The Afghan general in this area isn't going to wait for spring this time to throw the Taliban out of Farah. As soon as the weather clears, we're going in—"

Jason put his hand up, "Yeah, I know, you're going to throw down some serious hurt?"

"Throw down...what is a throw down...should I use this word?"

"Sure, Kaufer, it means a challenge."

"Okay, then we will throw down some serious hurt. Where are you heading?"

"To a place on the other side of Farah, a little village called Azau. I'm on a hunting mission with a client."

"You are on suicide mission, my crazy friend. You will get caught in the crossfire between the Afghan army and the Taliban—that is if the Taliban don't kill you. What is so important about this client?"

Jason looked around to see if they were being overheard. "My client is looking for her man. He's the guy being blamed for stealing the robe from Kandahar."

Kaufer lowered his head then raised it, staring into Jason's eyes. "Really, my friend. If this is the case, I will do what I can. I have some air support. But I can't send any helis to you if they are needed for the attack."

"I'll only call you if I'm desperate," Jason said.

Kaufer put his hand on Jason's shoulder. "My friend, you've been desperate all the time I've known you. Now, I will give you some maps you'll need." He looked around. "No one will miss these."

Reza, Almas, and Bernadette found shelter beside an outside heater under a tarpaulin. Three female NATO soldiers were huddled near the heaters smoking cigarettes.

Bernadette nodded to them as she put her hands towards the heater. The heat in the car wasn't great; she'd had to keep her hands in her parka to keep them warm. Almas had been cuddled up beside her to try to keep from becoming a popsicle.

The soldiers eyed Bernadette and her companions. At first they said nothing, smoking their cigarettes and drinking coffee. The female, a soldier with corporal stripes and an American flag on her shoulder, stared hard at Bernadette.

Bernadette caught her eye, nodded, and looked down at the heater.

"What the hell you people up too?" the soldier asked. Her nametag said Lacroix. She was tall and blonde with a distinct southern accent, somewhere between South Carolina and Georgia. Bernadette had heard that same accent in Charleston once.

"Oh, us?" Bernadette looked up as if she'd been noticed in the aisle of a supermarket. "We're just out looking for a lost relative."

"Likely freaking story," Lacroix said. "You some kind of spook?"

"You mean, CIA? Not me, I'm not smart enough to be one of them." Bernadette replied with a wink.

The soldier beside Lacroix, a black lady with a round face and short cropped dark hair, made a whistling sound. Her name was Smith. "Girl, if you're not CIA and you don't look army—then you're out of your mind being here. You best get in that little bitty car you came in and high tail your ass back to Kandahar. 'Cause this place is about to have the shit hit the fan with incoming Taliban." She rolled her eyes for effect. "Know what I mean?"

"Thanks for the warning, I appreciate it." Bernadette said with a forced smile. It was better to humor these two.

"This little girl doesn't get it, does she?" Lacroix said looking at Smith.

Smith lowered her head as if in mourning. "Nope, she don't get it." She raised her head up again, her eyes going wide. "Listen up, little missy, wearing the guns and knives and looking cool. There's a shit load of Taliban out there. When they catch a woman they make sure they get their fill. Those bastards form a line and call in all their pals. Then and only then, when they're done, do they kill the woman? No, they torture her first, just to make sure they got their kicks in."

Bernadette's face went red. Not from fear, but anger. These women were trying to scare her off. This was bullshit. She closed her lips tightly so she wouldn't tell them to screw off.

"And another thing," Lacroix chimed in. "Here's the one last thing we'll tell you if you go out toward Farah since it looks like that's what you're fixing to do."

"What's that?" Bernadette asked through clenched teeth.

"Save a bullet for yourself."

The third woman beside them wore an Australian flag on her shoulder. Her nametag was Brownlow. "Look here, mate, these girls are having a bit of a laugh at your expense, but it's real out there. All the women worry about getting caught outside the wire by Taliban. The thing about the bullet—that shits real. Never let yourself be taken prisoner"

Jason came out of the command center with some maps under his arms. He motioned to Bernadette and the others to follow him back to the car.

"You make some new friends?" Jason asked.

"Just some girl talk," Bernadette replied looking over her shoulder.

They followed Jason to the car. They climbed in and Jason turned over the ignition. There was an ominous clicking sound of the ignition.

"This is not good," Reza said from the front seat. His head was shaking from side to side as if he was willing the ignition to catch with the engine.

"Nope, not a good sign," Jason said. He jumped out of the car, opened the hood, and fiddled with some wires and got back in. "Now, let's see who's on our side."

The car turned over and Jason gunned the engine. Almas clapped his hands from the back seat and started to chant something.

Reza turned towards Bernadette. "Almas is singing a children's song of how things are going well for us…with the help of Allah, of course."

Bernadette smiled at Almas. His enthusiasm was infectious. She wanted to bottle it up and keep it inside her. She hoped it would be there when they met the Taliban.

The car pulled ahead. Just on the outskirts of town, Jason stopped the car and opened the trunk. "Okay, Bernadette, it's time for you and me to put on our disguises.

Bernadette opened the door and got out of the car slowly. She hated the burka, hated everything it stood for, and most of all hated wearing it. She took a deep breath and pulled the garment over her head. She felt like she was disappearing, the large blue garment covered her down to her feet. The only opening was for arms and a slit for her to look through

Jason did the same. He looked like one hell of a large and tall Afghani woman. He returned to the passenger side of the car. Reza took the wheel.

"We'll be okay until we hit Bayak," Jason said. "Reza will try to talk our way through to a sick relative in Farah. He has a big wad of Afghani bills to hand out as bribes or '*baksheesh*,' as it's known here."

Almas put his hand on Bernadette's. "I will protect you with my life."

"You learned more English, Almas?"

Reza laughed from the driver's seat." He has been asking me to teach him how to say that in English. He is good, no?"

"Yes, he is good," Bernadette put her arm around him. He folded into her side and giggled.

She checked where the shotgun was strapped to her thigh. The Glock handgun was on her leg, a combat knife on her left side, and an AK47 lay covered on the floor. In all of this, she wondered what she'd do in a gun battle with the Taliban. Would she have the sense to save a bullet for herself? What about Almas? She couldn't bear the thought of him being abused again.

The car left the outskirts of the town and resumed its slow journey on the highway. The snow increased. Big, wet, sloppy flakes attached themselves to the car windshield and didn't want to slide off.

Reza kept putting the windshield wipers on. After a time, the wipers streaked frost across the windshield and then ice built up on the wiper blades. The car's heater could not melt the frost fast enough; it kept building, making it hard for Reza to see.

"I need to stop," Reza said. "The windscreen, I cannot see…"

Jason rolled down his window. He leaned out the window, grabbed the blades and smacked them hard on the glass clearing the ice. "Do this on your side, Reza."

Reza slowed the car. He did what Jason told him. For a short while the windshield cleared. It had no ice in the wipers, then it came back, just as bad as before.

Bernadette sat in the back with her arms, cradling Almas. What they needed was some good old windshield wiper antifreeze. She carried stuff good to minus forty back in Canada, but here in this country, she doubted if anyone had the stuff except for the NATO soldiers.

"Jason, you carrying any high octane booze on this trip?" Bernadette asked.

Jason turned in his Burka. "You asking me to put some of my medicinal tincture on the windshields?"

"Since you don't have any de-ice in your windshield washer—then yeah."

"Ah, crap. Reza, pull over," Jason said dejectedly.

Reza pulled the car to a slow stop, watching carefully that he was not going too close to the edge of the road. He looked nervously behind him, hoping a tank or troop transport did not come barreling up behind them and crush them.

Jason got out. The wind caught his burka, volumes of blue fabric streamed outward and looked as if Jason had a parachute fall on him. He opened the trunk and pulled out a bottle of clear liquid. He opened the bottle, took a swig of its contents through the slit in the Burka and trudged forward. Pouring the bottle on the windshield, it instantly cleared.

He got back in the car, looked at the empty bottle with a sigh, and threw it out the window.

Reza chuckled in the front seat. "Allah has found a good use for this alcohol you covet so much, Jason. One day you will become a true Muslim. You will see the will of Allah. How he guides our destiny."

"Well, if Allah is running things, and this is his will, he owes me one bottle of really good one hundred-fifty proof vodka from the best bootlegger in Kandahar."

Reza put the car in gear, the car's wheels spun in the snow, caught, and moved forward. The snow increased and the wind blew harder. Reza leaned forward to see the road; it was starting to disappear in the blanket of white.

Bernadette sat in the back with Almas, who clutched her for warmth and security. A feeling of foreboding came over her. She felt there was something out there ahead of them. She couldn't see it. She could sense it.

She leaned forward, wanting to say something to Reza, but she didn't know what to tell him, to slow down—to stop? She hesitated.

A group of figures appeared out of the snow, standing with their weapons pointed at the car. They looked like snow statues, like someone had carved them. But Bernadette could see they were real. One put up a hand to stop.

"Taliban," Jason said.

Chapter Thirty-Two

Reza muttered under his breath, "What do I do?"

"Don't look at me or Bernadette. Remember we are your wives. You're heading to Farah to see your sick father. You remember his name?"

"Yes, yes, I remember. I will be okay."

Bernadette pulled Almas tighter to her. His tiny arms circled her like a vice. If anyone tried to take him away, they'd be taking her ribcage with them. At this point, Jason could give no more advice. Afghan men rarely spoke to their wives when talking to other men. If Reza looked to Jason in his burka disguise or back to Bernadette it would be a complete giveaway.

A man with his machine gun came to Reza's window. His face was barely visible from his wrapping of heavy wool around his face and over his head. He exchanged greetings with Reza. There was the usual hand waving between the two as they talked.

Reza's voice became agitated. He waved angrily at the man. Bernadette wondered what the hell he was doing. The man had an AK47, one burst of the thing would put everyone in the car in danger of being injured or killed.

The man backed away and called someone else to the car.

"Now, you've just pissed him off, Reza," Jason whispered.

"He wants one hundred thousand Afghanis for safe passage to Farah. I told him he is ridiculous. I offered him half that much," Reza said.

"You're right, if you did not bargain, he'd have thought you even more suspicious," Jason said, staring straight ahead.

A large man with a rocket propelled grenade launcher balanced on his shoulder came to the car. He smiled at Reza. They shook hands; Reza gave him a large wad of Afghani bills. A truck pulled out with flashing lights behind it and a man with a machine gun in the back. They followed.

"This is your average Taliban shakedown. Who says these guys aren't smart? They will guide us through about four more checkpoints. Bernadette, I hope you know that this is going on your account cause each Taliban checkpoint may ask for a cut. Our escort will profess they're doing it out of good will and the others won't believe them. This could cost fifty thousand Afghanis per checkpoint," Jason said.

"Really, there's no honor amongst these bastards, how odd," Bernadette said. She couldn't even think of calculating the money now. The money for this trip, the money for bribes. How much was Chris' life worth? Her bank account was draining, but all she knew was every day she stayed alive in this country felt like it moved her closer to Chris.

Progress was slow and just as Jason had forecasted,

several Taliban checkpoints got a payment, some fifty thousand Afghanis and the last one got only twenty thousand. Reza had put his foot down, telling the last group there would be nothing left to take care of his ailing father if they kept fleecing him. That seemed to strike a note with the Taliban; they let him through for the reduced fee.

The snow and wind let up as they entered the city of Farah. It was now late evening. The call to prayer from the mosques confirmed the time. People moved about the town, vendors put their prayer rugs down beside their stalls and joined in the prayers.

Reza pulled the car over in the square and Almas joined him in prayers.

Jason turned his head slightly towards Bernadette, "I'll bet you're wondering why I don't participate in this?"

"No, not at all," Bernadette said. "I'm a semi-practicing Catholic. I figure there are two camps of religion. Those who are scared of life after death and want to improve their odds, and those who don't want to be left here in limbo on earth after they die—because this place is pretty bat shit crazy most of the time."

Jason gave a muffled chuckled from beneath his burka, "I think you got a good handle on it. But I couldn't believe in Islam after I saw what they did to each other in Croatia."

"I hear what you're saying, but then that's not religion killing people. That's people killing each other over their religious beliefs. Big difference," Bernadette said.

"Sorry, not convinced. Everyone here and back in Croatia would constantly say that things were the will of Allah, from what I saw, Allah was pretty cruel."

"Again, you're judging the people being cruel. I don't see God doing these things."

"Really," Jason said spinning in his seat.

Bernadette put her head closer to Jason's so no one outside could hear them speaking in English. "I've spent years wandering the forests of Canada, and you know what I saw when people weren't screwing things up? I saw harmony. I saw things in order. So, yes, I do believe there's a force of God, but no, I don't like how the human race has personified him, her or it."

"Damn fine speech," Jason said.

Reza and Almas got back in the car. Their escort had left them at the square. They traveled on until they found a guesthouse that Reza knew.

They piled out of the car and Jason made sure that all the gear was brought inside. He was afraid of thieves stripping the car bare at night, as there was no courtyard to pull the car into.

Bernadette helped with the packs. "These are pretty heavy, what did you bring with you?"

"Just a few toys," Jason said with a wink. He threw the pack over his shoulder and walked into house.

None of them noticed the two men squatting by the wall across the narrow street. One nodded in their direction. The other took out his cell phone and took a picture of Bernadette and her companions.

They checked into the guesthouse. A little woman who was hunched over and walked with a limp gave Almas and Bernadette a room together.

Bernadette turned to Reza, "Do I have to stay in this burka the whole time we're in this guesthouse. Are these people friends of the Taliban?"

"Oh, no," Reza said. He put his hands to his mouth and began to laugh. He yelled to the hosts who came out of the kitchen. The woman was dressed in trousers, the man wore jeans, and a western shirt and a baseball cap. "Please let me introduce you my friends, Miriam and Azar. They run this guesthouse and do archeology on the side."

Bernadette peeled off her Burka, she watched Jason do the same. "I'm so glad to be rid of that."

Miriam shook Bernadette's hand. "So glad you could make it through the Taliban. Get yourself freshened up with a hot shower, and I'll be making some cocktails and hors d'oeuvres once you're ready."

Miriam was in her mid-thirties, thin and wiry with curly hair and a distinct polished English accent."

"You're British?" Bernadette asked.

"Yes, from London actually, and Azar here was born and raised in Dublin, Ireland."

"And you're here?" Bernadette asked in a puzzled tone.

"Yes," Miriam replied. "This was the original Silk Road from China to Europe. There's a wealth of history here. We're working with a university to preserve some of the sites before they are destroyed."

"Or looted," Azar added. He was stocky with dark features, wavy hair, and bushy eyebrows. His accent was distinctly Irish.

"Both of us have Afghan parents. We came here to preserve our culture and our heritage," Miriam said.

"And what about the Taliban. Don't they harass you?" Bernadette asked.

"You have to realize they've only been here a short while. The Afghan army will be here soon and shoo them out. Then we'll be back to our archeological digs in the spring," Miriam said.

Bernadette hit the shower and was delighted to find a caftan made of fine cotton in a bright pattern on her cot when she came back to her room. She pulled it over herself and went into the dining room.

Reza and Almas were sitting on cushions in the dining area, drinking tea and feasting on a tray of nuts and figs. Jason was lying on his side, swishing something in a glass with ice. He looked up at her. His grin told her he'd found some alcohol.

"Best damn G and T I've had since my time stuck in London's Heathrow airport waiting for a plane back to this place," Jason said, his words slurring a bit.

"May I fix you a cocktail of 'mother's ruin?'" Miriam asked.

"Mother's what?" Bernadette asked as she sat on the cushions.

Miriam laughed. "Ah, the English slang name for gin and tonic."

"Sounds wonderful," Bernadette said. Meeting the Taliban had unnerved her. A cocktail of G and T or 'mother's ruin' suited her just fine.

Miriam was back a few minutes later, handing her a large tumbler of gin mixed with tonic, a slice of lime and some tinkling of ice cubes.

Bernadette took a sip and let the delicious blend of juniper berries, botanicals, and fermented spirits roll over her tongue and slide down her throat. "This is wonderful."

"I'm glad you approve. This is the legendary Tanqueray TEN that we reserve for our special guests. Hopefully the road to Iran will open again soon once the Taliban are gone, and we can replenish our supply," Miriam said.

"What road is that?" Bernadette asked taking another sip of her gin.

"That road you came on to here was Route Six-oh-six. A few years back, India, Iran, and Afghanistan agreed to put through a new trade route that will bypass Pakistan completely."

"And, I guess, that's a good thing?" Bernadette asked.

Azar walked in with a plate of food. "Most Afghan trade is principally foreign aid and opium smuggling through the port of Karachi in Pakistan. But Pakistan simultaneously supports and hosts the Afghan Taliban rebels fighting the government in Kabul and its western allies. The Afghan president said he wanted to prove that "geography is not our destiny."

"Sounds noble," Jason commented from his semi-raised position. He looked like he was dropping lower onto the cushions. Either a magnet was drawing him down or the gin was having an effect on his gravity.

"You know, my wife never liked me drinking. Did I tell you that?" Jason asked with an amused smile.

Bernadette only nodded in his direction. She could see he was drunk. There's no reacting with a drunk. Nod and wave is the best practice, but he referred to his wife in the past tense. She'd save that information for later.

Azar put a large platter of food in front of them. A steaming bowl of rice pilaf was mixed with carrots and raisins. Beside that he placed a large plate of lamb kabobs with a pile of Naan bread dripping in butter.

They dug in. Bernadette ate every morsel. For some reason, the cold, the tension, the danger, it all increased her appetite. She swigged on her gin. When Miriam offered her another, she declined and drank tea instead.

Jason was shoveling in his food as if he had not eaten in months. Bernadette eyed him, wondering what kind of demons had presented themselves that was making him drink so heavily.

Jason waved his empty glass at Miriam. For a moment

she hesitated. She looked at Bernadette and the look that passed between them said it all.

"Oh, my word, so sorry, Jason. We are out of gin; may I get you a beer? Or how about some tea?" Miriam asked.

Jason dropped his glass on the pillow. "Beer—that be fine." His head slid down on the cushions. Seconds later, he was fast asleep.

"I think your man has had enough for this evening," Azar said. "Should I escort him to his room?"

"No, let him sleep. The tension of the past few days has put him on edge. Drink and sleep seem to be his remedies," Bernadette said.

Miriam moved over to a cushion beside Bernadette. "I heard from Jason you are going to the village of Azau."

"Yes, we are. Do you know something about it?"

"We did some digs there last year. The warlord there, Ramin…"

"Rasul," Bernadette added.

"Yes, Ramin Rasul. We had some dealings with him. He is ruthless. We had to pay him a lot of money to keep our people from getting harmed and to keep working," Miriam said.

"Is he more money focused than religious?"

"How do you mean?"

"I need to know if he can be bought off. If he has a price that will be greater than his religious ideals," Bernadette said.

Miriam nodded her head. "I see where you're going with this. Yes, I'd say he was more on the monetary side. We wanted to check on some ancient Buddhist temples in the area, to get to them and preserve them before someone destroyed them. Rasul didn't care about the temples. He wanted us to pay him protection money for our safe passage."

"Was it protection from other bandits or him?"

Miriam smiled. "Yes, it was safe passage from his men. He made it known to us that if we didn't pay him, he would either kill us or take us hostage. We had to come up with a price that made him feel like he had a win."

"Was it worth it for the Buddhist artifacts?"

Miriam sipped the last of her gin. "We were able to get the statues packed, crated, and shipped out of this valley, right under his nose. Had he known how many millions of dollars those artifacts were worth he would have been furious."

"It's tough when you beat a crook at his own game," Bernadette said.

"Can you tell me why you're going into that valley?"

Bernadette pursed her lips, "I think Rasul might have my fiancé hostage."

Miriam looked as if the air had been let out of her. "My dear girl. That is very bad, do you have piles of money with you?"

"No, that's the problem. Most of my cash is back in Kandahar."

Miriam looked over at Azar, then back to Bernadette. "Give me a minute, I might have something for you to bargain with." She left the room and came back with something wrapped in a cloth.

She unwrapped it revealing a small figure of a Buddha made of jade that sparkled in the candlelight. Miriam handed it Bernadette. "Show this to Rasul. Tell him there's another one like it here in Farah, but he'll have to give up your fiancé."

Bernadette took the figure from Miriam. It was smooth

and heavy. It felt like it was hundreds of years old. "Where is this from?"

"It's from the dig we did near the valley you're going to. We found two and brought them here. Rasul heard a rumor we have them; he'd like to get his hands on them. If you must bargain, start with this—you'll get his attention."

"But this is priceless," Bernadette protested.

"So is your fiancé's life."

Bernadette hugged Miriam. "Thank you, I'll do everything I can to bring this back to you."

"*Inshallah*, you will return with your fiancé," Miriam said. She looked at Jason who was snoring on the cushions. "I think it's time we got your friend to bed and turned in for the night."

They picked up Jason. It took all of them, including Almas who held his head, to carry Jason to his room. They rolled him onto his cot. He looked up at them. "What time is it?"

"It's almost midnight," Bernadette replied.

"Is it still snowing outside?"

"No, it stopped several hours ago," Azar said.

"We have to leave early in the morning. The Afghan army will attack the city in the morning," Jason said. He closed his eyes, his snores shaking the room.

"Is he serious?" Bernadette asked.

"I'm not sure," Miriam said. "People in a drunken state say many things when they are half awake."

"Let's err on the side of caution. How about we're ready to leave at first light?" Bernadette said.

Chapter Thirty-Three

Bernadette woke to the sounds of explosions. Miriam was knocking on her door.

"The Afghan and NATO Army attack has started. You need to leave now," Miriam shouted.

Bernadette rolled out of bed and quickly got into her military fatigues and strapped on her weapons. Almas was awake. He understood the urgency and began to dress.

"*Yalla, yalla*," Bernadette said to him, using the Arabic word for hurry.

Coming into the hallway, she saw Jason. "We got to get the hell out of town," he said, throwing his pack over his back.

"What about wearing our burka's?" Bernadette asked.

"No time and no need," Jason replied. "The Taliban will be busy at the gates of the city. The Afghan army is making a frontal attack. They'll send their A-ten warplanes and helicopters to the center. We need to be out of here before all the shit hits the fan."

Bernadette followed Jason to the car. Almas and Reza were right behind her. They threw the packs in. Jason hit the ignition—the engine roared to life.

"Hell, yeah. We're out of here," Jason said. He hit the gas, and the tires spun then caught, as the car lurched forward heading for the western gate.

Two men squatting beside the wall across the street had been there all night. The picture they'd taken was worth a small fortune to them. They were Taliban that wanted no more part of the war. The money offered to follow the four was more than they'd ever dreamed.

The price offered for the location of the boy was well known amongst many who surfed the Afghani Internet of Warlords. Mohammad Mirwais had posted a quarter million Afghani prize for information. When Din Mohammad, the older brother, sent the text with a picture to Mirwais, he thought he would be immediately rewarded.

His brother, Dost, had warned him that any dealings with Mirwais could be a problem. It was. Mirwais replied that if they did not follow the boy until Mirwais got there, he would hold them personally responsible.

Dost watched as the car headed down the street. "Now, my brother, we take our lives in our own hands in following them."

Din waved his hand at his brother's worries. "We'll be fine. In one day's time, we'll have our money. You can marry the prettiest woman of your choice in our village and I will head off to Germany to begin my life in business."

"Only if we catch them. How do you plan to do that? We have no car," Dost said, with his usual dour expression.

Din leapt to his feet and ran to the other side of the street. He pulled aside a canvas partition that revealed an old motorbike. Hopping on it, he hit the throttle and pushed the kick-start, the engine fired with a cloud of blue smoke. He rode the motorbike across the street, stopping in front of his brother.

"This is stealing. We could get our hands cut off for doing such thing," Dost protested.

"We are doing this to chase the *kafir*. This is sanctioned in the Koran," Din said.

Dost shook his head. "Only two of them are *kafir*. How would you explain this to the police and the imams?"

"That's easy. I would tell them I'm doing the work of Mirwais. His very name will strike fear in their hearts. And now, my brother, if you do not get on the back, we will not catch our prey. I would have to tell Mirwais you were the reason we failed."

Dost's face went pale. He hiked up his billowing Afghan pants and got on behind his brother. With a rev of the engine the little motorbike spun its back wheel and headed off in chase of the Camry.

In a few minutes they caught sight of it. Din slowed and kept his distance. The snow turned to wet slush on the road making it easier for the motorbike. Mirwais texted to them that they were to stay out of sight and confirm the movements of the car. Mirwais would meet them in twenty-four hours with the most money they had ever seen.

Bernadette had her machine gun racked and ready, and she left the side window down. Their progress was slow. People were running for shelter. Shops were being shuttered.

A group of Taliban ran past them. One carried a

mortar tube, the other the tripod for it; a third carried two mortar shells under his arm. They wore running shoes, no body armor, and no helmets.

"They don't stand a chance against the Afghan Army and the NATO air force," Jason said, watching them run by.

"Won't they make it a house to house fight?" Bernadette asked.

"Not if they want to live to fight again," Jason said, turning the wheel hard to avoid a street vendor pushing a cart. "They wanted to hold this city until spring, but they don't have the fire power to do it. I saw a couple of tanks, but they won't have enough shells for it. If they start firing it, the air force will take them out in minutes. They know that."

The car careened passed a truck packed with Taliban heading for the eastern gate. Not one of them noticed the westerners in the Camry. Their eyes were fixed on the explosions in front of them. Some looked up. Jet fighters swooped down over the city hunting for targets.

A few minutes later, the city thinned out and they made it out into the country. A blanket of fresh white snow covered the fields. The small mud and brick huts dotting the landscape looked serene. Smoke curled from their cooking fires. To Bernadette, it looked like a postcard. As if she was on a tour and someone had said, "Now, on your right, is a typical Afghan dwelling—would anyone like to take a picture?"

The road became rutted; the car's non-existent shocks sent every bump up into the passengers. Bernadette wondered how much her butt and tailbone could withstand this pounding.

Jason hit the gas. The Camry started to bounce over the

road. Then, it evened out. It seemed to find a rhythm on the road that worked at the speed it was going.

In the distance, a mountain range of brown with a dusting of white was silhouetted against the moon. It was still dark. The car sped west then made a turn after it crossed the bridge over the Farah River.

Bernadette looked behind her. A lone motorcycle silhouetted in the moonlight without its headlight on was traveling behind them. She watched for a while then turned back to look at the road ahead.

Almas stared out the other window. His gaze was fixated overhead, on the stars.

"Reza, ask Almas what he sees in the stars above us," Bernadette said.

Reza turned to Almas and translated. "Almas says he sees the stars that are above his village. We are not too far away. Maybe forty kilometers, only."

Bernadette looked at the boy; a change had come over him now. He'd said his name meant diamond in Dari when they first met. He was sparkling like one now.

They rode in silence; Jason fought the wheel of the car as he navigated the road. No military vehicles or aircraft came in sight. They had entered a desolate part of the country. The road forked, one west one north. Jason took the one going west.

"Reza, ask Almas if he knows if we are on the right road," Jason said.

"The boy does not know the roads, only the stars. Until the warlord took him, he had never left his village. You need to keep on the route you are on. He can see his star ahead."

A sliver of sun came over the mountains. The stars faded with the dawn. Reza motioned to Jason that they should stop by the side of the road so they could pray.

Jason did not want to stop the car. But they'd been traveling for over two hours. He could use a break and pee by the side of the road while they did their prayers.

The road they stopped on was desolate. It vanished up the valley into the mountains. The mountains bracketed them on both sides, with no trees. They seemed to go on forever. Bernadette imagined this was what the moon looked like if it was dusted with snow. The valley floor was strewn with more brown rocks and shrubs that made a feeble attempt at vegetation.

Bernadette got out of the car to stretch. Looking behind her, she saw the motorcycle again. They'd stopped about a kilometer back.

Jason was peeing at the front of the car and whistling softly while Reza and Almas did their prayers on the little rugs they had with them. A cold wind whipped up the dust and light bits of snow.

Bernadette walked to the car and pulled out her weapon. She wanted to be ready in case the motorcycle was another hit squad. She'd faced one, did not want to face another.

Jason came beside her. "You see something?"

"Yeah, that motorcycle's been following us for the past two hours. Now it's stopped," Bernadette said.

Jason stared down the road. "Damn, you can see that far?" He pulled out a monocular and put it to his eye. "Yep, you're right, they look like Taliban. And me without my sniper rifle."

"What should we do?"

"We can't outrun them. If I can find a narrow road, like a choke point, we could set up an ambush, until then we just keep an eye on them," Jason said.

Bernadette lowered her gun. A loud chugging sound erupted beside her.

The sound came from the car's engine, the car started to shudder. Jason ran to the driver's door and flinging it open, he hit the gas pedal. The car kept shuddering—with one final shake, it died.

"Shit," Jason yelled, pounding on the steering wheel. He waited for a few minutes then tried the ignition. There was nothing. He got out of the car and opened the hood.

"Can't we push start it?" Bernadette asked.

Jason slammed the hood and came back to the rear of the car. He stared down at the road, a river of oil bled from under the car, he shook his head. He opened the trunk, taking out their packs.

Bernadette came up beside him. "I take it we're on foot?"

Jason handed her a pack. "The engine seized from an oil leak. This thing is a pile of junk. We'll have to hoof it."

Bernadette stared at the barren landscape. She'd been in worse, but that was with wild animals around. This was with men with guns who wanted her dead.

Reza and Almas got the message. They put the packs they were given by Jason on their backs without complaint. To Bernadette, it was the Afghan way. No one seemed to complain, the weather, the fighting, it didn't matter—they persevered.

She did the same. Donning a down parka and adjusting her pack, she slung her A-K47 over her shoulder and checked the position of the handgun. She'd moved it to her waist so she could access it more easily.

"Where are we heading?" she asked, looking at Jason for some kind of answer.

Jason shrugged. "We've got to ask Almas."

Reza translated to Almas, and he pointed in the direction of the mountains.

Jason turned back to Bernadette. "Looks like we've got that mountain range to climb."

"Almas says that the village is just over that mountain range. His home was only some few kilometers from Azau. He saw the last star location just before the sun came up."

"Okay, that's where we're heading. Nothing like a bit of exercise in the morning," Jason said with a smile.

"Cheery bastard," Bernadette muttered as she fell into step behind Jason. Reza and Almas followed behind. Bernadette looked down the road. At least they wouldn't have to worry about the Taliban following them on the motorcycle. If they came after them on foot they would be fair game.

Din and Dost watched with amazement as their quarry left the car and walked towards the mountains.

"What can we do?" Dost asked. "We cannot follow with the motorbike on such rocks."

"We must follow them on foot," Din replied, looking over his shoulder at his brother in disgust.

"You are joking, yes?"

Din pushed Dost off the motorbike and got off. "Do you want to explain to Warlord Mohammed Mirwais how we lost sight of them because the ground was too rocky? That your precious feet were too tender to walk up the mountain? You will have to explain it very fast—he will have you hanging upside down before he guts you with his knife."

Dost stared at his brother, before looking at the mountain then down at his thin running shoes and felt how light his cotton and wool parka was. "You are right, my brother.

We could possibly perish chasing those four or die with a certainty at the hand of Mirwais."

They pushed the motorbike off the road, grabbed their meager packs with rations, and the two ancient AK-47's slung over their backs. Din walked with the steps of determined man. Dost walked with the steps of a man going to his own funeral.

Din held Dost back. "We must not get too close."

"Are you joking with me? I do not want to get within five hundred meters of them. That is the effective range of their weapons."

Din waved his hand in a knowing gesture, "My young brother, they are all carrying AK 47's that are most accurate at four hundred meters."

"And you know this how?" Dost asked with his hands on his hips. He hated his older brother's superior knowledge.

"I watched all of them enter the car. They only had the Russian-made automatics," Din replied with a grin.

"And how does this help us if we follow at six hundred meters, this alarms them, and they lie in wait for us in the rocks? How does your plan work when we are surrounded by them in an ambush?"

Din's pause spoke volumes. He hadn't thought of this. "Very well, we will keep our distance by traveling to the north and then west. They will think we are on another path, but we will travel on a parallel path. They will think we are going elsewhere."

Dost put his head down and followed his brother as he threaded his way through the rocks. There was a problem with his older brother's plan—his brother had no sense of direction.

Bernadette turned as they reached the base of the mountain. She climbed a small promontory to view the valley behind her. Two men threaded their way among the rocks in the valley floor. She wondered what kind of Taliban these were. She was glad they weren't professionals.

She walked back to Jason. "We can take these two anytime we want to tonight, pretty amateur."

Chapter Thirty-Four

Jason had them walk close together as the snow fell. The climb had become steep, the rocks so large, they could no longer step over them but had to walk around them.

Bernadette felt her lungs starting to heave with the upward climb. It was like the exertion on a treadmill with the incline adjusted to the max with the addition of a forty-pound pack on her back and fifteen pounds of weapons and ammunition.

They stopped beside a wall of rocks. Bernadette turned to look for their pursuers but saw no sign of them. Either the snow was hiding them or they'd dropped off the trail.

"They started going on a parallel path three hours ago," Jason said as he saw Bernadette scanning the valley. "Then, they dropped into a dry riverbed that went north up the valley. I haven't seen them since."

"What do you make of it?"

"Either totally crafty Taliban or stoned out of their gourds on hashish—or useless at traversing terrain."

"I think we still keep watch for them," Bernadette said as she massaged her burning calf muscles.

"Copy that. We'd best push on. I don't want to be stuck on this side of the mountain in the coming storm. We'll get to the lee side, pull out some tarps and hunker down for the night with some tasty MRE rations."

"What are MRE's?" Bernadette asked. She was hoping Jason had something fantastic for dinner as she had been munching on energy bars for several hours and the carbs and sugars were sufficient for her body but doing nothing for her taste buds.

"Oh, the famous meals ready to eat? Probably the worst food any army could invent and give to men or women who are putting their life on the line. The main thing is how you approach it," Jason said shouldering his huge pack.

"And how is that?"

"You have to use your imagination. Try to think of it as the best Chicken Tikka you've ever eaten instead of the taste of wall paper paste in your mouth."

Bernadette tried to laugh. She wanted to, but tiredness was folding in her legs, her back, and her arms. She needed to keep moving. With lungs hitting the bursting level, they crested the mountain and started to descend. While the wind howled and tore on the other side, they were now sheltered.

Now, the treacherous part of the descent came into play. Each step had to be planted well. One slip and a knee could meet with a jagged rock or a backside could slide down the path. Now her quads and heels were taking a beating.

As the sky darkened, they came to a halt at what looked like it had once been a dwelling for a shepherd or a Taliban hideout. Jason approached it first. He came at the doorway from the side, peeked inside and proclaimed it "all clear."

Bernadette barely made it inside before she dropped her pack to the ground and collapsed on top of it. Almas collected small sticks and Reza built a fire.

Jason boiled some water he had collected from the snow, putting some silver packages in the pot and stirring with great expectations. He finally nodded that the packages of MERs were done. He handed the packages around with a spoon for each person.

Bernadette sniffed it before tasting. It smelled like a curried chicken, but her taste buds told her it really did have the consistency of paste. She gagged, taking a large drink of water to get it down.

Jason looked up from his package, "Oh, yeah, water is an essential to getting this stuff down. Without invoking your gag reflex."

Bernadette held up the package, she tried reading the writing. "Who made this?"

"These are from the Israeli army. I get these as I'm assured they are okay for Arab's and their *halal*, or Islamic purity laws for food," Jason said, taking a big spoonful and shoving it into his mouth.

Bernadette eyed Reza and Almas happily eating the meals. They seemed content with anything slightly warm and nourishing on this bleak mountainside.

The hut they were in wasn't more than a few meters square in size. They finished their meals, put away the packages, and threw down some mats before wrapping themselves in reflective blankets to keep themselves warm.

"Shouldn't we set a watch?" Bernadette asked.

Jason, vvvvvv had gone outside to look for their Taliban friends, came back inside. "I set a trip wire both sides of the trail. It will sound a sensor I'll be keeping by my head."

"You think those two Taliban are still following us?"

"They may be trying. From what I saw of them, they were not great trackers. If they stumble upon this path, I'll be impressed," Jason said as he yawned and lay down beside Bernadette.

The four of them lay on the floor. Almas was beside Bernadette, Reza on his side and Jason on her other side. Reza was snoring in seconds. Almas wasn't far behind.

Bernadette lay there on her back. She could feel the heat of Jason beside her. He was moving back and forth. He pulled a hip flask from his vest pocket. The smell of the grain alcohol seeped into the air.

"You want a nightcap?" Jason asked.

"No, not really, and not with that shit-kicker stuff you're trying to pass as alcohol. You not afraid you'll go blind?"

Jason took a pull on the flask. He had to take a moment to catch his breath from the potent liquor. "Oh, I've developed a tolerance to the stuff over the years." He paused for a moment and rubbed his eyes. "My wife doesn't like me drinking the stuff much…"

Bernadette looked at him. "You want to tell me about your wife?"

"What do you want to know?"

"Did she pass away or leave you?"

"What the…how did you figure that out…?" Jason said, his eyes going wide as he stared at her. He wasn't more than thirty centimeters from her. His breath was hot.

Bernadette returned his stare. She didn't blink. "You've told two different stories about your wife. I'm a detective, remember, which means I'm very high on bullshit detection. You drink as if you're drowning something out and you're still living in the most dangerous country in the world instead of going home. So, now, you want to give me the real story of your wife or do you keeping feeding me your bullshit stories?"

Jason turned away. He put his hand under his head, taking a long drink of his flask. He let out a long sigh. "Yeah, you're a good detective. My wife died in a suicide bombing attack in her mosque. She was a hell of a good Muslim…so much better than me."

"Is that why you don't practice your religion anymore?"

"Pretty much. The bomber attacked the mosque because my wife was Shia, the bomber was Sunni. There you have it. A totally good reason to kill someone if I ever heard one," Jason said, raising his flask to the air as if making a toast to the insanity that killed his wife.

Bernadette said, "There's no good reason for murder. Never was and never will be. My Irish ancestors killed each other because of Catholic and Protestant. I have no way of reconciling that. But I know we move on."

"You didn't move on," Jason said. "You could have stayed in Canada, let the government deal with finding Chris, but you didn't. How are you different from me?"

"Because my guy isn't dead, at least I don't feel it. But you can be sure, if he is dead, I won't spend my time hanging out here living with his ghost."

"You think that's what I'm doing?"

"Aren't you?"

Jason turned his head. He put his flask back in his pocket and shut his eyes.

Bernadette felt like an asshole, maybe she shouldn't have said anything, let him ramble on about his wife, and drink himself into a hole. But that wasn't her. She was the saint of lost causes—her friends back home and in the force had told her that. She told herself she was also the saint of the supreme asshole as well. Wondering if there was a Catholic medallion for that, she went to sleep.

Dost trudged behind Din. Every twenty minutes or so, he wanted to catch up to him, tap him on the shoulder, and say in a non-judgmental way, "My dear brother, we are going the wrong way."

Each time he got up the courage, he fell back, hunching his shoulders and keeping his head down as the large snowflakes got in his eyes. They'd made a right turn over three hours ago. Din's idea was to go a similar path and follow their prey up the mountain. Dost knew something was wrong. They were not going up.

Din stopped ahead. He dropped his pack and looked at Dost as he came beside him. "How long?"

"How long, what my brother?"

"How long have we been going in the wrong direction?"

The hackles rose on the back of Dost's neck; he knew he should have endured his brother's wrath and told him sooner. Now it was worse. "I...I think for some time." He looked thoughtfully behind them.

"Why did you not say anything?"

Dost shrugged. "We were making good progress?"

Din raised his hand to hit Dost, and then dropped it by his side. "We need to get back to where we left them." He looked up the sky. The clouds hung low in the valley, hiding the moon. They needed to get out of this valley before they were trapped in snow. "Come, we must hurry."

Dost trudged after Din. Next time, he would endure the beating to correct his brother. His brother would beat him, when he was more rested and assured his blows had some energy.

Mohammad Mirwais had summoned his fighters the moment he got the call from Din and Dost. He had an idea where his prized Almas and the infidels were heading. It could only be one place. He'd heard through the other tribal leaders that someone was holding a foreigner hostage in Azau. He didn't care for Ramin Rasul, but he'd kill him if he got in his way.

He had six Toyota pickup trucks with five heavily armed fighters in each. He received the call from Din at 0700 hours the day before outside Kajaki. He wasted no time in getting his force of thirty on the road. They traveled south to Laskkar Gar, skirted the military base, and avoided all the checkpoints in Delaram by using the countryside. The Toyota trucks took the rough terrain in stride.

They went north, then shot back towards Farah using another little used road to avoid the aircraft and artillery. Mirwais did not want his men mistaken for Taliban and taken out by Blackhawk Helicopters. They even flew an Afghan flag.

On the outskirts of Farah, they took a sharp right, crossing the river, leaving the sound of shells exploding and gunfire behind them. Mirwais did not doubt that Farah would fall to Afghan troops.

They drove in a tight convoy driving as fast as the rutted roads would allow. After two hours, the lead vehicle stopped to investigate an abandoned Camry. Mirwais got out and looked the vehicle over.

Right then, he would have liked to shoot three of his fighters who had let this car pass them a week ago. But he needed all his men, maybe he would kill them later. He stood looking up at the mountain, eyeing the goat trail they would take to get to the next valley and to Azau. He could chase after them now, but it was risky. Too many choke points for ambush, he was better off heading to Azau.

He yelled at his fighters to get back in the trucks and continue. The engines fired up, the trucks took off.

Din and Dost looked on from some five hundred meters away. "Who do you think that was?" Din asked.

"I have no idea," Dost replied, "but the old man seemed angry. I hope we never meet up with him."

They moved from their hiding place and headed up the mountain.

Chapter Thirty-Five

Bernadette woke from a troubled sleep. Her dreams were of Chris with a knife to his throat. All those newscasts of prisoners of the Taliban pleading for their lives, dressed in red, kneeling on the ground as a man stood over them with a large knife had flooded her dreams. It gave her chills.

Jason was already up and outside. Reza was making tea using the small camp stove they'd brought along. Almas was looking over a battered Koran.

Bernadette got up, stretched, and walked outside. The valley below had been bathed in a blanket of white. It no longer looked like the surface of the moon; it looked soft, as if it wouldn't harm you. There was no danger there, just snow.

She found a rock to pee behind, washed her hands in the snow, and joined Jason looking over the valley.

"Do you know which way we're heading?" she asked, already knowing the answer but wanting to break the ice after last night's conversation.

Jason didn't look at her. He stared down the valley. "Almas told me this morning we need to walk down into that valley and up that other mountain. Our village is on the other side."

"Oh, okay then. I guess I best get moving," Bernadette said. She glanced at her watch, noting it was 0700 hours. "I thought we'd be starting early."

Jason looked at her. "You were kind of moaning in your sleep last night. Looked like you had an attack of bad dreams. I thought I'd let you sleep in a bit. We'll make the other side of that mountain in six or seven hours of steady marching."

Bernadette turned to go back in the hut, then stopped. "What about those two that were following us? Any sign?"

"Yeah," Jason laughed. "They sprung the trip wire last night. I went out to look. Two of the saddest Taliban I've ever seen were following us. They went to sleep some eight hundred meters up the trail. I took the liberty of relieving them of some weight." He held up two AK-47 machine gun magazines.

"And they didn't hear you?"

"Nope, fast asleep, all cuddled together with their weapons five meters from them. That's pretty dumb for Taliban."

Bernadette went back into the hut to drink some tea that Reza offered her and munched on a protein bar. In minutes she was ready, shouldering her pack and joining the others as they moved down the mountain.

As she walked down, she realized she'd woken everyone in the hut with her dreams but had no idea what she'd said or how mournful she sounded. She kept her head down and tread carefully as they descended.

They reached the valley floor in an hour. The valley was flat with snow-covered rocks, much easier than the mountain slopes. The only hazard was stepping the wrong way on a slippery rock and turning an ankle.

The sun had broken through the clouds making the snow a dazzling white. Bernadette put on her sunglasses and looked up at the sky. Would they be mistaken for Taliban and strafed by a NATO jet or helicopter?

The thought of the Taliban following them had her stop and turn around. She saw nothing behind them. But she knew they were.

Din and Dost stared at the receding figures. Dost was against following in the valley, with no cover and in broad daylight. And there was the unmentioned fact that someone had stolen the ammunition from the weapons in the night.

Din finally listened to his younger brother. They waited by a rock while Din texted to Mohammad Mirwais. He included his longitude and latitude from his phone app. He smiled as he received a "well done."

"You see," Din said, showing the cell phone message from Mirwais. "He is pleased with our progress. We will meet him soon and be well rewarded."

Dost turned back to watch their quarry walking across the valley. Most of the schemes of Din's were never any good. He didn't expect much of this one.

Mirwais was stuck. His trucks had reached a raging river with a bridge that some idiot Taliban had blown up. He yelled at the trucks to split up and look for a place to cross.

He was close. He could feel it. He should never have let those people leave his village alive. When he caught up to them, he would let his men torture them to death. And the woman would receive his special attention.

Chapter Thirty-Six

Lackey was not happy. The Taliban suspect she'd interrogated hadn't given up much information. She had obtained one piece of interesting intel. The foreigner, Chris Christakos, was now of importance to the Taliban. Two weeks ago they seemed uninterested, claiming the theft of the robe was a hoax staged by the tribal leaders to gain power. Now they wanted to find the robe, and Chris. She'd sent the information to Langley, and now they wanted her to act.

She was in a room with three of her other CIA agents waiting for a call from CIA headquarters in Langley. This meant that they'd made a decision based on her report.

The speakerphone rang in the center of the table, and Lackey gave her usual, "Good morning, Director," greeting and waited for the director to give her a sense of where they would be heading.

"Agent Lackey," Director Harmon began. He was in his late sixties, a tall man with a full head of silver hair and a stare from bushy eyebrows that could wilt the heart of the toughest opponent. He'd spent time in South Korea interrogating captured North Koreans. He was said to have the best 'interrogation' stats in the agency.

"I wonder why you haven't picked up this Christakos and Lund for the theft of this robe the country is upset over," Harmon said.

"We've put numerous assets out there to find them. So far we have nothing," Lackey said. She looked around the room; they all knew her words weren't true. The other agents did not meet her gaze.

"I want you to increase your efforts, Lackey. Put every available resource you have on it. The State Department is not happy with the diplomatic fallout of this. The Iranians are massing on the western border. With the tribes going at each other over this, this makes the situation worse than when we first walked into that damned country."

"Yes, sir, we will find them and bring them in for questioning," Lackey said.

"No, I want you to do more than that. Turn him over to the Afghan authorities as soon as you find them. This is an Afghan problem. We have enough on our hands. The moment we distance ourselves from this, the better off we are," Harmon said

"Yes, Director," Lackey said. There was no use in questioning the logic. The Canadian would be the scapegoat to diffuse this situation. The decision had been made.

Lackey took the elevator down to the basement. She walked into a large room, dimly lit with banks of computer screens that monitored all communications in the country. There she found the chief supervisor, Rodney Kowalski, a balding and overweight man in his mid-thirties. He lived and breathed the information in this room, working too many hours and suffering for it in a way that only someone addicted to data could understand.

Rodney nodded at Lackey. "What can my room of wizards find for you today?"

"I need every bit of traffic on these people," Lackey said. She handed him a written list that included the names of Bernadette Callahan, Jason Radic, Reza and the boy, Almas.

Rodney's bloodshot eyes looked up and down the list. "Sure, I can find them the moment I ping their phones. Anything else?"

Lackey was about to give her okay, and then she stopped. "You know, this Jason Radic was in deep with all the NATO forces here. I want you to check everything from our side as well. Anywhere he goes, any cell tower he pings off of and anyone in NATO he bumps into. I also want an alert anytime you hear the name Chris Christakos mentioned.

"Whoa, you want me to spy on all our friendly forces as well? Tall order," Rodney said, pushing back the few hairs he had on his head.

"This is top level priority, Rodney. I know it's going to task your resources, but this is direct from Langley, all our jobs are on the line. You read me?"

"Sure, boss, just trying to get it clear on how deep I got to go and how we have to cover our tracks," Rodney countered. He hated getting on her bad side. She could make life brutal for him, worse than this dungeon of screens in the dark.

"Hey, sorry to come down so hard, but we've got the big guys in Langley on our asses," Lackey said, putting a hand on Rodney's shoulder. He was a good guy who did a great job but asked too many questions.

Rodney turned back to his people. He would give the order to put out a troll of every bit of traffic that had the names or was related to the names of these suspects. He would also pull up any cell numbers they had in the country. Every conversation, every text, every email they'd ever made would be examined.

Minutes from now, he would know exactly where these people were and their movements. God how he loved his work.

Lackey walked back upstairs. If Bernadette Callahan was as good a detective as she claimed to be, then she had to be on Chris' trail. Tracking her would lead to Chris, and hopefully end the mess the country was in—for now.

Chapter Thirty-Seven

Progress up the mountain was slow. The sun had melted the snow on the rocks into icy obstacles. They stumbled and fell. Their six-hour journey was pushing into ten. Jason tried not to look at his watch. The sun overhead was telling him what he feared. They'd be cresting the mountain in the dark.

Pushing their speed wouldn't help. Safety and getting to the village without sprained ankles or broken legs was his greatest concern. At the midpoint, he halted the group and they found shelter behind the biggest rock on the mountain and pulled out some MREs.

"I'm sorry I can't heat these," Jason apologized as he handed the packets around. "I don't want anyone coming to investigate a cooking fire."

Bernadette took a packet and ripped it open, pulling a spoon from her jacket. "Are you kidding? Cold chicken curry on a mountainside with this wonderful view, it couldn't be better."

Jason sat beside her and tore his packet open. "You

know, we haven't talked about an extraction plan when we find Chris."

Bernadette set her meal on a rock and pulled out a small packet wrapped in cloth. "I was going to see if they might accept this in exchange for Chris." She unwrapped the jade Buddha, handing it to Jason.

Jason looked at the Buddha, it sparkled in the sunlight, and he handed it back to her. "This will give you about thirty seconds more time before he either shoots you or hands you over to his fighters to play with before they kill you."

Bernadette rewrapped the Buddha and put it back in her pocket. "I got it from our hosts last night. They thought it might work."

Jason shook his head. "Those two have been working close to Ramin Rasul for some time. They pay him not to kill them or take them hostage."

"And the Buddha isn't worth enough?"

"No, it's probably worth a small fortune to an Afghan warlord, but you have to understand something, none of the captives have been offered for ransom."

"That's a big thing?"

"It's huge. Everything is a bargaining chip here. If they haven't put out a note for ransom, it means someone else is in control."

"How do you suggest we play this?" Bernadette asked.

"Real hard, guns blazing, no prisoners," Jason said.

"What are you, the reincarnation of John Wayne?"

"Nope, but Clint Eastwood and me are best buddies—in my mind," Jason said with a smile.

"Okay, we do whatever it takes to get Chris free," Bernadette, said. She pulled out the papers that Lackey had given her. "This is a complete satellite image of the village with all the buildings named as to use, as well as all the names of the villagers."

Jason looked over the map, "I can see where they probably have the captives. It will be one of these two small huts in the main square. They can keep a watch on them." He looked at another larger building, turned the map sideways and smiled. "I just found our way in. Let's move out."

Sardar Agha crunched a pistachio nut between his teeth and drank his tea. Nothing in the room went unnoticed. He watched the Shia tribes, those pseudo-Mongols who claimed Afghani blood and were really the decedents of the Russians hordes. He watched the several smaller tribal leaders sidle up to them, seeking their favor.

Jamshed took a seat beside him on a cushion. "How is it with you, Sardar?"

Sardar looked around the room with a furrowed brow. "What I see disgusts me."

"Why?" Jamshed asked.

"I see the Hazara tribe trying to curry favor with some of our Pashtun brothers."

Jamshed looked at the leader of the Hazara tribe, Abdul Ali Balkihi. "Yes, I can see he is speaking to a Pashtou, but what else can he do? They are outnumbered."

Sardar saw his trap was set. "But for how long, my brother?"

Jamshed let Sardar's words sink in. "I spoke to the others in my family. They see the danger of the Hazara. But how do we stop this? If we are attacked by the Shias of Iran to aid the Hazara, we will not be able to defeat them if NATO doesn't defend us."

"There is a bigger picture, Jamshed. What if the Taliban could be convinced to join with the Pashtun?" Sardar said quietly, looking around to see if anyone had heard him."

"You speak of treason, my brother."

"How many times has the government approached the Taliban to make peace and offering them a seat in the council?"

"Yes, but they cannot be trusted."

Sardar swilled the tea in his cup and looked at Jamshed. "Who can you really trust in our government? The Taliban tried to stop the corruption. If they were given the right guidance, let's say by a strong leader such as you…"

Jamshed let his eyes focus on Sardar. He nodded. He understood what Sardar was saying. "The implication is death—if we fail."

Sardar let the smallest smile grace his lips. "We will not fail. I have a source that tells me the robe will be returned in a day. If you were the one to bring it to me at the mosque, this would increase your status among the tribes, many fold, would it not?"

Jamshed smiled. "You are more conniving than a desert fox, Sardar. Yes, it would be of great value for me to bring the robe back. I'm sure you'd have a convincing story of how I attained it?"

"Of course, enough for the faithful to have you become a hero to our country."

Jamshed stood, made a gesture of peace and walked out of the hall.

Sardar knew what he'd done was dangerous. Now, he had to put the plan into action.

Jason took the lead up the mountain. Bernadette brought up the rear. She kept having a sensation they were followed, that eyes were watching them. Every time she turned to look, no one was there. Then, night fell.

A three-quarter moon lit their path as they trudged up the mountain. Steam rose from their breaths and from their clothes. The rocks were now freezing solid again as the temperature dropped. Several times they stopped to rest. The going was slow. Then, the light went out as clouds covered the moon.

When Bernadette thought her legs couldn't take the uphill battle with her heavy pack, they came to the summit. As one, they stopped and rested.

Almas pointed to the stars above them. The clouds had moved to make an opening in the night sky. He kept repeating something.

"Almas says that he knows all these stars, the bright one to the east is the one above the village he visited with Mirwais," Reza said.

Bernadette looked up at the stars; the one she recognized as Sirius was shining brightly. She looked down—darkness had consumed the valley. She felt her heart sink, how could they descend the mountain in the dark?

Almas took her hand. "You see, moon." He pointed upwards at the sky. At that moment, a single cloud that covered the moon moved away. The three quarter moon shone down brightly, revealing a narrow and winding path.

Bernadette knelt and hugged Almas. "Yes, I see, we have a bright moon." His eyes were shining. To Bernadette it seemed Almas had ordered the moon. She shook her head to gather her thoughts and turned to Jason.

"Well, what are we waiting for?"

"You're right," Jason said. "We need to get started. I

figure we have about three to four hours to descend to the village. I have a topographical map that shows us coming to the end of the trail about two hundred meters above the village, which should give us a good viewpoint."

"Do we go in as soon as we get there?" Bernadette asked.

"No way," Jason said, shouldering his huge pack. "I want us to do our extraction at dawn." He checked his watch. "It's zero one-thirty hours now. If we arrive at the village at zero five-thirty that gives us a few hours shuteye before sunrise."

Bernadette turned away and put on her pack. She couldn't help but smile at Jason's focus. She hadn't seen him taking swigs from his liquor flask all day. Maybe the little talk they'd had last night had some effect on him?

Din and Dost left the rocks on the other side of the valley as soon as the sunset. The tracks in the snow were easy to follow. This time there would be no getting lost, no losing their intended target. Din texted to Mirwais several more times as they moved across the valley and then ascended the mountain. Each time he got a reply that made him smile.

"It is not every day that you gain favor with one of our country's greatest warlords," Din said.

Dost put his head down and trudged along. He picked one foot up and placed the other down as if he'd been called to his execution. From the moment Din had hatched this plan, he knew it was wrong. Just like he'd known the plan to enlist with the Taliban for money and to join the battle in Farah was wrong. Dost, the younger brother, had been a happy shop keeper in Kandahar. Yes, he would have had to marry a less attractive wife, but all of that was more appealing than this night of cold in these barren mountains. Dost said a prayer under his breath to Allah and moved forward. His reply to his brother would not be worth it.

The texts from Din only made Mirwais angrier that his fighters were not moving faster. It seemed hours before they finally found a way over the river. They sped up the valley, forded the stream, losing only one truck that bobbed its way downstream with five hapless fighters onboard. The other fighters cheered them on as they floated away, wishing that Allah would be merciful if they drowned.

Mirwais shouted at his fighters. "Do you think if they could not make it across a simple stream, they could make it across the bridge over hell? Those idiots will be doomed to *jahannam*."

The fighters went quiet. In the Quran, all Muslim souls must pass a bridge over hell. Those who are destined for hell would find the bridge too narrow and would fall below to their new abode, *jahannam*, and eternal hell.

The convoy assembled and resumed down the valley road. Mirwais checked his map; they were only ten kilometers away from the village, but there were three more bridges. He knew that the Taliban would have blown each of them up. He sighed deeply and yelled at his driver to hurry.

Bernadette felt the moonlight on her face as if it was an omen. Somehow her steps felt lighter. The pack on her back was no longer a problem and everything in her told her she would see Chris soon. She tried to suppress a smile.

She checked her watch. They'd been descending to the

valley for over four hours. They rounded a corner in the trail to see a ribbon of light sparkling below. It was the small creek by the village. Then the village came into view. Bernadette felt her heart race.

Jason brought them to a halt at a group of large rocks. They could see the village in the moonlight. It looked serene, but they all knew how dangerous it was.

Jason whispered, "We pull out our bedding and sleep here. I'll take the first watch, then Reza. At first light we'll see how we do our extraction."

Bernadette pulled out her thin foam pad and bedding. She was both too tired and too excited to eat. She lay down with Almas beside her and Reza beside him.

When Jason came over to get some water from his pack, Bernadette touched his shoulder. "I see you're taking a break from your liquid courage."

Jason nodded. "No, it wasn't liquid courage it was the liquid to forget. You were right to let me have it last night. I've been living with a ghost, and it's time to set her free."

He moved away to his sentry point. Bernadette could only make out his outline in the moonlight. She was glad she got through to him, however, maybe it was too late, as tomorrow, if things didn't go well, they might all be ghosts.

Chapter Thirty-Eight

Bernadette had fallen asleep. It could not have been for long, but long enough to have a dream of Chris. He was pointing a gun to his head. Her Grandmother Moses was standing over his shoulder. She had her hand up. What did it mean?

She woke with a start. Sitting up, she saw that Almas and Reza were gone. She was frantic, shaken; looking around, she saw them by the rocks with Jason. She threw off her covers and walked to them.

"There's some activity in the village," Jason said.

Bernadette looked down into the village square. Four Toyota Land Cruisers were parked and a group of Afghanis with guns milled around the square. Some leaned on the trucks, some squatted by the large tree, smoking cigarettes and chatting.

"What do you think is happening?" Bernadette asked.

"I got a feeling they're getting ready to move the prisoners," Jason said.

"What's our move?"

"I see about fifteen fighters. Now, we've got a great attack position, at two hundred meters above them, but the moment we open up, they'll start a flanking position and come after us. We'd maybe last a few hours before our ammo ran out," Jason said.

"Okay, scrub that. What's plan B?"

"Drone warfare," Jason said. "I brought just the thing." He pulled out a small drone that had been in the box on top of his pack.

"So that's what you've been packing all this time," Bernadette said.

"Yep." Jason smiled. "The Taliban have been using these effectively for some time. They attach a grenade to a drone and drop it on the NATO troops. Damn effective."

"You think one grenade is going to do it, dropped into those fighters? I mean great idea, but I'm thinking they'll scatter the moment they hear the racket from that thing. Little drones sound like a bunch of pissed off bees in stereo," Bernadette said.

"You're right," Jason said. "That's why I brought this along." He opened his bag and brought out a brown package of C-4 explosive.

"You'll blow up the entire village square with that, plus Chris and all the captives," Bernadette said.

"I'm not aiming for the square." Jason pulled out the map that Bernadette had given him. "You see this building just one hundred meters from the square? The CIA intel says this is their armory. I'm sure this little bit of C-4 dropped on the roof will spark a few grenades and give us the ka-boom we need to pull all the captives out."

"And when the Afghans find we're the ones attacking them? Then what?"

Jason winked. "We get down there during the explosions, shoot us some Afghans, take their weapons and give them to the prisoners. Those guys are all trained killers. Bingo, we have our own army."

Bernadette put her hand on Jason's shoulder. "You know, I'm sure every army guy has hatched a simple minded plan like yours. Napoleon and Hitler come to mind."

"Hey, trust me, once this loud ordnance goes off, those Afghans will head for cover. They'll think the entire NATO force is here."

Bernadette sighed. "Okay, do your thing, let's get this party started."

Jason attached the C-4 to the drone. He got out his remote and started it up. It did sound like a bunch of bees amplified by a stereo sound system. The little thing rose up in the air and dropped down towards the village. The Afghan fighters looked up. First in interest, then in horror—they raised their weapons and began firing at it. They knew what it was.

Jason moved the drone up and down then right and left to keep it from being hit. He swooped it low around the fighters and onto the building.

"Get ready for a little ka-boom," Jason said.

The next thing they knew, the earth shook. The C-4 exploded first, and then more explosions rocketed through the village. Missiles launched themselves out the building and exploded into the hills. The fighters ran from the square.

"What the hell did you hit?" Bernadette asked covering her head behind the rocks.

"They must have had a bunch of RPG's and landmines in the building. I'll be damned, it sure cleared the square," Jason said peering over the rocks.

"We'd best get down there before they come back," Bernadette said. She turned to Reza, "Where's Almas?"

Reza looked to his right, then his left. "Oh no, he said he could find a way to set the prisoners free and help you. I did not think he was serious."

"When did you last see him?"

"Just a few minutes ago."

Bernadette looked down the path, Almas was running full speed towards the village. He had a handgun in his hand. Bernadette looked at her holster for her gun—it was missing.

"Let's go," Bernadette said. She grabbed her AK-47 and launched herself down the path after Almas. Jason and Reza were behind her.

The path was narrow and rocky. It took all of Bernadette's skill to keep from tumbling forward. The path led into the side of the square. She stopped so quickly; Jason and Reza almost collided with her.

"I'll take the point," Jason said. "Cover me." He ran around Bernadette, through the square and into the first building. He came out and motioned it was clear. He went into a small hut. He stopped—his body went rigid.

Bernadette came in behind him. Her heart skipped a beat. Jason was standing in the doorway. His gun was trained on something. She peered into the darkness.

Chris was there. Behind him was an Afghani with a large knife at his throat.

Chapter Thirty-Nine

"Hey Bernadette," Chris said. "Glad you could make it."

His captor squeezed his neck, pressing the blade deeply.

"Sorry about this guy. He really doesn't like me. He's been threatening to kill me for some time. Looks like he's going to get his chance."

When Reza came in behind Bernadette, she turned to him. "Tell that guy we'll let him go if he doesn't harm Chris."

Reza repeated her words; he listened to Chris's captor, and turned to Bernadette. "He says this is the infidel who stole Mohammad's robe. By killing him, he will be assured a place in paradise."

"My god, I hate when they talk about that going to paradise crap," Bernadette said. "Can't you tell him that if he kills an innocent man, we'll shoot him and he won't go to paradise, he'll come back to earth as goat or a dog?"

Reza shook his head, "Wrong religion. Muslims do not believe in reincarnation."

Bernadette turned to Jason. "Do you have a shot?"

"No," Jason said. The guy's head is behind Chris. I'd try shooting Chris in the arm or leg but he's got him crouched, and this damn AK-47 would put too big a hole in him. Can't risk it."

A window opened in the back of the hut. A small hand appeared, then a leg. Almas climbed into the hut. He dropped down silently behind Chris and his captor with his handgun.

"Reza, ask the man what he wants, tell him we'll give it to him—tell him I have a jade Buddha." Bernadette pulled the small packet out of her jacket and unwrapped it. The figure sparkled as a beam of sunlight hit it.

Reza repeated Bernadette's words.

The man began to shout at Reza, he pulled the knife closer to Chris's throat.

"He says this is an idol of the infidels. All of these should be destroyed," Reza said. "I think we made it worse."

Almas crept up behind Chris's captor. Bernadette kept her eyes on the man, and tried to not look at Almas. One misstep, one glance, and the man would slash Chris's throat. There was no triage for such a wound. They wouldn't be able to save him.

Almas brought the barrel of the handgun to the back of the Afghan's head. He pulled the trigger. The gun clicked—a misfire.

The Afghan threw his head back to look at the noise. Chris felt his hold release. He threw an elbow in his face and hit the floor just as Jason shot the Afghan in the head.

Bernadette rushed to Chris. They collided into each other's arms, ignoring the dead Afghan who lay on the ground beneath them.

"I knew you'd get here, baby," Chris said.

"I was almost too late," Bernadette said.

Chris kissed her forehead, then her lips. "They were about to take me back to Kandahar."

"Where is the rest of your unit?" Jason asked.

"In the next building. I haven't heard much from them in the past few days, but I know they've been kept there," Chris said.

Jason left the hut and crossed to the building. He walked into the room and at first saw nothing. Then, looking at the dirt floor, he saw mounds of earth. He walked to them and moved some earth with his hands, revealing the faces of three dead men.

"You'd better come and take a look at this," Jason motioned to Chris.

Chris followed Jason. When he stepped into the building, he stared at the corpses, and then sat on his heels, putting his head in his hands. "They murdered them," Chris said with a heavy sigh. "These were good guys, they didn't deserve this."

He stood up and looked around the room, "but Lund, he isn't here."

"Wasn't he captured with you?" Bernadette asked.

Chris stood beside her. "Yeah, we were all taken at the same time. They separated us right away. I spent all my time in solitary. The past few weeks have been a bit lonely."

"You've been captive for a month," Bernadette said.

Chris shook his head. "My, how time flies." He looked at Reza, Almas, and Jason. "How big a team did you bring?"

"This is it," Bernadette said with a weak smile.

"Holy shit, are you serious? You know how many fighters this warlord has and how pissed he's going to be when he finds me gone?" Chris said.

"Speaking of that, we need to get gone," Jason said. "I think the fighters have figured out there's no NATO force coming. We best steal a truck and get moving."

Chris nodded. "Right, let's go."

"Wait," Bernadette said. "What about the robe. Isn't it here?"

Chris came beside her. "It was never here. The last I saw it was with Lund. The Imam had given to him to look at then he handed it to me for a second outside the museum, the lights in the square went out. Then he grabbed it back."

"Perfect move to frame you," Bernadette said.

They moved into the courtyard. Machine gun bullets strafed the wall behind them. They returned fire. Chris picked up an AK-47 from a dead fighter, racked it, and began firing.

"Get to the trucks," Jason commanded.

The four Toyota Land Cruisers were loaded with weapons. Jason opened the back hatch of one of them, taking out three grenades.

"Get in the lead truck," Jason yelled.

Chris jumped in the driver's seat, Bernadette got in beside him, and Almas and Reza got in the back. Jason pulled the pins on the grenades and threw them into the other Toyotas.

Jason jumped in the back seat, "Go!"

Chris threw the truck in gear, punched the gas, all four tires bit into the earth. They shot out of the courtyard as more explosions rocketed through the village.

"What the hell was in those things?" Chris asked, looking at the fireball coming from the village.

"They were loaded with RPGs and landmines. Those

bastards meant business. Keep sharp as we leave the village. There may be some stragglers out there."

The truck left the safety of the village walls and came under fire. Bernadette, Jason, and Reza returned fire until they made it into the hills.

"What road do I take?" Chris asked.

Jason had the map out. "Once we cross that small mountain we're almost in Almas's old village. From there we will find a little used road that will lead to Shindand. There's an airbase there. I can get us a heli lift back to Kandahar."

Bernadette put her hand on Chris's leg and squeezed it. They could be back in Kandahar that evening. She'd get all the charges against him dropped and she'd have him all to herself.

Chris looked at her and smiled. "It's great to see you too, baby."

The ground in front of them exploded. Chris threw the truck to the right. An explosion erupted twenty meters on the left.

"We've got company," Jason said, looking out the back window.

Chapter Forty

Bernadette and Chris whirled around to see four trucks with Afghan fighters. One was aiming a rocket propelled grenade launcher. Chris hit the accelerator, the Land Cruiser lurched forward making the crest of the mountain.

"Which way from here?" Chris asked.

"Head to the dry riverbed. This will give us speed, then we find a road on the right two kilometers ahead." Jason said.

The Land Cruiser bounced over rocks and become airborne several times heading downhill. When they reached the riverbed, Chris put the pedal to the floor, making the engine roar.

Their pursuers were falling behind. The fighters couldn't aim their RPG's with any accuracy as they bounced over the terrain.

"Only five hundred meters before we reach the next road to the right," Jason said.

"Is that what I think it is ahead?" Bernadette asked.

Jason looked up to see two armored vehicles seven

hundred meters ahead of them. "Oh shit. It's the Iranian army. We must have come too close to their border."

"Will they let us take the road we need to get over the mountain pass?" Bernadette asked.

"Not bloody likely," Jason said, shaking his head. We get any closer, they'll put a warning shot through our windshield."

Two trucks appeared to the right of the Iranians, blocking their escape. Chris brought the Cruiser to a stop. He pulled over to a collection of rocks that could act as a shield from all their threats.

"We need to head for the rocks," Jason said. "Everyone take as much ammo as you can."

They clambered out of the vehicle, Chris, Bernadette and Jason pulling out AK-47's and Reza and Almas following with rockets for the RPG.

Jason scanned the trucks behind them with binoculars. "We got Mirwais and his fighters behind us. Oh, and he's met up with the two that were following us." He handed the binoculars to Chris. "You recognize any of the guys in front of us?"

"Yeah, that's Rasul, our happy camp commander," Chris said.

A megaphone came on, first from Mirwais, then Rasul. There seemed to be much discussion over them.

"What's up?" Bernadette asked Reza.

Reza listened intently shaking his head. "They're fighting over us. Mirwais only wants Almas back. He'd like to torture the rest of us to death, but he'll leave the rest to Rasul if he gets Almas. Rasul only wants the infidel Chris to take him back to Kandahar. He'd like to take part in the killing and torture of us as well but has a deadline to meet."

Jason pulled out his satellite phone. "It's time I phone

a friend." His phone rang four times until Kaufer, his NATO contact, answered. "Hey Kaufer, you have a few helis free? I'm in some serious shit and could use a pickup."

Kaufer was in NATO's command room. "Jason, do you have the guy you told me about?"

Jason was taken aback. "Yeah, if you mean the guy who was accused of stealing the robe. Yeah, I got him, but not the robe. We don't have that."

"How many for extraction?" Kaufer asked.

"There are five of us. How soon until you get here?"

"I've got helis in the area," Kaufer said.

"I'll give you the coordinates."

"I got them, my guys are twenty mikes out. Stay frosty." Kaufer said.

Jason put his phone back in his vest. He turned to Bernadette. "I have some help coming. Strange thing is—they knew our coordinates…and Kaufer sounded strange."

"Someone's been tracking your phones. Any idea who?" Chris asked.

"If they're in league with NATO, it's got to be top level government, maybe Homeland Security or CIA," Bernadette suggested.

"We'll have to see who shows up. Look, they're twenty minutes away. We need to stay alive between the warlords and the Iranian Army," Jason said.

"What's the plan?" Bernadette asked. Looking up and down the riverbed she could see the men milling around the trucks unloading weapons.

"I doubt if they'd attack in broad daylight," Jason said. "Remember, Mirwais wants Almas alive. He'd rather have us dead, and Rasul only wants Chris—I assume that's alive?"

"—He wants me alive, bringing a dead scapegoat won't be well received." Chris said.

Jason looked at Mirwais's men getting out of their trucks. "I agree. I think they'll want to wait us out, do some feint attacks to get us to use up our ammunition then pick off the ones they don't want and each of them gets their prize."

"Sounds pretty cruel and straightforward to me," Bernadette added.

Almas tugged on Reza's arm and whispered in his ear.

"Almas says that he will die fighting rather than be captured by Mirwais," Reza said.

Bernadette knelt in front of Almas, putting her hand on his shoulders. "Tell him I will not let him fall into their hands."

"You must make that same promise to all of us, and to yourself," Reza said. "Being captured by the Taliban is automatic torture before death."

Bernadette looked up at Reza. "Is that why those women soldiers back at the NATO base said we needed to save one last bullet for ourselves?"

Reza nodded and his eyes went misty. "Yes, my sister. If you would do me the honor of shooting Almas and me before they capture us we would be eternally grateful."

"*Inshallah*, I hope it does not come to that," Bernadette said.

"If you two are finished with your suicide pact, I suggest we get to killing some Afghan fighters that are approaching," Chris said. He had his AK-47 trained on three fighters climbing into the rocks above them.

The three fighters Jason saw included the forlorn figures of the two men who had been tracking them. They ran up the hill above them, one of them trailed as if he was being pulled along against his will. The unlucky Din and Dost had met Mirwais and been told to join in the fight or be shot on the spot.

"I hate situations like this," Jason said. "They're doing a flanking maneuver. I guess I was wrong about them attacking in broad daylight—I've got to stop it." He ran to the base of the rock, picked up the RPG and shouldered it. "Okay, now, my boys, this is what happens when you stay too close together."

He pulled the trigger. The grenade made a whooshing sound out the back of the tube. The fighters looked up in surprise as the rocket approached. They had seconds to duck. They were too late. The rocket exploded in their midst.

Dost felt the explosion tear through his body. He fell to the ground beside Din, who was mortally wounded.

"We are lost my brother," Din said. "But we will go to paradise."

Dost shook his head. "No my brother, we will go to the place that Allah reserves for those who do stupid things."

Dost made an effort to reply, he couldn't speak from loss of blood.

Jason did a fist pump. "There you go, three down, a whole shit load to go. Everyone get to a position. Keep them at a distance."

Bullets ricocheted off the rocks behind them. They returned fire. A mortar round exploded near their truck. The fighters spread out, making them harder targets. Jason shot off three more RPG rounds, hitting one fighter and taking out a truck.

"I'm out of RPG grenades. I need to run back to the

truck. Give me some covering fire," Jason yelled. As he started toward the truck, it exploded and Jason was thrown against the rocks with the force of the blast.

Bernadette looked around the rock. "What the hell was that?"

"Sounds like a shell from the Iranian armored vehicles. Looks like they've joined in," Chris said.

"Damn, I hate an uneven fight," Bernadette said. She let off a burst of her AK-47 at a fighter, who jumped back behind a rock.

"Reza, check on Jason," Bernadette yelled over the gunfire.

Reza ran, crouching by the rock and put his hand on Jason's throat. "He is okay, just knocked out."

"Excellent. That really helps." Bernadette looked up to the sky, "Okay, here's the deal God, I need either a miracle or a helicopter. If you want, call the heli a miracle and I'll go to church when I get home."

In the midst of the gunfire, they heard the distinct thrumming of helicopters. Bernadette ran to Jason, took out his satellite phone, and pressed redial of the last number.

"Kaufer, here."

"Hey, this is Callahan here with Jason, but he's out cold right now. If those are your helis coming in, tell them we're the ones in the middle of the cross fire by the large rock with the burning truck. We'd stand up and wave but we'd get our asses shot off."

"Copy that," Kaufer said. "You have three Blackhawk gunships coming in and two medevacs. I'll let them know you have contact."

"If contact means a shit load of bullets—sure. And tell them there's Iranian armor on our three o'clock."

"Copy that," Kaufer said.

"Let's see how the Afghans and Iranians like a whole bunch of air power," Bernadette said. "Take cover under the rocks. There's about to be fireworks."

The Blackhawks came in low. They wasted no time in strafing the fighters of Mirwais. Rockets blew up their trucks, and the fighters ran for cover.

Turning towards the Iranians, the Blackhawks let off with their machine guns then fired rockets. One Iranian vehicle blew up, the other backed up in a hurry losing its taste for battle.

Rasul and his men needed no further demonstrations of the havoc the Blackhawks could bring. They jumped into their vehicles and sped away. Some had to run to jump into the trucks or be left behind.

Bernadette grabbed Chris, hugging and kissing him. "My God, we're saved."

"I never had any doubt that you had a backup plan, Bernie," Chris said, wrapping her in his arms. "I couldn't see myself having to put a bullet in your head to save you from those bastards."

"Oh my god, I forgot I said that." She buried her head in Chris's big chest. "So happy we didn't have to do that. I'm so not ready to be dead yet."

"Me neither."

"There's just one more thing," Bernadette said. "I had a call with your mother…"

"My mother. That's a buzz kill. What did she want?"

Bernadette bit her lip. "She kind of wanted me to promise her that I'd leave you once I returned you to Canada."

"Really? Did you swear on a whole stack of Bibles or spit?"

"Ah, no…"

"Then, it didn't happen. The Greeks have to do that to make an oath real…so no problem—you're clear."

Bernadette kissed him hard on the lips. "Thanks, because I was going to go back on my word anyways."

"Works for me."

The helicopters landed in the riverbed. A team of soldiers jumped out with their weapons ready. A woman with a helmet and flak vest was with them.

As Bernadette watched them approach, she recognized Sergeant Hammer leading the soldiers. Agent Lackey walked behind them.

"Don't we meet in the strangest places," Bernadette said as Lackey approached.

"Yes, we do. Is this Chris?"

"He sure is," Bernadette said hugging him. "I found him safe and sound."

"That's great." Agent Lackey walked towards Chris. "I'm here to take you into custody and deliver you to the Afghan authorities for the theft of their ancient religious artifact. You will be tried in their courts and sentenced accordingly."

"Bullshit," Bernadette said. "You know that isn't true. You know he's been set up. The Afghans need someone to execute for it. You've chosen him because he's expendable." She pointed her weapon at Lackey.

"You need to stand down," Sergeant Hammer said. His team of soldiers surrounded Chris and Bernadette.

"It's okay, Bernadette," Chris said. "I'll be fine. I'll get a lawyer from the Consulate. I'll be out in a week or two."

"No you won't. They'll make sure they prosecute you so fast, and they'll manufacture evidence. You know it's a sham."

"Sweetie. Drop your weapon. I don't want this nice big

sergeant to put a hole in your pretty body. I'm planning on doing all kinds of things with you when I get out," Chris said with a smile.

Bernadette dropped her weapon and stared hard at Lackey. "You bitch."

"I'm a bitch that gets things done," Lackey said. "We're taking Chris in the lead heli, you get into the other one. How bad is Jason hurt?"

Reza responded from beside Jason. "He has been knocked unconscious."

Lackey turned to Hammer. "Get the medics to put him on a stretcher."

Hammer pressed his throat mike, calling the medics from the heli. They came running out, putting Jason on a stretcher. Bernadette, Reza, and Almas followed Sergeant Hammer to the other helicopter.

Bernadette stopped at the entry of the helicopter and looked at Chris. He was in handcuffs; a soldier was leading him to his helicopter. Chris stopped and turned, he smiled that big dumb grin of his, the one that made her madly in love with him or made her want to kill him for something stupid he'd done. At that moment, her joy of finding him was shattered by the possibility she might lose him again. And this time, there were even greater forces aligned against both of them.

Chapter Forty-One

The trip back to Kandahar seemed a blur to Bernadette. Jason was on a stretcher with an IV in his arm in the center of the helicopter, Reza sat across from him, and Almas stayed by her side. He rested his head on her shoulder and held her hand. He knew what had happened, understood the consequences of what would happen to Chris.

The chopper landed at the Kandahar Air Force base. Chris was hustled into a waiting Afghan military vehicle. Police Chief Khan was there to greet them. He smiled at Agent Lackey as his men took Chris into custody. They spoke for a moment and parted.

Bernadette held back in the chopper, not wanting Khan to see her. She was an escapee from his custody. She couldn't do anything for Chris inside an Afghan jail. She watched Chris leave and got out of the chopper. Lackey approached her.

"I got the charges against you dropped by Police Chief Kahn," Lackey said.

Bernadette nodded at her. "You know, normally I'd thank you, but with Chris in custody, you know it's a pretty moot point."

Lackey shrugged. "I guess it is." She turned to walk away. "Oh, I had your things picked up from our compound. I'd thought you'd want them. Sergeant Hammer will have them for you."

Bernadette saw Jason on the stretcher. Reza was still beside him. He was awake; eyes clear, searching her face.

"Hey, Bernadette, seems I got my bell rung pretty good," Jason said.

Bernadette knelt beside his stretcher. "Hey, you need to take care of yourself. I'm sure they'll check you out and after some rest you'll be fine."

Jason raised his head off the stretcher. "Not a chance. Look, these NATO guys are going to drop me off at the Kandahar hospital and be done with me. I've had worse than this. I'll be fine in a few hours, then you and me—we're getting back to work. You hear me?"

Bernadette felt a rush of admiration at his determination. "Okay, it's on. I'm going back to the Continental Guest House. You can contact me there."

"I'm glad he's okay. I would have hated to have to report him as KIA, too much paperwork," Lackey said with her hand on the door of her ride. She got into a black Suburban and sped away.

Bernadette stood there with her hands on her hips as she watched Lackey's vehicle disappear and Jason being put into an ambulance. She needed a plan. She needed an internet connection and a phone…and a large scotch.

Sergeant Hammer came up beside her. "Can I drop you somewhere?"

"Yeah, that same guest house you found me at last week," Bernadette said. She turned to Reza. "I can take Almas again if you like."

"Maybe he should come with me," Reza said. "You have much to do. My wife would like it if Almas came to our home."

"Can you explain that to Almas?"

Reza spoke to Almas and the boy hugged Bernadette hard. "*Inshallah*, you set him free," Almas said.

"Yes, Almas, God willing I will set Chris free," Bernadette said, kissing Almas on the head.

Hammer sent Reza and Almas off in a Humvee and took Bernadette in another. They rode in silence. The streets seemed deserted. Little traffic was on the road.

"Is there some kind of religious holiday going on?" Bernadette asked.

Hammer looked away, then he turned to her. "The word is out that the infidel who stole the robe has been caught. The entire town is getting ready for a celebration tonight."

Bernadette didn't know what to say. Kandahar was excited that Chris had been caught. There was no robe, but somehow having him to vent their anger on would be enough. This was the worst case of frontier justice she'd ever seen. She was too numbed by the events to think—but she had to. Fatigue was wracking her body, her eyes wanted to close. She pinched her arm to pull herself awake.

The Humvee arrived in front of the Continental Guest House and Hammer looked at her for a second. "I'm sorry about your man."

Bernadette let out a breath. She spoke quietly, "Are you sorry he's being used? Sorry he's being set up? Sorry you're a part of this?"

"I...look...I'm truly am sorry," Hammer said, "I came here to defend my country and kill those Taliban bastards. The events of today? Well, I know they don't add up. Maybe it's too much for a soldier like me to understand." He looked down; his face had become noticeably red.

Bernadette put her hand on Hammer's arm. "You're a good man, Sergeant, I know you're just doing your job, but that's the problem, the whole world is doing their job and following the orders of some crazy ass politicians and bureaucrats who don't see what we see."

She got out of the Humvee, took her bag out of the back, and walked into the courtyard. She met Aaron and his Uncle Jangi Shah. They bowed with their hands over their hearts as she entered.

"Salam Aleichem, I need a room, a computer, a new untraceable phone, and a scotch if it's available," Bernadette said.

"Of course," Jangi Shah said. He turned to Aaron, giving him instructions, and in a few minutes Bernadette was in a similar room to the one she'd been a week ago.

Bernadette looked around the sparse room. "Same old, same old." She realized the first thing she needed was a shower, more to clear her head, but also because the smell that rose from her body was somewhere between barnyard and locker room.

She threw her clothes in a pile, put on the cool water, and did as much time under the shower as her body could withstand to make herself clean. Toweling off, she got some fresh clothes and felt ready to do battle.

A knock on the door from Aaron brought the arrival of a new phone, a small carafe of scotch, and some pistachio nuts.

Aaron bowed and brought his hand to his heart. "My

uncle and I are both saddened for the events. We are so sorry for your fiancé, Madame."

Bernadette smiled at Aaron. "I thank you for your concern. Please tell your uncle to add the phone to my bill."

Aaron shook his head. "No, this is complements of my uncle. Not all Afghans are in league with the devil such as the government is. Most of us are simple people who do not want to prosper on the shoulders of others."

"You are very eloquent, Aaron, I thank you for your words."

Aaron bowed and walked out.

Bernadette poured herself a scotch, chewed on some nuts, and went about looking over the phone. It had already been activated. She checked the time. It was 1400 hours, 2 p.m. Afghanistan time. What was the time change to western Canada? She did a quick calculation, realized it was really too early to be calling—then started to dial.

A sleepy voice muttered, "Hello?"

"Anton, it's me, Bernadette."

"It's two a.m. here. Who else could it be?" Anton asked.

"I need your help—I'm desperate."

"I saw the intel about Chris being picked up before I went to bed last night. I tried to call you but got no answer," Anton said.

"I was a kind of occupied," Bernadette said. She brushed the hair off her face, trying to block out the memory of the firefight.

"Yeah, I read the report. You were in a hell of a fire fight," Anton said.

"We made it out alive, but they've taken Chris prisoner on charges of stealing the robe. I need to clear his name before some imam decides to remove his head to make his followers feel better."

"What do you need?"

"You remember my request for information about Caprinski?"

"Yeah, yeah, I have it right here, I was reading it before I went to bed," Anton said.

"Looks like Caprinski parties hard in Dubai. He goes there every three months, spends a ton of dough at one of the finest hotels and casinos, and drops himself into a big vat of alcohol."

"Sounds about right for the guy I saw. Did you see any other names of people he traveled with?"

"Yeah, Agent Lackey," Anton said. "They came on separate flights but stayed at the same hotel. Sometimes the same room."

"Holy shit, now that's something." Bernadette let out a whistle and took a swig of her scotch.

"Here's the real down and dirty on this. I sent out a quiet enquiry to some of our friends in the field. You know, the ones who like to dish dirt. You wouldn't believe how much the German and French agents love scandal," Anton said.

"And?"

"Lackey and Caprinski were seen at many parties locking lips and doing the nasty on the dance floor, sorry that's code for almost consuming each other during the music."

"I'll be damned. Here I was, wondering who could find a hole in the satellite surveillance. Had to be Lackey giving Caprinski the times, he then had Chris and his men taken with no photos to trace them," Bernadette said.

"I have no idea. All I can see is that Lackey has been in a relationship with Caprinski going back to two months ago when they were both in Dubai last. I could send you pictures if you want," Anton said.

"Send them to this phone," Bernadette said.

"Sure, you got it, Bernadette. One other thing, you can use the Canadian Consulate. They don't have a lot of pull there, but a lady named Chandra Gupta is quite capable."

"That's the person I totally pissed off when I arrived. Remember you told me she was trying to get me booted out of here."

"I'll make it right with her. Reach out to her for anything you need. And Bernadette?"

"Yes?"

"Try not to piss off anyone else for the next few hours while I try to arrange some things for you—can you do that?"

"That's a big ask, but I'm about to get some sleep, so hopefully yes, there will be no further people contacts from me."

"Great, that's all I ask. Now that I'm totally awake at this ridiculous hour, I'll start to work on whatever I can do for you."

"Anton, you are amazing. Thank you."

She put her phone down, drained the rest of her glass of scotch, and felt a weariness descend over her brain as if a curtain had lowered itself. She realized in her trek over the mountains she had hardly slept. Maybe a few hours, or was it a few minutes in two days?

She decided she would allow herself a quick nap and then do some research on the hotel's computer followed by a phone call to Chandra Gupta to maybe patch over their misunderstanding.

Then she would write out her game plan for the next day. She had some hard questions for Lackey and Caprinski, and she couldn't wait to see their faces when she confronted them. A small smile formed at her lips when she lay on the bed. She looked at her clock, it showed 1415, she told herself she would power nap for twenty minutes.

Closing her eyes, she fell into a deep and dreamless sleep. Her eyes would not open again for sixteen hours.

Chapter Forty-Two

A constant knocking entered Bernadette's brain. She wondered why no one was answering the door. She called out to her grandmother, but she didn't answer. She called to Chris, and he said he was in the shower, couldn't get there. Her eyes opened like the aperture on a camera lens trying to find some light for a dim exposure.

Her head rolled over to the clock. It said 0800, which meant what? It dawned on her. It was 8 a.m.

"Holy mother of god," Bernadette shouted. "I've been asleep for…" She rubbed sleep from her eyes as it dawned on her. "…forever."

She pushed herself off the bed and went to the door. Aaron was there with a message.

"Madam, a gentleman named Jason has been calling you, he says he does not have your cell number anymore. He wants you to call him at this number."

"Thank you, Aaron," Bernadette said.

"I will have coffee for you and the special Afghani

breakfast you like as soon as you wish in the dining room, Madame."

Bernadette looked at the message from Jason. Do nothing, go nowhere until you've contacted me.

Bernadette dialed the number, Jason answered on the first ring. "Who is this?"

"Hey, Jason, it's me, I got a new phone. I realized that Lackey was tracking us using our phones."

Jason laughed. "Funny you say that, I got rid of mine. This is a new burner phone as well. Do you have a microwave in your room?"

Bernadette looked around her small room and noticed an ancient looking microwave in the corner, "Yeah, I do, why?"

"Put your old phone in there, it stops all GPS signals."

Thanks, I'll do that, so what's with the ominous message? Kind of scary before coffee at this hour."

"There's a *fatwa* on you."

"A fat—what?"

"A *fatwa*, it's a religious edict. In this case it's your death sentence. Sardar Agha doesn't like the fact that you're free. He knows you'll move heaven and earth to free Chris. He wants Chris executed for the missing robe. He's tying up loose ends."

"So, I'm a loose end?"

"Sorry, girl, that's the size of it. Any Muslim who kills you gets some special points for heaven. Kind of major bullshit, I want you to know that the mainstream Muslims don't believe in this crap."

"Really, Jason, when did you become a mainstream Muslim?"

"I had a vision from the prophet Bernadette while I was on trek in the mountains recently."

Bernadette smiled. "Can you get to my guesthouse? I'm about to chow down on some great Afghani breakfast with some really good coffee. You care to join me? That is if you can hang out with someone who has a *fatwa* hanging over them?"

"I'll be there in twenty minutes," Jason said. "Now, as I said, go nowhere. Stay in your guesthouse. I'll get you a disguise so we can get you around Kandahar."

"Oh great, that must mean me in a burka. Have I told you how much I hate those?"

"I think you have, several times. But just remember, we can put some pretty cool stuff under a burka. See you soon."

Bernadette closed her phone then headed for the bathroom to wash her face and comb her hair. Today, she knew, was going to be the day for one hell of a hunt for the truth.

Chris sat in his cell in the police station. He felt he'd gone up a notch in his confinement. The food was slightly better although the smell was decidedly worse. He missed the smell of goats and the mountain air already. A light came through the window announcing morning, the second call to prayer was sounding outside, telling him it was around 0800 hours.

He'd asked for a representative from the Canadian Consulate to visit him. In his own mind, he knew it was a long shot. Consulates replaced your lost visa or passport, let you call home if you ran out of money, but when it came to something important like trouble with another country's legal system, you were on your own. They could wage strong complaints to the government and that was about it.

Chris could see some foreign diplomat, fresh from

university, walking into an Afghan's office after Chris' head had been detached from his body and giving them a strong letter of indignation. The letter would be well written—and way too late.

He would ask them to get him an Afghani lawyer, although he knew no lawyer would be able to go up against an imam, especially one who wanted to use him as an example. But he would make an attempt, do his best, and hope that just maybe, Bernadette would be able to find some evidence that would clear him. He knew she was his only chance.

Chapter Forty-Three

Bernadette walked into the dining room to see that Jason was already there. He was smiling and looking sober, a welcome surprise. A large bandage covered his head, giving him a mystical appearance.

"Hey Bernadette," Jason said as she approached. "You're right about the coffee. This is the real thing." He held up his cup as if it was the finest liquid he'd ever tasted.

Aaron poured Bernadette a coffee, and she mixed in some milk and sugar. "Totally, thanks Aaron."

Aaron told them he would bring them both the Afghani breakfast of eggs swimming in a bed of tomatoes and spices with Naan bread.

"So much better that MRE rations served cold in the mountains, don't you think?" Bernadette asked.

"Copy that." Jason watched as Aaron walked away. "I have heard on the Afghani rumor mill the imam wants a real quick trial."

"How much time do we have?"

"I'd say forty-eight hours—tops."

"Doesn't he get a lawyer?"

"Sure, he does. The guy will show up, make a couple of arguments, the imam will quote a bunch of stuff from the holy Quran, and the lawyer will sit down and shut up," Jason said.

"So, we have to find Lund and the robe, or just the robe to get him off?"

Jason sipped his coffee. "That's it. No other way."

"I think I may have something," Bernadette said. "I found out Lackey and Caprinski were having an affair in Dubai."

"So? That shit happens all the time here. Dubai is the place everyone here goes to for sin and relaxation," Jason said.

"I've got a hunch. I think I see some dots that need some connecting."

Jason stared at Bernadette as if he could see something forming in her brain. He waited while Aaron placed their breakfast in front of them.

"Are you thinking of going after Lackey?" Jason asked.

"Let's say I've got a few pointed questions for her," Bernadette replied.

"She's one hell of a tough customer, and so is Caprinski for that matter. Make sure I'm with you when you see him."

Bernadette took a piece of her naan bread, dipped it in her eggs, and swallowed. She almost closed her eyes at the delicious taste.

"I'll be careful when I see both of them, but I need you to do something."

"Sure," Jason said digging into the breakfast.

"I want you to see the cleric at the museum of the robe. See if he'll give you the exact movements of Lund, the imam and the robe that night?" Bernadette asked.

"Okay, I can do that this morning. What are you going to do?"

"I'll need that burka disguise. I want to make a quick trip to see Lackey. I want to know how close she was to Caprinski. Someone gave up some surveillance patterns to him. I'm trying to find out who."

"You don't think it's far-fetched? I mean, shouldn't we be looking for the robe instead?"

"I got a feeling that whoever hid the exit of Lund is the same one who knows where the robe is. If I find Lund, I find the robe," Bernadette said.

"Well, it's a better plan than I have." Jason produced a bag from beside his chair. "Here's your lovely form-fitting burka, one size fits all. I'll have the same taxi driver take you anywhere you want to go."

"You mean the ancient warrior with the motorized rickshaw?"

"Yep, that's my man, Mohammad. He can get you anywhere in Kandahar and most Taliban and tribesmen fear him like he's the devil incarnate. Be sure to tip him well," Jason said.

"How do I get hold of him?"

"His rickshaw is outside. He's been there since midnight making sure no one tries to get into this place, and believe me, a few tried last night. They won't try it again."

"But I can't leave right away," Bernadette protested.

Jason put up his hand. "Don't worry, Mohammed is here to take you wherever you want to go. He'll also be outside this guesthouse to ensure no one tries to cash in on your *fatwa*."

"An ancient *mujahedeen* is my protection, that's comforting."

"Not to worry, he brought along a friend to help out. You'll be fine."

Bernadette finished what she could eat of her breakfast. The task at hand was more important. "I'm got to make a few phone calls, then I'll get Mohammad to take me on my quest to find some answers. Can you call me as soon as you've talked to the cleric?"

"Will do," Jason said.

Bernadette grabbed a coffee to go and went back to her room. With Jason helping her, and the old *mujahedeen* as her driver, she felt like she could be mobile. Her first task was to contact Chandra Gupta at the Canadian Consulate. She would have to use some finesse, as they had not parted company on good terms.

She found the consulate phone number on the room's computer and dialed the number. A polite French Canadian sounding woman told Bernadette that Chandra was out.

"It's really important that I speak to her," Bernadette said.

"I am so sorry, she is visiting someone at the police station," the receptionist said.

"Are you French Canadian?" Bernadette asked in her best French Canadian accent.

"Yes, I am," the receptionist replied.

Bernadette then asked the receptionist her name, — Monique—then in her best French, described in detail who she was and why she had to speak to Gupta.

"Mon dieu," Monique said with a loud rush of breath. "You should have told me right away who you were. Of course, Madame Callahan, I will put your call through to her right away."

Bernadette smiled. The French Canadians were the

greatest romantics of Canada and they wore their hearts on their sleeves.

Chandra Gupta answered her phone a minute later. "Gupta, here."

"Chandra, it's me, Bernadette Callahan, I need your help."

"I don't know if I can talk to you right now, I'm about to meet with your fiancé," Chandra said.

"Great, I need you to ask him some questions for me—please."

Chandra paused for a full minute, then Bernadette heard. "I'm walking to his cell right now. There's a policeman here, please be careful what you say, I can only give you a minute."

Chris was sitting in a chair in front of a table for their meeting.

"Ms. Callahan is on this phone, please talk to her quietly…if the guard finds out, our meeting is over."

"Hey, Bernie. Nice surprise," Chris said.

"Oh, my god, Chris!" Bernadette blurted.

"Hey, nice to talk to you too. Look, there's a jail guard monitoring this call," Chris said.

"Oh, yeah, I'll be quick. Look, who asked you to go to the museum of the robe? Lund or Caprinski?"

"It was Caprinski."

"And when Caprinski sent you out with Lund, did he have any exact time you had to leave?"

"Yeah, come to think of it, he was really pissed we were late. He kept telling us to hurry up. What's up?"

"That's all I need for now. I love you madly, you know that."

"Totally, baby," Chris said. "I'm giving the phone back to Chandra."

"Chandra, I owe you big time," Bernadette said. "Sorry for pissing you off a week ago."

"No problem. That's the least of your problems now," Chandra said.

"Can you get him a decent lawyer?" Bernadette asked. She closed her eyes at the request. She knew the answer.

"We'll be getting him the very best Kandahar has to offer." Chandra said, but her voice faltered slightly.

"Thank you," Bernadette replied. She heard the tone in Chandra's voice; she knew the tone spoke volumes. It spoke of despair.

Bernadette put her phone down. Part of her wanted to have a good cry from the conversation with Chris. "Get a grip on yourself girl." She shook her head and checked her voice mail on her phone she'd stored in the microwave.

There was a tirade from Chris's mother. The Canadian Consulate had informed her Chris was in prison and to be tried for the theft of a precious artifact. Bernadette could imagine someone from the government in the foreign office explaining all the things they were going to do for him.

The tirade was along the lines of you promised to bring my Christos back, why are you not the one in jail, then she finished off her phone call with how she wished Chris, had never met Bernadette.

Bernadette erased the message. There was no use calling Mrs. Christakos back. When you got a Greek mad, they stayed mad for a long time. His mother was not open to listening to anything Bernadette could say. She placed the phone back in the microwave and then took it out. She realized if someone was tracking it, they might as well think she was in the guesthouse.

She needed to make one more call. It would be her make or break one for the day. She hesitated as her finger poised over the cellphone. Breathing deeply, she pressed the dial pad and waited for the ring tone.

"American Consulate."

"Yes, I need to speak with Agent Lackey," Bernadette said in her most commanding tone.

"Who's calling?" the receptionist asked in a thick Southern accent.

"Detective Bernadette Callahan." She used her title, hoping it get her through to Lackey.

"One moment."

Bernadette tapped her fingers on the side of the little desk, wondering what Lackey would think of her calling. Would she have time for her or would she brush her off?"

"This better be quick," Lackey said coming on the line. Her voice was sharp and tense. But then, Bernadette realized she *had* called her a bitch. She could tell she was on Lackey's speaker in her office.

"I need to see you, it's important."

"No time. Look, Callahan, you need to accept the facts, your man was caught, he'll be tried—make your plans to take what's left of him home and move on."

Bernadette tightened her hand into a fist. She seethed over Lackey's words. "Thanks for the advice, but I have something to show you."

"Unless you have evidence that clears your man or the robe, I have no time for you." Lackey said. She sounded distracted. The sound of paper being shuffled on her desk told Bernadette how important this call was to her.

"No, but I have a video of Caprinski and you doing the lambada dance in Dubai."

"Where did you get that?" Lackey asked quickly.

Bernadette noticed the change in her voice; she wished she could see her expression right now.

"I have some great sources. Did you know that the French agents who took this gave you four likes? They even commented when you tried to consume Caprinski's back teeth with your tongue on the dance floor, now what's that word— how seductive you were."

"How do I know you're not bluffing, Callahan. Sure, I've been to Dubai, and yeah, I did a little dancing with Caprinski and I might have had too much to drink, but that's it. Rumors are all you have."

"No, I have pictures and videos, and wait—there's more. I have pictures of you doing some cool ass grabbing of Caprinski as you fall into your hotel room. Now, that one is nice," Bernadette said.

"You can't blackmail me with this. I can do whatever I want in my free time," Lackey said.

"You sure can. And once your bosses at headquarters see all these videos that I'm going to post on Facebook, Instagram and Twitter of the Kandahar CIA station chief having an affair with a security contractor who is part of the ongoing investigation of the missing robe—I'll bet they see things your way."

"You bitch."

"Now, we're speaking the same language. When can we meet?"

"What the hell do you want?"

"Simple, you answer some questions about your affair with Caprinski and these videos and pictures never see the light of day," Bernadette said.

"Be here in a half hour." Lackey said, hanging up abruptly

"You got it," Bernadette said into the dial tone. She blew out a breath. "Now, you best not screw this up or you'll be in a deep dark room with Lackey holding a rubber hose," she reminded herself.

She took her burka and put it on. Standing in mirror, she saw two things—how ridiculous this garment was and how it made complete cover for anyone wanting to hide their identity.

Grabbing her new phone, she made her way out of the guesthouse. Aaron and his uncle watched her leave with interest. As she was the only female in the guesthouse, they knew who she was.

The red motorized rickshaw sat in the street. Mohammad was there, puffing on a cigarette. Beside him stood a man who looked much older than Mohammad, if that was possible. He had few teeth, one eye, and one leg. A peg leg protruded from where the leg had once been. His face was a mass of wrinkles that cascaded into his beard. When he saw Bernadette he bowed, pounded on Mohammad to get his attention, and hobbled towards Bernadette using the butt of his AK-47 as a crutch.

Mohammed came forward, greeting her with a "Salem alaykom, Madame Callahan."

Bernadette was stunned. "How did you know it was me?"

Mohammed smiled. "Afghani women in burkas do not travel on their own. They must be with a man, either a husband or a relative. Jason told me you would be in disguise."

Bernadette had to grin under her burka. She wished that some of the police officers she knew had the same instincts.

"Where do you wish to go?" Mohammed asked.

"The American Consulate," Bernadette said.

"No problem, this time I have my friend Jebran for added protection."

Jebran bowed low, placing one hand over his heart. Close up he looked even older than Bernadette had previously thought.

Mohammed directed her into the cab of the rickshaw. Jebran sat beside her, resting his AK-47 across his lap. The muzzle pointed out the cab, which made Bernadette very happy.

Mohammed pulled the cord on the rickshaw. A cloud of blue smoke engulfed it. He put it into gear, which produced a screeching sound confirming the drive belt was engaged. It lurched down the street with one backfire for good measure.

Bernadette felt like she was in a fantasy story that she hoped she would wake up from one day or hopefully really soon.

The streets were quiet. She could only assume it was because Chris had been captured. All of Kandahar was waiting to find out where the robe was. The speculation would be running rampant as to why the infidel had taken it, how soon he would be found guilty, and, how long until he was executed.

The rickshaw made its way past the shops, the teahouses, and the few people in the streets. Jebran gazed from side to side, sweeping his gaze for any threats. Bernadette couldn't imagine how a man of his age and disabilities could defend them.

A column of Afghan army military vehicles passed them. They blew past the little rickshaw as if it were standing still. Bernadette tensed up. She hoped that Lackey had been right about the Afghan police no longer wanting her. Would Lackey go back on her word? How would she be received?

She realized she should have sent a text to Anton before

she left. She could have told him that if he didn't hear from her in twenty-four hours, that the entire video of Lackey should be posted to Facebook. Was that too paranoid?

The rickshaw careened around a corner and they were there. In front of them was a maze of concrete barricades that vehicles had to navigate to get to the American Consulate.

No vehicle could drive in a straight line. It would have to make a serpentine path, losing speed as it navigated the obstacles. All the while, three machine guns on three heavily armored vehicles tracked their every movement.

Mohammed drove the rickshaw slowly, taking each turn with care and waving his hand towards the machine gunners and the marines at the front gate. The way he waved and smiled you'd have thought he was coming home for Thanksgiving dinner.

Some fifty meters from the front gate they were stopped. A large marine looked inside the rickshaw. "You speak English?"

"Yes, I do." Bernadette replied.

"The burka comes off," was the terse reply.

"You don't need to ask me twice," Bernadette muttered under her breath as she pulled the confining garment over her head and placed it beside Jebran.

She was wearing jeans, a sweatshirt and light down jacket under the burka. Feeling relieved to be a semi-civilian again, she gave her name to the marine and followed him into the consulate.

The pat down was more stringent this time. Everyone at the gate seemed more on edge. She hadn't remembered three armored vehicles last time. This heightened security meant a threat was imminent.

The marine was large, imposing, smelling of gun oil and

Old Spice aftershave. He marched her briskly to Lackey's office and then stood at attention outside.

Lackey motioned Bernadette inside and shut the door. She turned on a small stereo system to drown out their conversation.

"So, here you are, Callahan. Just what the hell do you want for my transgressions? I'm not religious—so no mea culpas," Lackey said. She pulled out a bottle of scotch from her desk drawer and poured herself a glass. She didn't offer Bernadette any.

"I need to know if Caprinski compromised you in any way," Bernadette said.

Lackey opened a drawer and pulled out a 9 mm handgun. She placed it on the desk beside her scotch. "Easy there, Callahan. It'd be easy for me to say you jumped me and I shot you."

Bernadette stared at Lackey. She could see she was rattled. This entire conversation could turn bad in a second.

"What I need to know, is if Caprinski could have gained any knowledge from you about satellite and drone surveillance times on the roads in Afghanistan," Bernadette said.

"Why?

"I learned from Chris that Caprinski wanted the team to leave at an exact time, as if they had a rendezvous with someone—but it was the surveillance times. At the time they were captured, no drones or satellites were overhead. It was the perfect way for Lund to escape with the robe. They then took Chris's unit hostage. Kept them in a small village, and then murdered his unit. When we arrived, they were about to bring Chris back to Kandahar to face the courts—for his crimes—the perfect set-up."

Lackey took a long pull of her scotch. She took the gun,

sighed and put it back in the desk. "Aw shit, I can't believe I didn't see through Caprinski."

"Enlighten me," Bernadette said.

"When we were in Dubai, he kept asking me about the surveillance times. He said he was worried his men would be out without cover. I told him not to worry about it. There's only one time of day on one road that we have a hole, other than that his people would be fine," Lackey said putting her hand to her forehead.

"Did you give him that exact location?"

Lackey nodded her head. "Look, I might have. I'm a highly functioning alcoholic; Caprinski filled me with some of the best god damned scotch I've ever tasted. I was with him for an entire weekend. It was kind of a haze." Lackey pushed her scotch away. "When the shit went down, and his men were taken…"

"You wondered if you were the one that had given him the intel?" Bernadette asked, leaning forward a little. She could see the desperation in Lackey's eyes. She could tell she was hurting.

"Christ. If this gets out—and that video, I'm done—I'll be a security guard in a mall in Wisconsin."

"I'm not releasing the video. And no one needs to know our conversation. Are you still tight with Caprinski?" Bernadette asked.

"No, we broke it off… Okay I lie; he dumped me a few weeks ago. He said his ex-wife wanted to get back with him, he said he owed it to his kids to give it a shot."

"And you know that was a lie too. He was never married," Bernadette said.

"Aw shit, yeah…I did. I realized I was better off without him and the booze fueled weekends," Lackey said, staring down at her desk. She raised her head. "Are you going to see him next?"

"Yeah, I think he's hiding something. I got a feeling he's in on the stolen robe. You want to come along?"

"I can't. I have a conference call with my bosses from Washington in a half hour," Lackey said. "I wish I could be there when you ask that son of a bitch some questions." She reached into the other drawer in her desk. "You might need this."

Lackey took at a Sig Sauer 9mm handgun, checked the load, and slid it across the desk to Bernadette.

"Nice gun," Bernadette said.

"I took it off a Taliban last week. Made in Germany, full clip of ten bullets," Lackey said, narrowing her eyes, "If you happen to shoot Caprinski in the head after you've found Lund and the robe, I won't miss him." She looked back in her desk. "And take this with you." She pushed across a mini tape recorder. "He'll deny everything unless you get him on tape."

Bernadette checked the safety on the gun. She placed it in the front pocket of her jacket with the tape recorder. "I'll let you know what I find."

Bernadette walked out of the consulate checking her calls as she got back into the rickshaw. There'd been one from Jason. She dialed his number.

"You have anything from the cleric?" Bernadette asked when Jason answered.

"Yeah, he said there was a night watchman in the shrine that night."

"Why didn't he mention him before? He's not even in the police report."

"The imam told the cleric not to mention him."

"Did the watchman see anything?"

"The cleric said the watchman told him he saw Lund take the robe back from Chris after he handed it to him. He said he was standing by the front door when the lights went out. But he could still see the exchange," Jason said.

"Did he say where the imam was standing?"

"He said the imam was standing by the front door. Then the lights went out and he couldn't see much after that."

"How'd you get him to tell you, he wouldn't tell me anything?" Bernadette asked.

"That's simple. You are a non-believer, and to some Muslims it's okay to lie to you," Jason said. "Now, I'm a Muslim, and to lie to another Muslim is very bad—but there's something else."

"What's that?"

"The cleric thinks the imam is up to something from what the watchman said."

"What was it?"

"I'm not sure how to explain. He said that the imam stood with Lund by the door and then came back in. The watchman thought it was some kind of a game. He kept saying it looked like rugby."

"Did he say if the imam was carrying anything? Did he have anything in his hands, a bulge in his cloak?"

"No, that's just it, he said the imam had nothing in his hands. The watchman was at a loss to explain it."

"I wonder why the cleric would tell you that?"

"He is more afraid of losing the robe than the wrath of the imam. He's been guarding that cloak for most of his life. To him, everyone is a suspect until his precious robe is back," Jason said.

"Sounds like a sequel to the Lord of the Rings," Bernadette said.

Jason chuckled. "Yeah, I guess it does. What are you up to?"

"I had an interesting meeting with our Lackey. She confirmed my suspicions about Caprinski. He's my next stop."

"I'm on my way. I can be there in a half hour," Jason said

"Okay, I'll meet you there," Bernadette replied. She ended the call and put on the burka, then gave instructions to Mohammad. The rickshaw erupted into its blue cloud of smoke and they were off. Bernadette felt the outline of the handgun under her garment. It felt good.

Chapter Forty-Four

Sardar Agha surveyed the room. It was packed. The tribes had sent their imams. This morning he would be swift, the infidel must die. He directed everyone to watch the video, the two men stood at the entrance of their sacred museum. Many an imam gasped as they realized infidels had held Mohammed's sacred robe—to them an obvious death sentence.

The video ended, and Sardar rose from his chair, clearing his throat. "You have seen with your own eyes that these men stole the sacred robe."

"Why has the robe not been recovered?" Abdul-Bari shouted.

Of all the imams to ask a question, Sardar hated Abdul-Bari the most, he had to take a breath before he answered to calm his anger.

Sardar raised both his hands. "We have offered the man a quick death if he tells us the where the robe is. He seems to hold his tongue for his compatriot. We think the other man, Lund, has taken the robe to Europe to sell it to the highest bidder."

Shouts of "outrageous, a sacrilege, criminal," filled the room.

Sardar nodded his head in agreement. He waited until they quieted down. "It is my opinion, and I await the approval of my esteemed brothers, that this man be put to death immediately."

An imam, stood up in the back. "But what of our rule of law? Will this man not be tried in court?"

The room erupted in a general condemnation of his suggestion.

"I know that normally this would be placed into the hands our country's legal system. The trial could drag on for months, while in the meantime, the criminal, this infidel would remain unpunished for his crime." Sardar surveyed the room and lowered his voice. "And, as we all know, in many cases these criminals are let off on a legal technicality."

"Death to the infidel," an imam shouted in the front of the room. His words were taken up into a chant in the room.

Sardar tried not to let his lips show a smile. He lowered his head and placed his hands on his chest at the simple command the room had made.

Chris sat in his cell. He gazed at a stream of sunlight on the floor, trying to imagine its warmth. He had just had a visit from his lawyer. It was the strangest conversation.

The lawyer came in. He wore an ill-fitting suit and his beard was sparse. Chris couldn't recall his name. All he did remember was that a religious tribunal had met. They had reviewed the evidence. Chris was to be sentenced to death.

"Is there an appeal?" Chris had asked.

"No, there is no appeal in the case," the waif of a lawyer said.

"When will the sentence be carried out?" Chris asked. His voice had sounded surreal, as if he was asking about someone else.

The lawyer gulped, his skinny neck with its too large Adams apple bobbed. "I fear…as soon as tomorrow. But, you must know, something…" The lawyer said. "The imams will not allow you to be drugged for your execution." His tone was apologetic.

"Well, I hate drugs anyway. Tell them thanks if you see them." Chris replied. He remembered Cameron telling him of men he'd seen in Saudi dragged in a daze to a place called 'chop chop' square to the executioner. He didn't like the idea of his last moments on this earth being in a fog.

The little man had left, his baggy suit wafting out of the cell, leaving behind only this stream of sunlight.

Chapter Forty-Five

The rickshaw barely made it up a small incline to Caprinski's security office. Jebran was making motions with his hands to will the little contraption to make it. Somehow it did. Jebran turned to Bernadette with a toothless grin, as if he had something to do with it.

The same two large-scale security guards were outside. The one named Vince eyed them with disdain. Bernadette threw off her burka. There was no way she was going in with that restricted garment. She turned on the tape recorder and felt the gun in her pocket.

She scanned the street and saw no sign of Jason. Checking her cell phone, she saw a text message from him. He was having trouble getting through a checkpoint and would be there in about an hour. Could she wait? That was obvious—not possible.

Walking towards Vince and his large bookend partner, she smiled. "Hey guys, mind if I just see Caprinski for a minute. I need to do a little follow-up."

Vince raised his size X-Large hand with the half leather

glove. "No way. Caprinski is moving house. He's got a lot of work to do."

"Oh, so the security outfit is closing down?" Bernadette asked.

"Yeah, but that's none of your business. Now leave." Vince replied. He stuck his hand back in his web belt and stuck his chest and his chin out in a defiant stance.

Bernadette smiled. "Now, Vince, I know you're real busy, but I just need a minute with your boss, I promise I won't be a problem."

"The problem is you don't listen. Now shove off," Vince said, his voice rising.

Bernadette almost moved her hand to her jacket. If she pulled a gun on them she might have to use it. She needed to think of something to get by these two doorstops.

Mohammed brushed past her. "You no speak to lady with such words." Jebran limped beside him.

Vince laughed. "Really old man? Maybe you're all *muhajadeen* and all, but you got nothing. Now take your crippled friend and this silly bitch in that little piece of shit—"

Bernadette couldn't believe how fast Mohammed and Jebran were. Mohammed threw a throat punch into Vince. He stumbled back. Jebran swept the legs from the other one by balancing himself on his AK-47 and sweeping his peg leg under his feet.

Within seconds, both guards were on the ground with the business ends of AK-47's pointed at them.

"You must show respect to this woman," Mohammed said.

"Sure, sure," Vince said with his hands up.

Bernadette looked down at them. "As I said, I'll just be a minute. Sorry, but my guys can be a bit rough." She stepped over them unable to keep the grin off her face.

The hallway was the same, musty, messy and the cat hadn't moved. It looked just as uninterested as before. When she got to Caprinski's office, she found him hunched over a box as he filled it with files.

"I hear you're leaving town," Bernadette said.

Caprinski's head shot up and his eyes went wide. "How'd you get in here?"

"Your guys outside, they had a change of heart on letting me in," Bernadette replied as she took a chair in front of the desk. "How about if you take just a moment to answer a couple of questions I have."

"My flight leaves in three hours. I got a lot of stuff to do." Caprinski said. He continued to fill the box.

Bernadette pulled out her gun and chambered a round with a loud click. "I think you can spare a few minutes."

"Wait—there's no reason to get all violent," Caprinski said.

Bernadette arched an eyebrow as she raised the gun in line with his chest. "Really, Chris is in jail and chances are the imams will sentence him to death for something he didn't do. Something I'm pretty sure you helped manufacture—"

"Now hold it. How are you bringing me into this?"

"Simple. I had a talk with Lackey. She's pretty sure you got the surveillance times for satellites and drones from her. You helped Lund slip away. He wasn't there by the way, when we found Chris. But then you probably knew that."

"Lackey is a drunk."

"Yep, she sure is, she admitted it and told me you used her. So here we are, me with this nice German handgun with big ass bullets and you with answers. What's it going to be answers or bullets?"

"You can't coerce me to talk with a gun. That would never hold up in a court of law."

"Really? What law are we talking about? The law of this country where everything is done by a bullet?' Bernadette laughed. "You know the courts here are mostly bullshit. They get the answers and verdict they're looking for. I'm here with you and ten bullets. Each bullet is seeking an answer; each bullet is a juror of your peers. Now start talking."

Caprinski raised his hands. "Look, I'll answer anything you want. Just don't kill me. I got a family."

"That's a lie," Bernadette said with deadly calm. She raised the gun in line with his head. "That kind of bullshit will get you a head shot instead of shot in the arm. Now, do you want to tell the truth or do I end this interview and your life?"

"Whoa, okay, you got me. I have no family," Caprinski said, putting his hand in front of him.

"Better answer. Now, why did you let Lund escape the warlord's village?" Bernadette said lowering the gun down to his chest line.

Caprinski let out a sigh of relief. "This whole plan was Lund's idea. He planned to steal the robe and take it out of the country. He figured he'd set up Chris for it, him being the Canadian and all. That way we wouldn't have any big search from the American Forces. Sorry about that."

Bernadette shook her head. "Yeah, life's a bitch, now where is Lund…and where is the robe?"

Caprinski shrugged. "Lund is probably in Paris right now, sipping champagne, quaffing oysters and laughing at how he screwed all of us. I was supposed to pick him up a week after, but he paid the warlord off and had someone take him out through Iran."

"So, you're saying he double crossed you?"

"You got it," Caprinski said with a nod of his head towards the box on the floor. "Look, I can show you the tickets I had booked for Lund and me."

"Pick them up slowly," Bernadette said getting out of the chair. She wanted to see exactly what he was getting out of the box. "If you pull a gun out of that box, I put a bullet in your head."

"Yeah, yeah, I get it," Caprinski said in a pissed off tone. He knelt down to the box rummaging around in it. "I know I got it—yeah here it is."

Bernadette heard a loud alarm bell beside her. She turned towards it. A projectile came at her head. She fell backwards.

Chapter Forty-Six

Bernadette opened her eyes. Caprinski was sitting on her chest with her arms pinned. Her feet were under the desk and a gun pointed at her head.

"So, how's it feel? I've planned that little distraction for some time. Best thing I ever did, everyone looks at an alarm. Now, my little bitch, I can put a bullet in you, dump your body in the street, and go catch my plane. Some Afghani policeman will find you, file a report, and you'll be one of the many killed in a day in this god forsaken country."

"You should have left when I had that welcome committee blow up your truck at the airport. But no, you had to stick around. And the guy on the motorcycle, you didn't get that message either." He cocked the gun. "Maybe now you'll get the message."

"Tell me the truth, Caprinski," Bernadette pleaded. "You owe me that at least before you kill me. Where the hell is Lund, where is the robe? I know you're feeding me bullshit—at least tell me the truth before you kill me." She was stalling him, hoping Mohammed and Jebran would come in.

"Ah, the real truth. Why not?" Caprinski laughed. He pulled a set of keys from around his neck. "I hold the key to everything right here. I always have. I had everything put together until that damn imam decided to screw it all up—"

Caprinski was stopped in mid-sentence by the butt of Mohammed's AK-47.

Bernadette rolled to her side and got up. She bowed to Mohammed and thanked him. She wanted to say, "Where the hell were you?" but timing is everything. Bending down, she took the keys off of Caprinski's neck. There was writing and a symbol on the keys, plus a number. She needed a translator.

With Mohammed's help, Bernadette found some rope to tie up Caprinski. She'd have Lackey pick him up and give him to Kahn. Walking out of the office, she saw Jason get out of an old Toyota Camry. The car looked more beat up than the last one.

Jason walked up to Bernadette "I take it you missed Caprinski?"

"No, I met him."

"And it went okay?"

"No, not at all, but I'm alive. Look, I've got to find out what these keys are all about," Bernadette said, showing them to Jason.

"This looks like the name of a company. I'm not good at reading Pashtou. Let's go ask Reza," Jason said.

She walked out into the sunlight; it felt good to be alive. Taking out her phone, she dialed Lackey. "Hey Lackey. I found Caprinski and I got his confession on tape…but here's the thing. I can leave the tape here, but you might want to doctor it a bit."

Lackey chuckled. "Thanks for covering my ass. Did he tell you where Lund is?"

"No, but I got a lead. Hopefully I'll find out soon."

"Callahan, there's something you need to know."

"What's up?"

"The court of the imam's gave Chris the death sentence."

"How long has he got?"

"Tomorrow morning." Lackey said.

Bernadette gripped the phone. "Those sons a bitches. They want him dead in a hurry."

"Yeah, someone wants Chris's death to prove they have punished the thieves, but they still have no robe," Lackey said.

"I'm going to find that robe," Bernadette said.

"Look, I know I've been a bitch by helping bring Chris in, but I was acting under orders. I have no orders now. If you need help in finding the robe, if you need some muscle, I'll send you a team. Sergeant Hammer and his guys are good. Let me know if you need them."

"Thanks, I'll let you know," Bernadette said, ending the call. She turned to Jason. "We need to find Reza and get the answer to the keys, now!"

She ran with Jason to his car. He fired it up, and spun the tires as they hit the road. Mohammed and Jebran would stay with the suspects until the police arrived. Lackey had assured Bernadette that one of the policemen was in her pay, and he would make sure the tape came to her first.

They arrived at Reza's place. It was a little place in a row of mud-washed houses on a narrow side street. The usual dogs and chickens wandered in the road, looking for food.

Jason and Bernadette got out of the car and Reza met them at the door.

Bernadette thrust the keys towards Reza, "We don't have much time. They are executing Chris tomorrow morning. What do these keys mean?"

Reza took the keys, putting them up to the light. "I know of this place. This a storage facility near the airport."

"Let's go there," Bernadette commanded.

"One second," Reza pleaded. He ran inside, told his wife where he was going, and put his hat on.

Almas came running out and rushed into Bernadette, hugging her hard. "Bernadette, me go with you."

Bernadette knelt down and brushed his hair. "Sorry, not now. We'll come back for you."

"You promise?"

"Yes, I promise."

Bernadette got in the car with Reza and Jason, turning to look at Almas as they left. She couldn't believe how fast the boy was learning English and more importantly, the feelings she had for him.

The journey to the airport took too long in Bernadette's mind. Every check stop, every traffic jam, was a nightmare. They finally pulled up to the gates of the compound. Reza told the guard they wanted to enter their storage container and showed the key.

The guard looked at the key, nodded, and pointed for them to turn right after entering the compound. Jason put the car in gear and followed the directions. A minute later, they were driving down row upon row of storage containers.

Reza checked the numbers, directing Jason to drive to the very end. He put up his hand to stop.

No one else was around as they got out of the car. Bernadette took the key, pushed it in the lock, and turned. It moved slowly then the lock clicked open. The large lever groaned as the door slowly swung open.

The first thing that hit them was the smell.

Chapter Forty-Seven

Jason put his hand up to his nose. "What the hell is that smell?"

Bernadette turned to him. "The smell of death." She found a light switch on the side of the wall and opened it. A large watt light bulb illuminated the space.

The storage unit had been converted into a living space. A cot was in the back, with a table and chairs in the center. On the side was a camp style washbasin with a water tank and propane stove. A portable toilet and shower occupied a corner.

"Someone has been living here," Bernadette said as she walked into the container. Something crunched below her feet. Looking down she saw the remainder of pistachio shells.

"All the comforts of home," Jason said. "But where is that smell coming from."

Bernadette saw something glistening in the far corner of the room. She found a flashlight by the side of the sink and turned it on. "Yes, I think we have source of the smell…"

She walked towards the corner, as she did the glistening became a large plastic garment hanger suspended from the ceiling. Inside was a body.

"Is that Lund?" Jason asked peering at the figure in the bag.

"Yes, it is," Bernadette replied. "I can make out his features from the pictures I've seen on his website." She turned to Jason and Reza. "Now we know he didn't double cross Caprinski. Looks like they had Lund here all along. Probably brought him back from the village and had him hiding here."

"But why?" Jason asked.

"Lund probably thought he was going to get hold of the robe after they hung the theft on Chris. Someone screwed up the plans."

"Any idea how long he's been dead?"

"I'm no medical examiner, but my years of being around the dead tells me he's been dead about twenty-four hours. This container is pretty warm, that produces a pretty quick smell to a dead body. Looks like Caprinski was tying up all the loose ends with Chris being caught," Bernadette said. She could see fresh ligature marks around his throat.

"Let's look for the robe, it's got to be here somewhere," Jason said.

"Sure," Bernadette replied. "I don't think it's here, but let's give it a try."

Reza, Jason, and Bernadette went over the storage container, turning over boxes, looking under the mattress. It took all of twenty minutes to exhaust every inch of the place.

Jason sat back on his heels. "It's just not here. Sorry, Bernadette."

Bernadette wiped sweat off her brow. She looked back

at the garment bag with Lund turning silently in it. "It was never here."

She got up and walked to the front of the container and took out her phone. She dialed Lackey. She picked up on the third ring, "I found Lund dead in a storage container by the airport."

"And the robe?"

"Not here."

"I assume Lund didn't die of natural causes?"

"You got it, he was murdered about twenty-four hours ago. Someone was cleaning up. My guess is Caprinski."

"What are you going to do now?" Lackey asked.

"You said you'd give me back up, is that still on?"

"Sure, what do you need?"

"I need Sergeant Hammer and a whole bunch of his kick ass team. Have them locked and loaded for early tomorrow."

"Where do you want them?"

Bernadette turned to Reza. "Reza, when and where will the imam execute Chris tomorrow?"

"They will do it after the second call to prayer in front of the main mosque," Reza said in a solemn tone.

"Have them in the street in front of the main mosque at zero-seven hundred hours. I'll meet Hammer there."

"What have you got Callahan?"

"One crazy ass idea on how to save Chris. Can you send me the video of the night Lund and Chris were in front of the museum to my phone?" Bernadette asked.

"Sure thing, I'll send it right away—anything else?"

"Yeah send a body collector to storage container two-fifteen at the airport and have Kahn lean on Caprinski hard, then bring him to the party at the Mosque tomorrow if he has anything good."

"You don't ask much do you?" Lackey said with a note of sarcasm in her voice.

"I'm looking for a bona fide freaking miracle tomorrow. Everything helps," Bernadette said. She ended her call and took a deep breath.

"Where too now?" Jason asked.

"You can take me back to my guesthouse. Both Reza and you need to get a good night sleep tonight. We got a big show tomorrow."

The ride home took over an hour. Traffic in the street was building. People were out shopping preparing for a feast tomorrow after the execution. The imam had promised a great new revelation, and the city was buzzing with speculation.

Jason dropped Bernadette in front of the guesthouse. The red rickshaw with Mohammed and Jebran was there. They bowed in recognition of her and resumed their posts of watching over her, their AK-47's leaning up against the rickshaw as if they were waiting for batting practice or a cricket match to begin.

When Bernadette walked into the guesthouse, Aaron greeted her, and bowed low. "Would Madame care for another carafe of scotch?"

"Thank you, Aaron, but no, I'd like some Afghani tea, and could you go to the market and get me a few things?"

"Of course, it would be my pleasure." Aaron said bowing again.

Bernadette found a pen and note pad on the hotel desk and quickly wrote out a list, then pulled out a wad of Afghani notes. "I hope this will be enough?"

Aaron looked at the list. "This is a strange list. I'm sure this money will cover it."

Bernadette went to her room. While sipping the tea

Aaron brought to her room, she reviewed the video Lackey sent her, watching it several times. Lund walked out with a package, he handed it to Chris, and then the lights went out. Someone in the shadows was in the background.

There was no way to enhance the video on the phone. She'd have to use her instincts. Setting the phone down, she knew there was one person she had to call. She dialed the number.

After a long series of rings, her Grandmother Moses picked up. "Hey Bernadette I wondered when you'd call."

"You knew it was my ring again?" Bernadette asked incredulously.

"No, I got a new phone. This one has caller display, and it says Afghanistan right on the screen," Grandmother Moses said.

"Oh...that's great," Bernadette said.

"What's wrong?"

Bernadette held back tears; her grandmother always knew what was going on with her. "I've got to take a gamble tomorrow. It's the only way I can save Chris."

"Bernadette you've lived your life by taking chances, don't let anything stop you now. Don't you remember the time you saved your grandfather from that charging grizzly bear?'"

Bernadette thought for a moment. "I did? I don't recall that."

"You were only two years old. Grandfather and you were out for a walk. The grizzly came out the bush, mad as hell, charging down the path. Your grandfather turned to grab you and shield you. He fell down."

"I don't remember..."

"You might have blocked it out. You got in front of grandfather, you stood tall with your arms raised and roared. That grizzly stopped in his tracks. He turned and walked back into the bush."

"I did that?"

"Yes. Now, whatever chance you need to take, you take it." Grandmother Moses said.

"Thanks, Grandma Moses, I will." Bernadette closed her phone and fell back on the bed. Tomorrow she would have to stand up to an executioner's blade. How tall could she make herself, how loud could she roar?

Chapter Forty-Eight

Sleep did not come to Bernadette that night. There was too much at stake—Chris's life. She drank a large amount of tea while reviewing the video numerous times. Then, she'd pored over the internet to look at every file on Mohammed's sacred robe to see the last time it was worn and when.

The Taliban had worn it once in what was called a brilliant propaganda move. The Taliban leader, Mullah Omar had taken Mohammed's shroud out of storage and wore it in public to identify himself with the prophet and to give him legitimacy.

Bernadette had read that around three a.m. "What was that Caprinski had said about everything was fine until the crazy imam's got involved? What are they up to?" she asked herself.

By 0500 hours she was beyond sleep and her whole being was buzzing with energy. She felt like she could have taken on the entire Afghan army. At 0600 she got herself ready. She showered and put on the clothes she'd asked Aaron to get for her. The tricky part was the final touches.

She walked out of the guesthouse at 0630; Jason and Reza were already there with Mohammad and Jebran. They probably hadn't slept either.

As Bernadette walked up to them, Mohammad and Jebran raised their guns and shouted warnings in Afghani.

Bernadette raised her hands, "It's okay. It's me, Bernadette." She was wearing the traditional Afghan men's pants, long shirt with the hat and parka overtop. She wore her own boots.

Jason's eyes went wide. "Why are you dressed like a man, and what's with the stick-on beard?"

Bernadette chuckled. "Women are rarely invited to the front row of executions. I need to be front and center to save Chris."

Reza nodded in agreement. "You are most correct, the women have to be in the back. Even in a burka you would not get close."

"Okay, we're ready to roll then," Bernadette said. "I'm hoping Hammer and his team are in the side street I told them to be on."

Chris stared at his breakfast. The guards had made sure he had a good meal of porridge and chicken with some Naan bread. He pushed it aside. He couldn't eat. The guards had told him in sign language that he would not be hanged. His fate was that of an executioner's blade.

This was the one time he was not so proud of the large neck he'd developed from all his years of weight lifting in the gym. A size eighteen neck was an accomplishment but not when someone wanted to chop your head off. Chris's hand went instinctively to his throat. He let it drop away.

He'd been awake all night, thinking of his last moments

with Bernadette back home. How the time ended with wild love making, but then he could see they were drifting apart. This crazy idea of his coming to Afghanistan was his way of proving himself worthy. Now, if something didn't happen in the next few hours, his head would be removed from his body. He closed his eyes to shut out the vision.

The guard came to the cell; it was time for him to go. They gave him an orange coverall to wear. He looked at it, and then put it on. There was no use in arguing or fighting. He'd only delay his date with a large blade.

Bernadette rode with Jason and Reza. Mohammed and Jebran putted behind them as fast as they could in the red rickshaw. Somehow, they kept up. The traffic moved slowly this morning. Numerous vehicles were heading in the same direction.

"What's with the all the traffic?" Bernadette asked

Jason looked ahead, clearly reluctant to answer, then he looked at Bernadette, "The rumor is…that Chris will be executed by a ceremonial sword."

"Holy Christ! Are they serious? What the hell kind of people do this?" Bernadette said. Her fists clenched and unclenched. She wanted to grab something—punch something.

Reza spoke up from the back seat. "The imam is trying to make a show. He wants a grand spectacle. Remember, he said he has something grand to show afterwards. This is his way of drawing a crowd for his purpose."

Hammer moved his unit along a side street. He was in the lead unit of four armored personnel carriers with a manned

50 MM turret and a complement of six fully armed marines in each vehicle. They were almost in position. One more street and they'd be there. An Afghan Army tank came around the corner and stopped. Their way was blocked.

Bernadette's little convoy of two came to the side street where Hammer was supposed to be. Bernadette jumped out of the car. "Where the hell is he?"

Mohammed came up from behind in the rickshaw. "I will look for him." He pulled the rickshaw around them and was gone.

Bernadette stood by the car. She heard the second call to prayer. She knew that in a half hour from now, the faithful would be filing out of the mosque and into the square to see Chris' execution.

Her only hope was Hammer and his men. The plan was to have Hammer's team surround the execution site, pointing their weapons at the imam, while she tried to find the robe. She only hoped she was right about where she thought the robe was—Chris's life was on the line.

Mohammed came back in a cloud of blue smoke, the rickshaw screeched to a stop in front of her. "Afghan Army tank blocking the street," he said, shaking his head. "The Americans no get through."

Hammer got out of his vehicle. He grabbed his interpreter, Aziz, and went forward to the tank. The tank hatch opened. An Afghan officer peered down at them from behind the hatch.

Hammer looked up at the officer and smiled. The man

looked all of twenty years old with a stubble of beard. "Aziz, tell this officer that my unit must go through this street."

Aziz bowed to the Afghan officer and repeated Hammer's words, then turned to Hammer. "This officer says that no one is allowed to go into the square today other than Muslims who wish to witness the execution. All NATO personnel are forbidden to enter."

"That's bullshit. What kind of dumb ass would make such a command?" Hammer said.

"You want I should translate this?" Aziz asked. He looked up at the officer who was waiting to hear what Hammer had to say.

"No, damn it." Hammer whirled and walked back to his vehicle. His cell phone rang. He took it out of his pocket and answered it, "Hammer."

"You've got to get through to the square," Bernadette demanded.

"My personal carriers are no match for a tank," Hammer replied.

"Without your backup, Chris will be executed."

"There's not much I can do."

"Figure something out. We've got twenty minutes." Bernadette said.

Hammer stared at the phone and punched the end button. He put the phone back in his pocket. He had twenty minutes to move a twenty-ton tank.

Chapter Forty-Nine

Chris sat in the back of the police van, staring down at the floor. Two police officers sat across from him, two more were by his side. He didn't feel like eye contact and they spoke no English. What was there to say?

They marched him to the van in his orange coveralls with his legs and arms in shackles. He looked briefly at the sky; it was a pale blue with a few clouds. He missed his bright blue skies of home, of Canada.

As the van rocked and bounced over the uneven streets, he wondered what he'd feel before he died. Part of him felt loss. No one ever wants to die, especially when you're thirty-seven years old and innocent. But he realized the crime he'd committed was trying to make more of himself than he was.

Had he stayed in Canada with Bernadette and been content, had found another way for their relationship, he wouldn't be here now. He tried to reconcile himself to his stupidity. His only crime was being in the wrong place in time, in taking a wrong turn, and not having the sense to go back the way he'd come.

The van came to a halt. He could hear a lot of voices. The door opened. A cordon of police lined the way towards a dais with a block—and a man with a large sword.

The crowd cheered as Chris stepped out of the van. He realized he was the main event. It felt odd that the spectacle of his death would be of interest to these people. Part of him was angry at this, and another part sad that they should find joy in his death.

He shuffled along in his chains towards the dais. As he got closer, he saw the man with the sword. That's when he became really pissed. The guy had scrawny little arms.

"Aw, for Christ sake," Chris said out loud, "at least you guys could have found someone who could put some muscle into it."

Chapter Fifty

Bernadette heard the cheer from the square. She knew it meant Chris had arrived to be executed. She turned to Jason, "What can we do?"

Jason looked at her. "I don't know, he's going to be surrounded by police…"

Mohammed pulled a canvas bag out of his rickshaw and walked towards Bernadette. He pushed it towards Bernadette.

"What is this?"

"Makes you a big voice," Mohammed said.

Bernadette opened the soiled bag and took out an old battery powered megaphone. The thing looked like it was ancient technology.

"But what am I to do with this?"

"You must be louder than the imam, you must speak your truth to the crowd," Mohammed said.

Jason turned to Bernadette. "He's right. If you can prove Chris is innocent, you need to do it in front of the crowd. Reza will translate for you and speak—you have to give him the words.

Bernadette looked at the megaphone. She turned it on and gave it a quick test. It worked.

"You're right. I need to stand tall with a big voice. Let's go."

They ran to the square. The place was packed. Men of every age lined the square, shoulder to shoulder to see the spectacle of a westerner having his head chopped off.

The imam stood close to Chris on the dais with Jamshed beside him. He surveyed the crowd; he had them in his hands. Today would be a turning point in Kandahar, once the infidel was executed, he would tell the crowd that a miracle had happened, the man had confessed before death. He would produce the robe and place it on himself for all to see. He'd promised it to Jamshed, but he knew he must have it for himself. He would have power over this city and soon, the entire country.

He had chosen his own son to be the executioner for the day, hoping that this would make him into the man that he sorely lacked in being. He'd had him wield the large blade many times in their courtyard chopping melons.

When Chris arrived on the dais, the imam realized to his own horror what a large neck he had. He quickly sought out a big policeman, asking him to assist, that it was his duty. The policeman reluctantly agreed.

Sergeant Hammer heard the loud noise from the square. The hair raised on the back of his neck. He hated this feeling. The tank in front of his unit was going nowhere. He couldn't convince the tank commander to back up.

A group of kids played soccer on the side of the road, kicking the ball back and forth and watching the tank with interest.

Corporal Mendez came up beside him. "You'd think that cheer was for a soccer match and not an execution."

"That's it," Hammer yelled slapping Mendez on the back. "We need to play some soccer."

Mendez looked at Hammer as if he'd just lost his mind. "Sure, Sarge, if that'll make you happy…"

"Get the men out of the vehicles. I want a quick meet," Hammer instructed. He ran to the kids in the street with Aziz by his side. "Tell the kids I'll pay them for the use of the soccer ball for five minutes."

Aziz translated and turned to Hammer. "They think the privilege of their soccer ball is worth many Afghanis."

"I'm sure they do—is this enough?" Hammer asked, shoving a wad of bills towards the kids. The kids grabbed the money and handed over the ball.

Hammer jogged back to his men who were forming in a circle. "Okay, men, any of you know how this game is played?"

Three of them nodded, the others shrugged, and one said, "I think it's with your feet and not your hands, isn't is Sergeant?"

Hammer nodded, "You're going to kick this ball around until all those Afghanis in that tank come out to play. There are four of them in there. I figure they won't be able to stand watching you Jarheads mess up their beloved game." Hammer pointed to his other men. "You guys stay on the sidelines, cheer like hell, make noise, and when the guys come out—take them down—but no rough stuff. This is going to be a peaceful tank takeover—you copy that?"

The men yelled in unison, "Copy that, Sergeant!"

The men started to kick the ball around. Others cheered on the sidelines. Hammer stood with his back to the tank watching his men. Mendez stood to the side of him so he could watch the tank.

"Anything happening?" Hammer asked.

"The tank commander opened the hatch, he's watching," Mendez replied.

"We need some action," Hammer said. "Okay you guys, play rough, and let's see some tackles and some checking."

"There's none of that in soccer," Mendez protested.

"There is today," Hammer said. "Come on you guys, a little hustle let's see some contact."

The marines gladly complied. They found kicking the soccer ball boring. Private Olsen threw an arm block into Private Sawchuck, who responded by kicking the feet from under Olsen. The men squared off ready to have a fistfight.

"Is that what you're looking for?" Mendez

"Anything from the tank?"

"Yeah, the commander is climbing down and the other three crew are coming out. They are yelling something."

Hammer looked to Aziz. "What are they saying?"

"They want to show us how the true game of football is played. They do not call it soccer."

"Is that so, tell them they are welcome to show us," Hammer said with a smile.

The Afghani tank crew came down from the tank, and the marines grouped around them. In seconds, every one of the tank crew had their hands bound behind them in nylon zip ties.

"Okay, Aziz, tell the Afghan tank crew they have possession of the ball, we have the tank. Men, get that damn tank moved, we got a mission to do."

The men yelled, "Aye, aye, Sergeant." Two of them

jumped in the tank, threw it into reverse and backed it into a side street. Hammer and his men got back in their vehicles and headed for the square.

The imam put his hands up to silence the crowd. He took the microphone and started to speak. "This infidel dared to steal the cloak of the Prophet for his own gains. He has tarnished the good name of our country and our faith. For that he must die."

The crowd cheered.

Bernadette stood behind Reza. "Okay, here goes, just translate everything I say."

"Yes, *inshallah*, we will set your Chris free," Reza said. He picked up the megaphone in a shaking hand.

"Imam Sardar Agha. How can you execute an innocent man?" Reza translated for Bernadette over the megaphone.

Sardar looked up from his microphone. He was incredulous that someone would dare to challenge him in this crowd. "Who speaks this nonsense?"

"He says you speak nonsense." Reza said to Bernadette.

"You say this man is guilty of stealing the cloak of the prophet—is that true?" Bernadette said to Reza. He translated, somewhat haltingly. He couldn't believe her words.

"Yes, that is true. This man stole the cloak. He must die for it." Sardar commanded by pointing his hand to Chris. "Place him on the block. There is no delay."

The crowd cheered again.

Reza translated Sardar's words to Bernadette, and shook his head. "He does not agree with you." Reza said.

"But you know the cloak is here. It never left," Bernadette said and Reza translated.

The crowd of men looked at each other. There was silence.

Sardar looked to both sides of him, as if he could not believe this insult. "Who makes this accusation? This falsehood? Surely we will seize this person and have them cut down with this infidel."

Reza's hand shook even more. He turned to look at Bernadette. "You have his attention. I'm not sure if this is good."

"Keep going, you're doing fine," Bernadette said.

"Yes, and I'm going to be very dead very soon," Reza replied.

"If I can show you the cloak of the prophet will you admit this person is innocent?" Reza translated for Bernadette.

The crowd started to talk amongst themselves. Men started to yell, "Show us the cloak—show us the cloak!"

"Do you want to see the cloak of the Prophet my brothers or do you want to hear the words of an imam who is attempting to use the cloak for his own means?" Reza translated.

"We need to move forward, Reza." Bernadette said. She pushed Reza through the crowd. The men parted. Some looked angry, some looked baffled and amused by Reza's words.

"Where are we going?" Reza asked.

"Move towards the shrine. We're only fifty meters away." With Bernadette behind Reza they pushed their way through the crowd to the steps. They climbed quickly and reached the entrance.

The large black urn was in the corner. Bernadette took off the top. It was dusty and dirty. She peered down into the bottom.

"There's nothing there. I can't believe it's not there," Bernadette said. She pulled back in shock.

"You see," the imam yelled into the microphone. "This person has nothing. Nothing but lies—seize them."

Men rushed up the steps towards Bernadette and Reza. Jason tried to get to them. The crowd pushed him back.

"This is bullshit," Bernadette said staring at the men rushing towards her. "It has to be here." She took the lid and smashed it on the steps.

A cloth fell out.

The men stopped on the steps.

"Is that it?" Reza asked.

Bernadette knelt down and picked it up. She unfolded it and held it up. "My God, it's the sacred cloak of Mohammad.

A cheer went up from the square. Men started to clap and cheer.

"This is blasphemy," Sardar yelled into the microphone. "These men have planted this robe here. They knew it was there all along. They are in league with the infidel. Bring them here and we will execute them all with their partner in crime."

"What's he saying?" Bernadette asked Reza.

"He's not buying it. He's saying we planted this cloak. He wants us to suffer the same fate as Chris."

"That slimy son of a bitch," Bernadette said. "Where's your megaphone?"

Reza looked to his side, "It is gone. Someone tore it off me."

Men surged forward, grabbing Bernadette and Reza. They pushed them towards the dais with Sardar and Chris. Other men picked them up, placing them beside Chris.

Bernadette was forced to kneel beside Chris. Her head was down. She turned slightly, "Hey, sweetie, it's me."

"Bernadette! Oh my god, what the hell…" Chris said turning his head. "Why?"

"I had to try, honey. Sorry…I had to try…" Bernadette said, stifling a sob more from frustration than fear.

Chris shook his head. "I wish you'd stayed out of this. You should have gone home."

"You knew I wouldn't."

Chris sighed. "Yeah, I knew I'd see you here. This is really a bad way to have death do us part. And we never got to our wedding vows."

A loud roar of vehicles came from outside the square. The crowd moved as NATO armored vehicles pushed into the square. A man on top with a megaphone yelled something to the crowd.

"What's he saying, Reza?" Bernadette asked Reza who was kneeling beside her and wondering why he'd ever become her interpreter.

"He is saying that the imam must let everyone go. They must stop this execution immediately," Reza said.

"Wonderful news. Hammer made it through with his men," Bernadette said.

Sadar took the microphone and began yelling something.

Reza turned to Bernadette, "The imam says that NATO has no authority here. This is the business of the religious council."

The crowd started to yell.

"How's that going with the crowd?" Bernadette asked Reza.

"Not good. The crowd believes the imam."

Bernadette blew out a breath. "Damn, no one wants to miss a triple header."

A sound of sirens came from the other side of the square. Bernadette looked to see armored police vehicles entering. A man jumped out with a microphone and started shouting. One word was understandable—Caprinski.

"I hope this is about Caprinski's confession," Chris said.

"This is Police Chief Kahn. He says he has a confession from the leader of the security team, Caprinski. He says that the imam, Sardar Agha, he convinced the infidels to steal it then double-crossed them. The imam was going to use the cloak of the prophet for his own gains. He was going to collude with the Taliban and help bring them back to power."

Jamshed pushed Sardar out of the way and took the microphone. "People of Kandahar, this is true what the chief of police is saying. This vile imam wished to fool you all. He's had the robe all along; he wanted to enslave you to the rule of the Taliban."

Jamshed turned to Sardar. "I will not hang with you, Imam, you will hang on your own."

"What's going on?" Bernadette asked.

"This was a plot to overthrow the government by the imam. He was in league with the Taliban."

"Holy crap," Bernadette said. "I thought this was all about money."

"The chief is telling the police around us to set us free immediately or be judged as criminals in league with the imam," Reza said.

Bernadette, Reza, and Chris were immediately brought

to their feet. The imam tried to grab the sword to make good his promise of a beheading. His own son grabbed it from him.

Chief Kahn made his way through the crowd to the dais and released Chris from his shackles. He looked at Bernadette in her disguise. "I should have known you would be here."

"Just trying to delay the proceedings until your big entry. Glad you could make it," Bernadette said.

"I hear you found the cloak. How did you know where it was?" Kahn asked.

"It was from an interview Jason had with the night watchman. He said it looked like Imam Sardar, Lund, and Chris were in a rugby match at the door. I had to look it up on the Internet. You can keep passing the ball laterally from one player to the other. Lund passed it Chris, and then the lights went out. Chris told me he had it for only a few seconds then Lund took it back. He gave it back to the imam who hid it in the top of the jar."

"And they used me as the scape goat," Chris said, massaging his wrists from the shackles.

"Yes they did, sweetie. I think Sardar got Caprinski to convince Lund he was going to get the robe out of Kandahar. But it was all a double cross. Sardar needed some non-believers to steal the robe to incite the tribes and turn them against each other. He was then going to come out the leader…with the cloak." Bernadette said.

"We are in your debt," Kahn said. "You have saved Kandahar from much bloodshed."

"You are welcome. And I'm most happy that we saved Kandahar from shedding our blood. Now, maybe I should take off this disguise," Bernadette said.

"Do not do that just yet," Kahn said.

"Why is that?"

"You were handling the robe of the Prophet, you are a woman. Perhaps you should not surprise this crowd even more," Kahn said.

Chris put his hand on Bernadette's shoulder. "Don't worry, honey, I'll be happy to get you out of that disguise when I get you back to our room."

Chapter Fifty-One

Bernadette and Chris were in luck—the shower had some hot water. They took advantage of it by showering together to save water. It wasn't until several hours later that they came up for air from their lovemaking, or as Chris called it…getting reacquainted.

"I'm sorry," Bernadette said as she traced her hand down Chris's chest.

"You're sorry? For what?" Chris asked.

"I should have seen the signs that you were unhappy. I was too busy being a cop. I know we kept making fun of you being the house husband, but I know deep down it was eating at you."

Chris kissed her on the forehead and placed his large hand on hers. "I should have been more vocal about it. Instead, I took this security job in Afghanistan to show you I was a big boy."

Bernadette chuckled and squeezed Chris. "Yeah, you showed me alright."

"So, what do we do now?" Chris asked.

Bernadette looked into his eyes. "I think we love the hell out of one another and get on with our lives. Sure, we're going to have some hard times figuring things out, but that's what marriages are for."

Chris kissed her on the lips. "That works for me."

Bernadette pulled back from him. "Oh, just one more thing, I may want us to adopt a boy I found."

"Say, what now?"

"It's kind of a long story, but this boy, Almas…he's how I found you. If it wasn't for him, you'd be either lying in a grave in that village or sent to the imam so fast I'd never have had a chance to save you."

Chris picked up her hand and kissed it. "If this little guy made such an impression on you, then I've got to meet him."

Later that afternoon, Bernadette called Reza and left a message. She wasn't sure how to broach the subject with Almas. She knew they were somehow connected by the events they'd been through, but would Almas want to be adopted? Would he want to leave his country?

It was not until late in the evening that Reza called back. He seemed excited. "Bernadette, you will not believe it."

"Try me," Bernadette said, as everything that happened in this country was somehow one step beyond her experience.

"You remember the people we met in Farah?"

"Yes, Miriam and Azar…the guest house…."

"Yes, that is the ones. I received a phone call this morning. They were back in the region to collect religious artifacts of Buddha and they came across a group of villagers that had been hiding in the hills from the warlord."

"Ramin Rasul?"

"Yes, he was pushed out of the region and left for Iran. Miriam found this out from the NATO troops. That is why she and her husband could resume their work."

"Okay, that's nice to know about Reza. But how is this unbelievable news?"

"Miriam found Almas' parents."

"What?"

"Yes, praise be to Allah, they asked Miriam if she knew of their son. They told him what he looked like. Miriam realized it was Almas. She had my number and called me; I put Almas on the phone with his parents."

Bernadette held back tears. "That is wonderful news. How soon does Almas leave? I want to see him before he goes."

"Oh no, he is already gone. My cousin was leaving for Farah this morning. I was able to catch him before he left and Almas went with him. How fortunate for all."

"Yes, how fortunate. Did Almas happen to leave any message…you know…maybe…?"

"Oh yes, he said *inshallah* he will meet with you again. He said he sees many happy things in your stars. And he left you a small picture that he drew," Reza said.

"Thank you, Reza." Bernadette put down the phone.

Chris came into the room. "What is it? You look like someone just died."

Bernadette shook her head. "No one died. It was just a dream that got shattered." She brushed away a tear. "They found Almas' real family and he's gone home. I, meanwhile, will give myself a reality check."

"So, we don't have an adopted son to bring into the family?" Chris said. He winked. "Well, we can always make a boy from scratch you know."

Bernadette punched him in the arm. "Don't get any bright ideas big boy."

Reza and Jason saw them off at the Kandahar airport a few days later. Reza bowed, placing his hand over his heart. It was the most affectionate he could get with Bernadette as his culture would allow no touching.

"Thank you, Reza, you were wonderful," Bernadette said.

"I have learned much about courage," Reza said.

"I think you learned you found your courage, Reza. You were a very courageous man—"

"...In the end," Reza said, finishing her sentence.

"No one knows the end. We are all many works in progress," Bernadette said.

"Ah, yes, works… That reminds me, I have something from Almas for you," Reza said. He took a small piece of paper out of his parka and handed it to Bernadette.

Bernadette unfolded the paper. "Oh my…." She clutched at her chest as she stared at the paper.

"What is it?" Chris asked, staring over her shoulder.

"It's a picture of a little fox. Almas has printed in English that his father called him the little fox."

"Okay. Really nice. Why are you so shocked."

"My grandmother had a dream about a fox. She told me one had come by her cabin to tell her something, she said it would lead me to you."

"Okay, now I'm doing the wow move," Chris said holding a hand to his chest.

Reza smiled. "There are many things done in this country that so few understand. One must look to the stars sometimes and other times to the Prophet."

Bernadette bowed deeply. "Thank you for bringing this to me. Now, there's one more thing I hope I can ask of you, Reza."

"Yes, whatever, just ask."

Bernadette waited a moment then stared into Reza's eyes. "When I was thrown into prison, I met many women who cannot get out of prison until a male relative comes to get them."

"Yes, this is true. This is a very bad Afghani system, but this is the way."

Bernadette nodded her head. "Yes, I know, but if I got the resources to provide many relatives, would you help with this?"

"Of course, but how would you do this?" Reza asked.

Bernadette handed Reza a small packet. He opened it to find the Jade Buddha sparkling inside.

"What am I to do with this?"

"Call Miriam. She has a buyer for it. She will help you set up a network to aid the women in prison," Bernadette said.

"This will be my greatest pleasure," Reza said.

Bernadette turned to Jason, "I have your final payment." She pulled out an envelope with five thousand American dollars and handed it to him." A deals a deal and you came through.

"But you were the one that actually saved Chris, I was only your guide." Jason protested.

Bernadette shook her head, you were one hell of a guide, and no one else could have navigated that journey. She looked around, "You know I'd give you a kiss on both cheeks and hug in true Canadian style, but I'd blow a bunch of Afghan's minds here."

Jason smiled, he opened the envelope and peeled off five

one hundred dollar bills, "Here's for your wedding. I won't be able to make it, even if you did invite me."

"What do you intend to do?" Bernadette asked.

"I was going to head to Africa to help a friend with water treatment for villages, but I think I'll stay here and help Reza spring women out of jail. You've got a great idea, Bernadette."

"Now, I have to go. Paris is waiting." Berandette said with a bow to Jason.

Chris had upgraded them to first class for their Lufthansa flight and once airborne they were offered champagne.

After they clinked glasses in a toast, Chris looked at Bernadette. "How exactly do you think you'll have all these women released from prison?"

Bernadette's eye's sparkled. "Last night, while you were sleeping, I called Miriam and she agreed the Buddha could be put to good use instead of in a museum."

"And how does she intend to do that?" Chris asked.

"Kind of easy. We're setting up a bunch of safe houses for these women to return to society. To do so, we'll have men show up posing as relatives to take them to the safe houses."

"And how do these men convince the guards they are relatives, who will show up to the prison in mass?"

"Simple, they will bribe the hell out them. Money and greed works just as well here as it does in London or New York City or Toronto, my love." Bernadette reclined her seat and finished her champagne.

Chapter Fifty-Two

Bernadette and Chris walked everywhere in Paris. They climbed the Eiffel Tower, drank café crème with a *pain au chocolate* outside the Louvre, and dined in the unassuming streets of Le Mouffetard in the Latin Quarter on a dinner of braised duck leg with star anise, figs and winter squash that had their eyes rolling with pleasure.

In three days, they'd eaten enough butter, cheese, pâté and baguette, washed down with copious quantities of good French wine to make all of Afghanistan and their brush with death a mere memory.

They sat quietly at a table on a side street with the sounds of the numerous cathedrals ringing their chimes. The chimes bounced off the ancient walls and cobblestones making them seem like everything was in tune with their world once again.

Chris moved a piece of baguette slowly through the last morsels of the cassoulet they'd ordered for lunch. He was going to order the crème brûlée for dessert. His weight was coming back on; he enjoyed every mouthful of it.

Bernadette checked her phone. She'd promised to return to work in a week. She was looking forward to it, but a feeling of anxiety crept over her, as if there were an issue in her life that needed to be dealt with. She told herself it wasn't the wedding plans they'd been talking about, there was something else, but she just couldn't put her finger on it. She read down her list of emails until one jumped out at her.

"What the hell?" Bernadette said, staring at her phone.

"What is it?" Chris asked, swallowing the last of his Chateau Laroix wine.

"I got a text from my chief. He says they have someone in custody who claims he knows me."

Chris chuckled. "I thought everyone in town knows you. Hell, you've arrested half of them."

"This guy claims he's my uncle, Cahal Callahan from Ireland."

"Do you have an uncle in Ireland?"

"My dad told me about him, but I've never spoken to him."

"So, what's he in custody for?"

"Attempted murder."

Next in the Bernadette Callahan Series

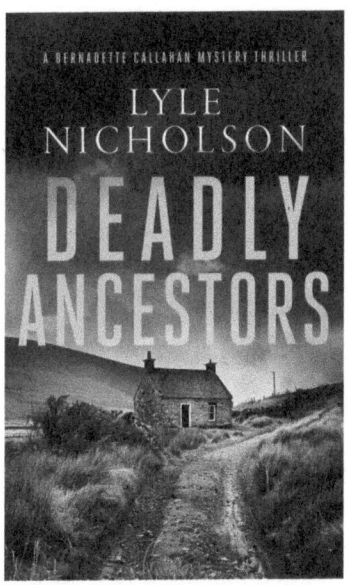

vinci-books.com/deadly-ancestors

A shocking attack. A long-lost uncle. Sinister links to ancient Irish Folklore.

When an Irish priest narrowly escapes an attempt on his life at a remote Canadian seminary, Detective Bernadette Callahan finds herself entangled in a mystery that hits unexpectedly close to home.

Turn the page for a free preview…

Deadly Ancestors: Chapter One

48 Hours Ago

Father Dominic entered the chapel. Two candles flickered on the altar, throwing shadows onto the statue of Jesus Christ above it. A beam of moonlight shone through the stained glass windows, making a narrow path of light from the doorway.

He lit a votive candle and walked towards the altar to say his prayers, the old wooden floors creaking as he shuffled forward. This was his speed at seventy-five years old. His body, wracked by arthritis, moved at its own rate; the good Lord would take him in time, but now he would kneel in prayer.

A sound made him stop. Was that a click he heard? It sounded familiar—but why? He searched his memory for that sound and in a flash of recognition; he knew. A round had been chambered in a gun.

How long had he been expecting this? He knew they

would come; they'd find him. He was thankful for one more moment in prayer before being sent to his everlasting life.

He moved faster, pushing his old bones forward. Determined to get to the altar to prostrate before the bullet entered his body. If he was to die—it would be before God. Father Dominic couldn't ask for more.

He reached the altar and sank to his knees when the shot rang out. The sound reverberated, bouncing off the simple wooden pews and making a wave of sound from the front to the back.

Father Dominic fell forward. His head hit the front of the altar; his arms splayed in one last worship to God. A trickle of blood flowed onto the floor. The moon cast a glow onto the blood as it made its way down the aisle as if it was searching for an exit.

Dominic waited for his spirit to leave his body, for the light, the angels, the sound of trumpets and the heavens to open. A door slammed; he heard footsteps. Was it Saint Peter? Was someone coming to take him to the pearly gates?

A hand touched his head. He expelled his breath, "Yes, I'm here Lord, I'm ready."

"Father Dominic, it's Father Frederic. You're hurt! I've called the ambulance."

"I'm not dead?"

"No, but you're losing blood. I'll put a compress on your head. Please stay still, the ambulance will be here soon."

Father Dominic looked up at the altar. The figure of Jesus stared down at him. Was that a frown on his brow? He'd never seen that before. Had he disappointed him? He wasn't sure... his mind fogged over. He slipped into unconsciousness to the sound of sirens coming up the hill to the seminary.

Constable Stewart picked up the call of gunshots at the seminary. A strange call on a cold February night, the seminary was ten kilometers on the outskirts of Red Deer, a small city of one hundred thousand in western Canada, two hours east of the Rocky Mountains and five hours north of Montana. It was an estimate that locals used when driving a car in the summer; in the winter they doubled the time. Gun violence, though rare, happened downtown where the drug dealers fought over their turf.

Stewart was a tall, muscular man with a dedication to the gym that made his biceps and triceps a thing of wonder to those who'd never spent time there. His other passion was the law and the Royal Canadian Mounted Police. His father had been a sergeant and his grandfather an inspector. His red hair and freckles made him look much younger than his late twenties, but no one dared call him 'kid.'

The other units and paramedics had arrived at the scene. Stewart was sweeping North Road looking for suspects. Another cruiser was doing South Road. The countryside was flat, with large expanses of farmers' fields covered in deep snow.

If he had to leave his car to follow tracks, this was the perfect night for it. A meter of snow lay on the ground, little wind, and a full moon. He could find just about anything or anybody in these conditions. He turned his headlights to high beam and slowed his speed to scan the surrounding fields.

Everything lay covered in a blanket of snow. The harvested fields of stubble lay frozen on the ground, waiting for the spring and summer heat to bring them back to life. There were few trees; someone had cut them down years ago for crops. The few trees left standing became property markers or windbreaks. They stopped the howling winds blowing in from the Rocky Mountains that could tear off a layer of topsoil in a day.

Stewart looked at the outside temperature gauge; it read minus twenty centigrade. Damn cold, but nothing like last month when a cold front had moved in from the Arctic and pushed the temperature to minus fifty at night.

Stewart looked out onto the field. Nothing was stirring. Then he saw something moving along the tree line.

"Is that an animal?" he muttered to himself.

He watched it move from tree to tree; it ducked behind a large stand of bushes when it saw the police cruiser.

"That's no damn animal, no frigging animal moves like that." He picked up his radio, "This is unit two niner, I got eyes on a person wandering in a field over here on Township Road four two one, just four klicks past Range Road, do you copy?"

Dispatch copied the message and replied that backup was on the way.

Stewart stopped the cruiser, letting the engine idle. The figure went still for a moment, then ran across the field.

He switched on his microphone, "This is the police. Stay where you are," he commanded.

The figure ran faster.

"Of course, that never works," Stewart said, climbing out of the car. He spoke into his shoulder mike, "Unit two niner in pursuit of a suspect on foot."

He was going to unlock the shotgun from the dashboard, decided against it, as it would be cumbersome to jump over the barbwire fence in the field with it. He put on his thick gloves and pulled his woolen cap over his ears. He hated chasing people in the winter.

He launched himself over the fence and trudged through the deep snow. He'd wished he'd time to pull on the snowshoes from the trunk but suspects never gave you that luxury. They ran at the most inconvenient times.

The figure in the snow ran slowly, as if the effort in the snow was more than he or she could handle. As Stewart caught up to it, he could see it was a man. He'd fallen into the snow and lay on his back with his hands in the air.

"For the love of god, please don't shoot me, I'm just an old man lost in the fields."

Stewart stood over him, shining his flashlight on him. The man looked a mess; maybe from the effort of walking in the fields. His long gray hair lay matted in strands. His face hadn't seen a razor in days. His eyes rimmed in red. His breath came in long puffs as he exhaled clouds of steam into the icy air.

"Do you have any weapons on you?" Stewart asked.

"No, just a penknife," the man answered in a thick Irish accent.

"I'm going to check you, anyway. Stand up. Can you do that, can you stand?"

"I'm not dead," the man answered with indignation in his voice. He stood up and raised his hands in the air.

Stewart frisked him. He pulled out an object with a bone handle. He felt a small button on the front. He pressed it; a switchblade knife shot out. Its sharp edges gleamed in the moonlight.

"You're carrying a switchblade knife, sir. These are illegal in Canada."

"I told you it's only a penknife. I use it for my protection and to clean my teeth once in a while."

"What's your name?"

"Cahal Callahan is the name. And what's yours?"

"Constable Stewart. You want to tell me what you're doing out here in this field tonight?"

Cahal looked around. "That's easy to see, isn't it? I'm lost. Why else would a man be wandering about on a miserable night like this?"

"Then why did you run when I hailed you?"

"You hailed me? On what now did you do that?"

"On the car's speaker; it has over two hundred decibels. You can hear it kilometer away. You didn't hear it?"

"I'm an old man, I'm near deaf, I am. Not a young buck like yourself."

"Why did you run when you saw my police cruiser lights on?"

"How am I supposed to know you're the real police? Here I am in a foreign country, maybe you're one of those masquerading police types like they have in South America." He huffed out a breath. "I was running for me life."

"This is Canada, Mr. Callahan…"

"Better safe than sorry, I always say," Cahal said with a nod.

They walked back as the other police cruiser came to stop on the road.

Stewart put Cahal into the back of the cruiser and walked over to the officer. It was Constable Marie Jelenick. She was new to the force and good at her job. In her mid-twenties, she had dark brown eyes and platinum blonde hair with an attitude that said all business. Stewart liked that about her.

"What have you got there?" Jelenick asked, nodding towards the suspect in the cruiser.

"The guy's name is Cahal Callahan, says he got lost. Told me as we walked back here that he hitched a ride to the seminary to see one of his old Irish friends, then he got lost on the road. Oh, and he says he's related to Detective Bernadette Callahan."

Jelenick smiled. "I'm sure Callahan will love that when she gets back from vacation."

"Well, that's all I got from him."

Jelenick squinted as she investigated the back of Stewart's cruiser. "Well, that's a delightful story, but the footprints in the snow led from the seminary to this field. I think we've got our prime suspect in your car."

Deadly Ancestors: Chapter Two

Detective Bernadette Callahan arrived at the RCMP detachment early. She was in her mid-thirties, taller than average, with red hair, green eyes, and freckles with a bronze skin tone that revealed her mix of Irish and Cree heritage. She had a lot to catch up on. Was it two weeks since she'd been away? One day seemed to collide with another, then there was the stopover in Paris; so nice being there with Chris, but here she was back at work. It was good to be back. She almost hummed a tune.

She found Jerry Durham, the chief of detectives in his usual place, at his desk with his all-day cup of coffee by his side and a stack of files. Jerry was mid-forties with a receding hairline he valiantly tried to comb into something that looked like hair on top but failed. His body was revealing the pressure of his desk by growing a paunch on his tall frame. It made him look like he could tip over when standing up.

He motioned for Bernadette to take a seat, pushing several files to one side and sitting back in his chair.

"Hey, Chief, how're you doing?" Bernadette said as she sat down and sipped her coffee.

"I'm fine, but how are you? I'm amazed you're back at work. I thought you needed more time in Paris. Hell, I would have cashed in my chips and stayed there."

Bernadette looked at Durham's tired eyes. He looked older than his forty-four years, but two kids and police work can age any man, and there was no way he'd ever 'cash in his chips,' to leave this.

"Yeah, Paris was nice, but I was getting chubby on the food, and I got a job to do."

Durham looked at the files on his desk. "You sure do. A bunch of drug dealers are having a war over who controls the fentanyl supply in the city."

Bernadette shook her head, "Damn. Don't tell me the dealers are muscling in on the pharmaceutical companies again."

"Still with the terrible sense of humor." He pulled two files from the top of the stack. "Take these two; it's a good place to start. There's an armed robbery and a drug dealer to chase down."

Bernadette took the files and leveled her gaze at Durham, "And… what about the suspect in custody who claims to be my uncle?"

Durham shook his head. "You know the rules. We can't have you tainting any testimony with personal conflict. The prosecutor would be all over us, so would the judge."

"But his statement is hearsay. I've no recollection of an uncle named Cahal Callahan. He could use this to get around us and pull me off the case."

Durham got up from his desk to pour himself a cup of coffee from his personal coffee machine. He'd brought it in because he drank so much of it. He filled his cup and looked at Bernadette. "I can't risk having you in the same room with him. He's in the Remand Center; the judge took his passport and denied him bail."

"Who has he got for a lawyer?"

"Joe Christie. He's beating the drum to have Cahal released from jail. I don't think I've seen more motions in my life," the chief said, pushing the files to one side.

He pulled some paper clippings from under the files. "These are a bunch of newspaper headlines from our local paper and some in Ireland. They're all saying we have an innocent man locked up, and an old one at that."

Bernadette scanned the pages. "Looks like the old public opinion poll works well for Cahal. How about I see him in an unofficial capacity?"

"What'd you mean?"

"I leave my badge at my desk and wander over to see if this guy is my uncle."

"You promise not to mention the case? If you do, his lawyer will have him out of jail in seconds, and this department will experience the pain and so will you."

"Chief, I'll just drop by to see someone as a potential family member, the blood thicker than water thing," Bernadette said. She knew the defense attorney, Joe Christie, when she was a constable in another province. Back then he was a crusader for his clients. He'd do everything he could for Cahal Callahan. She'd have to watch herself to not cross him.

Durham threw up his hands. "Okay, go, but if you sign in over there as Detective Callahan by mistake, I'll hand your ass to you on a platter."

"I got it," Bernadette said, getting up and taking the files with her.

She walked out of the office and over to the serious crimes division room where she worked. Two other detectives, Marsha Evanston, and Brad Sawchuck were busy at their desks.

Evanston was ten years older than Bernadette. She'd been with the RCMP detachment for five years, pulling herself up the hard way from constable to detective. She was also a girl from the far north, just like Bernadette. Sawchuck was a recent addition from Winnipeg; they had brought in him to form a task group on drug dealers. The way the users were dying on the streets, the dealers were winning.

Bernadette sidled up to Evanston and stood beside her, dropping a pair of ice hockey tickets on her desk.

Evanston pulled her head up from her computer screen and looked at the tickets and back to her screen. "Are those for tonight's game against the Edmonton Oil Kings?"

"Yes, they are. I got other plans; thought you might use them."

Evanston swept the tickets into her desk drawer. "I love the Red Deer Rebels. I don't have to kill anyone for these, do I? I have to draw the line somewhere."

Bernadette smiled; she loved her sense of humor. Always dry, always good. "Evans, I'd never cause you grief. I just need a peek at the Cahal Callahan file, just to get up to speed."

"Aw shit, I wish you'd asked me to kill someone. I'd be better off. If the chief finds out my ass is grass and he's a lawnmower."

"Look, I said a peek, I just want to see what they have on him. I'm not on the case, I'm only… an interested party."

Evanston reached into her desk and pulled out the file. "Take it to your desk, read it, and bring it back here. You have ten minutes."

Bernadette found a desk in the corner, far from the prying eyes of Sawchuck. He claimed he'd transferred to the smaller City of Red Deer to be closer to the Rocky Mountains and fishing, but in the time, he'd been there, no one heard him talking of fishing. The squad room rumor mill pegged Sawchuck as a demotion for some screw up or a divorce. The guy didn't talk much outside of work or go to the pub on Friday. You can't trust what you don't know is a detective's best defense.

The file had the arresting report of Cahal Callahan, a photocopy of his passport from the Republic of Ireland. Birthplace registered as Kildare on February 12, 1945. He claimed he had two siblings, Aideen Callahan his sister and Dominic Callahan his younger brother, which was Bernadette's deceased father. He had the birthdate of her father and his birthplace correct.

The interview with Evanston and Sawchuk showed little. Cahal kept saying he could not remember much of the night. He'd stated that with his age and the long flight from Dublin to Calgary, he'd become disoriented.

When Evanston asked him why he visited the seminary so late at night, he claimed the jet lag from the long flight and the fact that he hadn't changed his watch from Ireland made him forget the time.

The file had a copy of the ticket from his flight. He'd left Dublin at 0835 on a flight to Frankfurt, Germany, and then a direct flight to Calgary that arrived at 1455. The flight was nine and a half hours. On arriving at Customs, Cahal gave Detective Bernadette Callahan as his contact in

Canada. He'd written in her home address but not her cell phone number. Instead, he'd given the phone number of the RCMP headquarters in Red Deer.

How he made the two-hour drive to Red Deer from the airport in Calgary was another mystery. He said he found a ride with some good people he met at the airport who dropped him at a gas station on a major road into town. From there, he claims he found another lift to the seminary.

His reason for going to the seminary was that he'd tried to reach his niece, Bernadette Callahan, but was told she was away until further notice. He decided he'd go to the seminary to wait for his niece, Bernadette, to return.

Evanston had asked why Cahal didn't leave a phone message for Bernadette. He said he didn't want to spoil the surprise.

He claimed he was going to make a surprise visit to his old friend Father Dominic instead. They'd been in a boy's orphanage together at one time. Father Dominic couldn't corroborate the report, as he was not lucid.

There was also the charge of an illegal weapon. Cahal claimed he had no knowledge that his knife was illegal. The knife had been a gift. However, he couldn't recall who'd given it to him.

Bernadette sighed as she read the report. This was the most confused old man or the perfect alibi.

She pulled out the incident report and found little to work with. No witness to the shooting and no weapon. They had a bullet from the chapel, but no shell casing.

From running the bullet through the IBIS, the Integrated Ballistics Identification System, from an uploaded scan of the bullet and an exhaustive check, Evanston had determined the gun as a Sturm Ruger pistol and the bullet a twenty-two caliber.

Bernadette let her finger rest on the information. Who the hell brings a twenty-two to kill someone, unless you get close in? The chapel was small and the range close, but if you wanted to knock someone off, why not bring along a nine-millimeter?

The report went onto say that the bullet grazed Father Dominic; had it been a millimeter more to the right, he would have been dead. The injury had resulted in a concussion. Something he would recover from, but at his age it would take time. There was also a note on the report about a screw up at the hospital but it only mentioned, "a misdiagnosis resulting in a lack of being able to speak with the victim."

The last remark on the report was no GSR found on the suspect. That meant no gunshot residue on Cahal's hands. But they found him without gloves. Had he dropped them somewhere?

She rubbed her forehead; she had more questions than answers. She closed the file and dropped it back on Evanston's' desk.

Evanston looked up at her as she slid the file back under her pile. "You satisfied now?"

"Not really. How long before you have to spring him on what you brought him in on?"

Evanston raised an eyebrow. "Wow, that obvious, huh? The Crown Prosecutor asked for another thirty-six hours for us to recover any evidence."

"Is the judge going for it?"

"I think so. Cahal's all we got. Unless a ghost fired the gun, he's the only man around. We have a team of officers with a dog searching for the weapon today. Maybe something will turn up."

Bernadette walked out of the office. The mention of the

word ghost sent a chill down her spine. This man who claimed to be her uncle had the weirdest story and had appeared in her life at the strangest time. She needed to see him face to face.

Grab your copy...
vinci-books.com/deadly-ancestors

About the Author

Lyle Nicholson writes crime and mystery books you will find hard to put down. His first book in the series, *Polar Bear Dawn*, takes place in the high Arctic of Alaska in the unforgiving winter.

The series is based on Detective Bernadette Callahan, who readers love for her hard-nosed style, and failure to follow the rules. As a female detective, she is a phenomenon in Canada's Royal Canadian Mounted Police. You will enjoy her style as she solves crimes that will take you on a world journey.

He lives in Kelowna, British Columbia with his wife, and spends much of his time cooking, enjoying fine wines and writing novels. Somehow, he calls this work!